Sasha

Book Two

Infectious Rhythm Series

TONYA PLANK

Copyright © 2016 Tonya Plank
All rights reserved. No part of this book may be used or reproduced in any manner whatsoever without written permission except in the case of brief quotations embodied in critical articles and reviews. For information, address Dark Swan Press, 8721 Santa Monica Blvd, #335, West Hollywood, CA 90069-4507.

ISBN paperback: 978-1-942289-12-8
ISBN ebook: 978-1-942289-13-5
Library of Congress Control Number: 2016956193

Edited by Julia Ganis, Juliaedits.com
Cover design by Marisa-rose Shor, Cover Me Darling
Cover photo from istockphoto.com, photographer: konstantin32
Author photo by Bruce Heinsius

DEDICATION

For all of the wonderful readers who loved *Fever* and
wanted the story told from Sasha's perspective. This
book is for you!

CHAPTER ONE

Now I didn't give a shit about stepping on hands. Of course I didn't want to hurt anyone, but I warned everyone I was coming, and to get out of my way. Fast. I needed to get to Rory.

"Look out, keep your hands off ground," I yelled in my panic-induced crappy grammar as I rushed toward my love. Pepe was bent over her. Without saying anything, I brushed him aside, placed one arm under her legs, the other around her back, and in one scoop picked her up. Cradling her in my arms, I walked to the nearest sofa in the back lounge area and gently set her against a plump pillow.

"It's okay. I think I can walk, Pe—" she began to murmur. But then she looked up and let out a little gasp when she saw it was me. Her eyes were beautiful, serene and beatific, and her lips curved into a slight, sweet smile, despite the pain she obviously felt.

There was a great deal of commotion, so many bodies rushing toward her, surrounding her, asking if she was okay, what had happened. Everyone on her mambo team, her friends who'd cheered her on, other teachers and students at the studio who knew who she was—and they all cared. Right now, I couldn't help but be annoyed by them even as I was grateful for their support of my love. She needed physical help first. I needed to figure out how badly she was hurt.

"Could you get me some ice, please? And a bandage?" I asked Pepe.

"Yeah, of course."

"I'm so sorry, my love," I said as I laid her down onto the cushion. "This is…this is my fault. And I'm so, so, so sorry." I kissed her forehead. "We'll get this fixed. We will, my sweet. I'm so sorry." I was shaking with anger, at myself as much as at Cheryl. I should have known the woman was a psycho. She was my student. All the signs were there. My refusal to see them made me impotent to protect the woman I loved.

I knew I was making a scene, calling Rory "my love," "my sweet" in public, at the studio. But right now I couldn't give a serious shit about who all knew. In fact, I wanted everyone to know about our love. About our partnership.

"Oh no, it's not your fault," she whispered.

I shook my head adamantly, so angry at myself I couldn't speak.

"That was pure craziness. Everyone was all screwed up by that stupid stage layout," one of her teammates, an older blonde woman with a Southern accent, said to her. "Don't feel bad at all, honey. Important thing is your knee." She held Rory's hand tightly. Rory nodded, squeezing her eyelids shut, holding back tears.

"No," I said, more harshly than I'd intended. Rory wasn't about to take any blame whatsoever. The teammate looked at me, a confused frown taking shape on her face. "I'm sorry, I didn't mean to startle... You were dancing. You didn't see it. The problem wasn't the stage layout—"

"Oh my gosh, Rory! Are you okay?" Samantha yelled, out of breath. She was followed by Kendra and Rajiv.

We'd all hash it out later, I thought. Now was the time for her friends to show their support, not for me to make it clear to the world that I would take down a certain former student of mine, make sure she never hurt anyone I loved—anyone here at all—ever again.

"Is it bad?" Samantha said, looking back and forth between Rory and me. And I knew she knew the truth.

"Honey, honey, I was watching from the wings with Maurizio. You looked absolutely fab and then...you were down. What happened?" This was from Paulina.

Mitsi and Bronislava followed her. Bronislava shot me a knowing look, followed by a rapid shake of her head. She'd seen the whole thing too.

"Oh no, it is!" Samantha said as Rory's eyes teared.

"No. I mean, it hurts, but I've honestly never had so many people just...well, just care about me before." Rory looked away and blinked, not wanting her friends to see her so emotional. I knew she'd been in a bad relationship with that ass of an ex she had, but this made me feel like she didn't have a lot of support from family and friends either. We'd have to talk about that.

"Oh, geesh, of course we all care about you, silly!" Samantha squealed, rubbing Rory's arm.

Pepe returned with a big bag of ice, a beach-sized towel, and a large Ace bandage.

"Thanks, man," I said to him, taking the ice bag and towel and gently placing the towel on Rory's knee, which was now purplish. On top of the towel I placed the ice pack, and held it there. I looked her in the eye. "I love you," I said. Not mouthed, but said. For everyone to hear.

"I love you too," she said with a surprised laugh, now unafraid to let the tears flow.

I felt an excited silence all around us. I could tell people were smiling, whispering, giggling. Yes, everyone knew. And soon, so would Alessandra, who was out of the studio on a two-week vacation in Sydney. And I didn't care what she had to say to me when she returned. She couldn't prove I'd violated her no-fraternizing policy, because I hadn't. But Cheryl was a serious liability to her now. She couldn't be allowed back into the studio. I knew I had witnesses. It would be Alessandra, not me, who would be on the defensive at our next talk.

We decided to move our after-party to my place. We ended up inviting everyone who stayed around instead of just Rory's few friends. My place was a lot bigger than hers, and she wouldn't have to do the work of entertaining this way. She'd be able to soak in my tub knowing everyone was downstairs dancing the night away. I'd be lying if I said it wasn't a huge deal to me. I was a private person and didn't really like people knowing my business. But I had to remind myself these were studio people, our friends, and they weren't about to go off and rat on me to my family. They knew nothing about my family.

I loaded my tub with Epsom salts, gave Rory four Ibuprofen—prescription strength, I knew as a dancer—and a glass of sparkling water, which I jokingly told her to pretend was champagne.

I wanted more than anything to stay with her but she insisted I go downstairs and be a good host. The laughter wafted upstairs. She was right; there'd be plenty of time for more tub action later. Plenty.

"As much as my knee hurts, I am so happy, Sasha."

"Really?" I frowned.

"Yes! All of my friends are down there dancing their hearts out on your private dance floor to that awesome surround-sound stereo and views of that gorgeous canyon below." She swooned.

"So this is why you love me. For my house," I said, rolling my eyes.

"No!" she said, sitting up to play-slap me, her beautiful breasts bouncing up, nipples peeking out from the bubbles. I raised my eyebrows but before I could say anything she cried out and grabbed her knee.

"Okay, be careful. Let's not get too wild," I said.

"Seriously. Go down. We have all night." She wore that sweetly naughty smile I'd so grown to love.

I raised my eyebrows and flashed my wicked grin right back at her.

We'd agreed not to talk about the details of what had happened tonight, though I'd indicated it was Cheryl, which she now knew from all the commotion. She wanted to enjoy her party, her bath, being in love, and having our love open to all who cared about us. We'd agreed to put off how to deal with Cheryl's evilness until later.

I made a hospital-like bed for her, with all manner of cushy pyramid pillows and long Styrofoam roller pins ideal for massaging aching muscles and keeping your leg elevated while you slept.

"Of course you have all these things designed for an athlete—you're the world's greatest dancer." She beamed. "And I am determined to help you prove it in Blackpool come May, injury or not."

I kissed her on the forehead. "For now, we will think only of your recovery." I knew then that Cheryl, in her own totally warped way, had actually helped us. Rory was just like me; this experience crystallized that. She was bound and determined more than ever to let absolutely nothing get in her way.

Despite the free-flowing champagne and the raucous hip hop beat, Rory's friends couldn't help ranting about Cheryl. Kendra had seen everything. She was standing on the other side of the floor, and had the exact opposite view of the stage area as I did.

"Crazy bitch reached right out and grabbed Rory with her nasty claw," she spat. "She even had to lean over some bodies to get a good grip. People were like, 'What the fuck?'"

My bottom lip trembled. I could feel my face contorted with anger. This was the most angry I could ever remember being.

"I'll totally be a witness, if, you know, you want to go to Alessia, or she wants to sue or whatever," Kendra assured me.

"Me too," Samantha echoed.

"Me three," Rajiv added.

I nodded. "That would be very helpful. Thank you very much," I managed to relax my facial muscles long enough to say.

***

The next morning, I took Rory to the urgent care center. They took some x-rays and thankfully, so thankfully, pronounced nothing broken or torn. It did, however, look like the ligament was stretched and could tear if she didn't heal properly. The doctor told her to stay off it for at least two weeks. She could walk short distances, but no dancing. And do the RICE thing—rest, ice, compress, elevate—every day and night with prescription doses of Ibuprofen for the first five days. He advised her to see her regular doctor as soon as possible, who might want to send her for physical therapy in the event it didn't heal properly.

"It could have been so much worse," I said on the way home, one hand on the steering wheel, the other cupping her shoulder. "Two weeks is nothing. You can prepare mentally. You'll be healed just in time for your mambo team competition."

I honestly wasn't worried. The old me would have been. Most definitely. The old me would have been beyond pissed. Mostly at Cheryl, of course, but at the whole situation. The old me would have let Rory feel my frustration and might have even taken it out partly on her, making her healing process all the harder. But I wasn't the least bit panicked. Because I now knew Rory was driven to win Blackpool just as much as I was. She would heal easily.

***

Over the next two weeks, Rory did as the doctor ordered and took the time off from dance, which also allowed her to show Gunther and his partners how committed she was to her job. She worked late most of those nights, but each night when I picked her up, her main complaints were that she'd been assigned only to draft boring wills or search random documents for a key word or phrase in a large, unrelated case, and that Gunther wouldn't assign her any part of her innocent client case no matter how often she asked. I suspected he was doing it out of punishment for her having a life, but didn't say anything to her. I just hoped the bastard got his head on straight and realized he'd only be helping himself win by putting her on the case that so impassioned her.

After I'd pick her up, she'd spend the nights at my place where she could take a bath, use my arsenal of healing devices, and watch Greta and me practice, taking careful note of everything Greta did and said.

"I feel like an invalid," she complained.

"Don't," I said. "You're still training, just in this slightly altered way."

***

Alessia's two-week trip to Sydney gave me a good amount of time to calm down and organize my thoughts, my demands. We'd agreed to talk in person as soon as she returned. It was perfect that the studio was on a two-week hiatus as well, so I didn't have to deal with the Cheryl question immediately.

Alessia's office door was open. I tapped anyway, before walking in.

She looked up and flashed me a worried smile that contrasted sharply with her tanned, just-back-from-a-vacation physique.

"Who all have you talked to?" I started before she

could say a word to me.

"I've talked to Cheryl," she said, raising an eyebrow that indicated I was in trouble.

And there went my calm demeanor. "Half the studio saw her reaching out, trying to trip Rory, to make her fall, to hurt her. Immediately beforehand several students witnessed her smack me across the face more than once and try to do the same to another student. They also heard her scream obscenities at me, accusing me of cheating on her and declaring that she owned the studio and could assault whomever she wanted. The woman is deluded, has a tenuous grip on reality at best. But more seriously, she is violent, and if you keep her in the studio, you will risk liability. You have a duty to the students who take lessons here, and to your teachers, to provide for their safety as best as you can."

Alessia sighed, closed her eyes and rubbed her temples. After several long seconds she began. "Sasha, she said you kissed her during one of your private lessons. She said you asked her out repeatedly but she told you she was married..." Alessia's tone sounded more weary than accusatory, as if she knew without even hearing from me that Cheryl was a liar.

I tried to look her straight in the eye but she still had her eyes closed. "And you believe her? Over me?" I asked.

Now she placed her elbows on the desk and cradled her head in her hands. She finally opened her eyes and looked me straight on. "Did you violate the no-fraternizing policy, Sasha?" Her voice was nearly a whisper.

"Absolutely not," I said. "As I said, Cheryl has a very unhealthy relationship with reality."

"Not with Cheryl. With Rory?"

My heart pumped. But I had nothing to deny. "Absolutely not," I repeated. "I am now involved with Rory, it is true. But that did not happen while she was my student."

Alessia nodded. "Okay," she said, voice still weary, then returned to rubbing her temples with her fingertips.

I could now see lines of creased makeup around her eyes and lips, under her eyelids. I pulled out a chair and sat down. I'd been so pissed about what Cheryl did to Rory, I hadn't even considered what she might try to do to Alessia.

"What did you tell her?" I asked.

Alessia exhaled deeply. "She demanded I fire you. I told her I needed to talk to you first, hear your story. She said if I let you stay on, she would make things very difficult for me. For both of us."

I felt a sharp stab to my gut. If Alessia fired me, I could easily get a job at another studio, but I'd legally have to go back to Russia and apply. And that would ruin things with Rory. It would destroy our chances of Blackpool. But more than that even, I needed to be here to take care of her. It was my fault she was injured. She could hardly come to Russia with me with her job and all. I felt my heart race. No, Alessia would not fire me.

"Did she say exactly how she was going to make things difficult? Is she going to sue us because Rory stepped on her hand after she tried to grab her leg and twist it? I have many, many witnesses, Alessia." My voice was rising.

"She said if you stay, she'll not only leave the studio but convince others to do the same."

"Good!" I yelled. "I won't ever have to see that crazy b—" I wasn't one for cursing. I caught myself, and Alessia's grim face. She was really worried. "As I said, she's a liability to you, Alessia. And no one else will leave. We're the best studio in town. You know that. These are the rantings of a madwoman."

"What about Holly?" Alessia said.

I sighed. It was true; I hadn't expected her to leave simply because I made one of her weekly lessons available to another student. I was dumfounded someone could be so offended by something so minor. "That was different. I did something directly to her. Who's going to leave because another student is mad and tells them to?"

"I don't know, Sasha." Alessia put her head back into her hands. "Another student canceled her one weekly private—it's unclear if that's related—and Luna said she'll be on vacation for the next two weeks and will call me after she returns. It appears Cheryl has had some influence."

I closed my eyes and took a deep breath. I just wanted to dance, and teach dance. Why did studio politics have to make that so difficult?

"And, yes, she also threatened to sue the studio. As you know, her husband is a big-name lawyer," Alessia added.

"For what?" I laughed. Alessia didn't.

"She didn't say. But I assume sexual harassment, the way she was talking."

I wanted to punch my fist through the wall. But no. I could control my emotions and let reason rule. I wasn't a violent person. "As I said, there are plenty of witnesses who saw, who know how insane she is. You can't seriously be scared of her? How is everyone so scared of her and Luna?"

She rubbed her fingers together, indicating their money was their weapon. I looked through the window that opened onto the lobby. No one was there. The school was still on vacation for two more days. I wasn't even sure I wanted to continue teaching here. I had my students I liked, who had promise, whom I was helping advance, possibly to their own professional careers. I liked teaching. But the politics were ruining it for me.

"What are you going to do?" I said, still gazing out the window, not looking at her.

She hesitated as if she knew I wasn't going to like what she had to say. Or maybe she was waiting for me to look at her. I didn't avert my gaze. "Sasha," she finally began. "I want you to try to make amends with her. I don't mean you have to continue as her teacher. But just apologize for the misunderstanding. Try to get her to come back, and bring her friends back. Or just…just try to make things right, give it closure."

I couldn't believe what I was hearing. I was disgusted. After what Cheryl had done. If she could harm my partner, she could do the same to another teacher. Alessia cared only about her business. I suddenly had no desire to work for this woman anymore.

"I need…I need you to make things right with her. Please, Sasha. I've worked hard to build this…" I could hear the tears threatening to overtake her voice. She wasn't a whiny person, definitely not one who cried in public. She was a hard-ass businesswoman. She really was worried. But damn her for not trusting me.

I stood and looked at her straight on. I wanted

badly to quit. But instead of stomping off like a child, I said simply, "I will continue to work hard with my students, teaching and taking them to championships. I will continue giving showcases and performing at events outside the studio for the studio's benefit. I will not, however, have any dealings whatsoever with Cheryl. I will not teach her, I will certainly not apologize to her, I will not speak to her at all. Ever. If you would like, you are free to fill the hours left vacant by her, Luna, and this other student you think she has convinced to leave, with some of the students on my substantial wait-list." With this, I turned and left without waiting for her response.

***

"So, what did Alessia have to say?" Rory asked me from the tub, where I'd just served her a glass of chilled white wine. She looked slightly worried. I could tell she was trying to figure out from my body language if it was good or bad.

I smiled. "I can see your brain working. My little lawyer," I said kissing her rosy cheek. "My smart, very, very smart, beautiful, lawyer girlfriend."

"Stop it! You're making me want to pull you right down into this tub with me!"

I raised my eyebrows. Sounded enticing.

"Seriously," she said. "What happened?"

I told her what Alessia had said, and what I said in response.

"Oh, wow. I can't believe she wanted you to do that," she said, looking off in the distance, shaking her head.

"I think she's just worried. She knows Cheryl's

crazy. I don't think she was serious."

Rory shook her head, a haze in her eyes. "But that makes it worse. I could see if she truly believed a student's claim. But it's like she's letting her get away with what she did. And what she can do. And what she can do. I mean, she scares me now. I'm proud of you," she said with a flirty smile, though there was still worry in her eyes.

"Please stop worrying. I will never, ever let her touch you again. I prrrromise," I said, rolling the r's and making her giggle. I squeezed her soapy hand.

"I know. I'm just mad at Alessia now. I know it's her business but she should be above that. I mean, what if she insists you make amends? And she doesn't make Cheryl leave? She's out to sabotage us. It could just get really…bad. I can't believe she cares so little about her employees."

I took a breath. I'd been thinking about other work possibilities a lot lately. Especially since this happened, but really starting with Alessia's insistence that I persuade Rory to do pro/ams, and turn her into another cash cow. I squeezed her wet hand again. "In the event I decide to leave the studio…there are other possibilities. I can't imagine it seriously coming to that. I think Alessia knows how bad Cheryl is, and she's not going to let go of me. She'll come to her senses. But, you know, there are other possibilities," I repeated.

"I just don't want you to have to leave the country," she said, her voice almost a whisper now.

"It's not going to come to that." I laughed. "There are different types of visas, or other studios where I can work that will make me eligible for the same visa I now have."

"But that would still entail you having to leave the

country for a time," she said. We hadn't talked about this in detail. She must have done her own research.

I nodded. "There are also others ways to qualify for U.S. citizenship." I said this before thinking about the exact words coming out of my mouth. In my heart and mind I thought of us getting married. But I certainly didn't want to ask her in this way. I wanted her to know I wanted to marry her because I was so beyond in love with her, that she was everything to me, that she was half my soul, not for some stupid political reason. What had I said?

Her big doll eyes widened and her cheeks grew rosy red. *Sweet.* Then she gulped, breathing in some of the bubbles that had inched up her neck, resulting in a minor coughing spell.

"Are you okay?" I gently patted her back. But I could read just what was going through that beautiful, powerful mind of hers. We were on the same wavelength. Of course.

She looked away, obviously embarrassed. "Mmm hmm," she mumbled.

I nuzzled my nose into her hair. "That's a very serious possibility," I whispered, without elaborating further, just leaving it in the air. I kissed the nape of her neck. I would marry her in a heartbeat. But right now we really needed to focus on the competition.

She giggled. She understood. She could read my mind as well.

***

Rory's two weeks of doctor-ordered rest were officially over and we were both psyched to make up for lost time. Luna's temporary and Cheryl's permanent departure from the studio worked out well. It freed up a lot of my time to work with Rory and Greta. Alessia wisely dropped the apology-to-Luna issue, and I asked her to wait to replace Luna and Cheryl until Blackpool was over so I could work hard with Rory. I convinced her that if Rory and I won, and were Blackpool champs and not just finalists, it would mean all the more honors bestowed on the studio, all the more demand for privates and pro/am comps, and all the more demand for local performances, for which the studio would receive a good share of our fees. I knew it was hard on her temporarily. She needed to bring money into the studio on a regular basis. And I was her main source of income in terms of the privates and the pro/ams. But she agreed with me, and so yielded.

Now we just had to work on getting that bastard Gunther to let up a little on my love. He was becoming a bigger pain in the ass every day, telling Rory he'd never had any employee work less than eighty hours a week. But she was a trouper. She struggled hard to do well at both her job and our training. I worried it would eventually take its toll, though.

Greta and I, despite our usual resistance to doing so, made little videos of our rehearsals so that Rory could watch during breaks at work. There were too many times we'd made a tweak to a tiny bit of choreography and forgotten to tell her. Rory was getting so serious about Blackpool, she'd get as upset as I did when she made a fumble. I didn't want her too anxious. Especially when it was my fault. But Gunther caught her watching a video on her phone at her desk. Even though she was eating lunch and obviously on break, he'd made a reference to her not taking her job seriously. So she stopped "practicing" during breaks. She continually assured me that if it wasn't for the case she so believed in, with the innocent potential death-row client, she would seriously be entertaining my earlier suggestion about leaving this job.

The man's asshole-ishness came to a head the Friday of the weekend she and her mambo team were to have their first competition in Irvine, when he conveniently forgot that she'd be away Saturday and Sunday and insisted she spend the entire weekend working on Jamar's case. She called me from the ladies room of her office, very upset.

"I just asked him this morning if he had any more work and he totally blew me off, told me he was too busy to talk. So, I was getting ready to leave a little early to come home to get mentally prepared for everything and Samantha called to wish me luck. And right when I'm on the phone he stops by as if he suddenly has something for me to do. Then he stomps his foot, like a friggin' child, Sasha! And shakes his head and leaves, looking very pissed. So I tell her goodbye and run down to his office and he tells me he needs the memo before I leave. I'm like what memo?" She was crying so badly I couldn't hear her well.

"Calm down, sweet. Just take a breath. I can't understand well."

"I'm sorry," she said after a pause. "Apparently there's hearing for Jamar on Monday and he told me I'd agreed to write a memo for him. I was like, what hearing? He never told me about any hearing! He totally excluded me. And now…" Now she sounded pissed. Her crying had turned to anger. I didn't blame her.

"Rory, the bastard is totally playing mind games. Is there really a hearing that you know of? I'm really starting to think this guy is whacked."

I could hear her working to catch her breath. I could practically hear her pulse racing. "I don't know. The courts are closed. I swear he said nothing about any hearing, about any memo, the entire week. He told me I was totally irresponsible. He acted like he was genuinely mad. I think in his mind he thinks he gave me the assignment. And now…he's making me question myself. Have I been that out of it with all this training and the injury and Cheryl and everything that I totally—"

"No," we both said in unison. She knew she wasn't the problem. She had a psycho for a boss. My heart sank for her. It was impossible to deal with these kinds of people. I should know. My family, Cheryl… I tried to think of something helpful I could do about it besides going downtown and beating the living shit out of him, which wouldn't do any good.

"Anyway, he says I have to work all weekend to get this memo done. Sasha, I just don't know what to do. The team's counting on me. And I know my job comes first, but I'm not even entirely sure what he wants from this memo. He was so pissed, he stomped off and I only have a vague understanding of the research."

"Because he made it up, Rory. There is no memo for you to do or he definitely would have had you do it. He's setting you up to fail."

There was brief silence on her end. I knew she didn't want to hear that. I knew she wanted to trust her boss. Who wouldn't? But this was simply the truth as I saw it. "I know," she said after a lengthy exhale. "But if I don't at least try to give him something, he can fire me. And that will look very, very bad from my very first legal employer."

"Do you really think he would do that? He needs you."

She laughed through tears. "Yeah, he does. But we're talking about a guy who's nuts, remember?"

"Well, I'm no lawyer, but if you want my advice, I'd go to Irvine tomorrow, think about nothing but mambo until you kill it! And then I'll drive you back early Sunday morning and you can work all day on his memo." I immediately regretted what I'd just said since Sunday was our practice.

She took a deep breath. "Sasha, that would be perfect. Would you mind?"

And now, of course I had to say no.

***

I picked her up at her office, her briefcase overflowing with file papers, her face still a little tearstained, though I could tell she'd tried hard to wipe off all of the mascara.

"Feeling better?" I said, enveloping her in my arms and giving the crown of her head a long kiss.

"Mmmm. Yes, thanks to you. My ever-so-understanding man with all the answers!" And with that, she giggled for the first time that night.

We didn't even try to practice. I knew it would be pointless, we were both so wound up. Instead of giving in to frustration-induced panic all night, I decided she needed more than anything to relax before the team comp. So we sat in my backyard in the warm bubbles and cool breeze of the jacuzzi. We were way past having uncomfortable silences, and she mostly just sat in my arms as I kissed her head and neck and massaged her shoulders.

When it began to grow late, I prodded her to let me drive her home. Of course I wanted nothing more than for her to stay the night. But we both knew she needed to get a good night's sleep, which meant we needed to sleep separately. We'd decided she'd drive down with the team for camaraderie. I'd give my private lessons at the studio, then drive down in the evening to join her and watch. It was nice to have everyone know about us. No hiding our love. I couldn't believe I'd once even considered doing that.

"Mmmmm, don't wanna go home," she murmured sleepily.

"I know. Someday…we will…have to stop doing this… I mean, every night," I said, again stopping when I realized what I was trying to say but shouldn't. Yet. She should just move in with me so I didn't have to keep driving her back. But was it time for that? Would we kill each other while training?

She giggled, knowing exactly what I meant.

CHAPTER TWO

I checked into my room at the hotel, and had a glass of cognac in the bar. It was much more quiet, more sane, than the last time we were here for the student pro/ams. Cheryl, Luna, Arabelle—it all seemed like a lifetime ago. I sank into a back corner booth and tried to relax. But I was filled head to toe with Rory's anxious energy. We were sending each other vibes even when we weren't in the same room. *Calm down*, I mentally told her. *Don't think about anything going wrong. Nothing will. Don't worry about your knee, don't worry about letting your team down—you're hardly going to be the one to do that if anyone does. And for God's sake don't think anything the least bit negative about that beautiful body of yours.*

I'd noticed last night in the hot tub that she was still losing weight, despite my efforts to get her to eat more and drink my juices, and to make her feel better about herself naked. I wasn't doing enough to convince her. I hadn't wanted to pester her, with her Gunther problems and her injury. But that was going to have to change. She needed to listen to me better about that body image of hers.

"So excited about this!" It was a voice I

recognized but couldn't quite place. I was sitting in a darkened corner, actually hoping no one would see me, just wanting to be alone with my thoughts for a while. Plus, this was Rory's show. Not mine.

"She's going to rock it! She's such an awesome dancer. Without that über bitch Cheryl around to spoil things, she's going to kill the others!"

I could now see them. It was Kendra and her girlfriend. The one who'd gotten into that absurdist costume tiff with Luna.

"Totally!" This was Rory's other good friend, Samantha.

They'd all shown up to cheer her on. Sweet, good-souled Rory, making so many genuine friends in the studio. It was more than I could say for myself. I was too much of a perfectionist, slave-driving pain in the ass to win people's hearts on that level. I mean, I knew they liked watching me perform and looked up to me as a dancer role model. But that was from afar—totally different from making connections with people who knew you as well as you knew yourself, capable of lasting a lifetime. Well, I had that with Greta. And Sadie. And now I had it with Rory. Maybe I wasn't such a bad guy.

Samantha eyed me. I gave her a little wave. She seemed to know I wanted to be alone. She smiled back, without pointing out my whereabouts to anyone else in the crowd.

I sat by myself for a little while longer. About half an hour before the competition was to begin, I texted Rory.

Merde, my love. Don't worry about complete perfection. You can't help but be spectacular and that's far better. I love you.

Merde was just a French curse word that, for some reason, ballet dancers used to wish each other good luck. It was a dancerly way of saying "break a leg." Ballroom dancers didn't use it but Rory liked it and I'd overheard her teaching it to her friends. She hadn't taught it to me, probably because I'd been so pissy about her ballet background when I first met her. I was far over that now.

I made my way to the ballroom and watched the team warm-ups. It was odd. The teams were dancing all different styles, and had different numbers of dancers. Some teams were composed of more pros than others. Rory's had only one. Well, two: Pepe plus Rory. They were by far the team leaders. But then, Rory was all I could see.

Mambo Caliente was the second team up. *Good*, I thought. She wouldn't have time to watch the other teams and get nervous or lose her confidence. Adrenaline pumped through my veins, as it likely did hers, as she and her teammates took their places. Rory and Pepe were center stage, as well they should be. My woman looked absolutely divine. Of course. The bright red costume looked brilliant on her. But, yeah, it was loose-fitting. She really had lost weight.

Pepe gave her hand a soft squeeze, and whispered something in her ear. She smiled and squeezed back. Words of encouragement. Pepe was my man.

The pulsing beat of the music blasted on and for a split second my Rory froze. As did I. But I knew it wouldn't last. And it didn't. First-time nerves. Rory was far above all that. Pepe started, right on the second beat, and she followed him perfectly. Yes, I knew she could follow. Maybe she just had to be

27

nervous to her core in order to do so. They began a high-charged series of underarm turns, getting faster all the time, working up to practically the speed of light. Rory's skirt flowed around her. Her spins were simply spectacular.

Pepe whispered something in her ear again. The judges would never notice. It was just something I spotted because I was so focused on her. Then I saw it. Something was wrong. Rory was struggling. I could see it in her eyes. She was dizzy. Blinded, even, by the lights. But her spins remained spot-on, feet landing in perfect position, form immaculate. You'd never notice anything unless you were connected to her, either physically, like Pepe, or mentally, like me.

Then, a series of super-fast spins in a line. Pepe whispered to her again.

She opened her mouth in an O shape, and drew in substantial breath. She was feeling faint. But why? Her spotting was perfect. It wasn't lack of skill. Dizziness simply didn't happen to her during turns.

Thankfully, the spins ended and they went into the tricks, beginning with the snake. She slithered down his leg, wrapping her legs around his ankles, a subtle look of relief in her eye. Momentarily seated, she caught her breath. But the music caught up with her. Pepe pushed her between his legs, and she ducked and slid through. Then he pulled her up to take her into the pot stir—where she'd hurt her knee before. But she couldn't seem to pull herself up. She sat in the stir spin, now closing her eyes, not even trying to spot. Did her knee hurt? It didn't seem so. It was a dizziness issue. I felt it.

But Pepe didn't. When he pulled her up again, this time all the way up into standing position, she lost it. Her face suddenly turned beet red. And her breaths intensified, like she was gasping for air. What the hell? I knew I'd embarrass the hell out of her but I didn't care. I'd gotten up and was about to run toward her when she collapsed and fell into Pepe's arms.

"Rory, Rory," I called out, running to her, yelling for someone to call 911. When I reached her, and took over from Pepe, cradling her in my arms, for some reason, I started babbling in Russian. It was her eating issues. I knew it. She'd fainted for lack of food, energy. I guess I didn't want anyone else to know that, so I spoke in Russian, telling her how sorry I was that I hadn't helped sooner, how I'd selfishly been too focused on our training and the practices we'd missed because of her boss, rather than her health. I knew what was happening. Her anorexia was out of control. And I'd done nothing.

I promised her, still in Russian, that I'd make everything right, and how beautiful and brilliant she was and how she had to know that soon. *Now.* Pepe caught my vibe and spoke in Spanish. I couldn't tell what he was saying but it was likely the same. She briefly opened her eyes, and looked right into mine.

"Sweetheart," I said. But then she began to squint. "What is it?"

"The light behind you. That halo. It's so bright," she said.

Halo?

The lights were really distorting her vision. "I love you, my angel," I said in English, then pressed my lips to her forehead.

She cocked her head and looked at Pepe, and then sideways at Rajiv, who was now standing next to me. I kissed her forehead again.

"Thank God, she's awake," Pepe said.

Rajiv breathed a sigh of relief but the look in his eye said something different. He seemed deeply worried, actually, which scared the hell out of me. She'd told me he was a doctor.

Then I heard another familiar voice I couldn't place coming from behind me.

"Can I please see her? Can I please see her?" It was a male voice.

"Step back, sir, please. We need you all to clear away," someone else said. When I forced myself to look away from Rory, I saw that this speaker was a paramedic. He pushed the man behind me away, then addressed me. "Sir, I need you to stand back so we can help her. Please."

I nodded and released her. "I'll go with you wherever they're taking you, Rory," I said.

"Excuse me, sir, I'm a lawyer, and her fiancé. I would like to accompany her to the hospital."

Now I knew exactly whom that first male voice I'd heard belonged to. *Her fiancé? Please.* They'd broken up months ago now. I turned to see the smug, ruddy face of that bastard boyfriend she'd somehow been unlucky enough to ever meet. He narrowed his eyes at me, but took a step back.

"Uh, this man is actually her boyfriend," Rajiv said, pointing to me. "The one who was holding her and kissing her and telling her he loved her?" Rajiv sounded just as pissed as I was.

"Yes, I would like to accompany her to the hospital," I said to the paramedic.

"Doctor, please. I care greatly about her," squeaked the asshole. I badly wanted to haul off and punch him in the gut but I knew that wouldn't do a damn bit of good. Other than make me feel a lot better.

"Ror—" I began. But no, it would be ridiculous to ask her to choose.

"Okay, you can both get yourselves to the hospital on your own," the paramedic said, squinting back and forth between us. "Please, just stand back while we load her."

"Rory, sweet, I'll be there when you get there. I promise." I gently let go of her hand, begrudgingly doing as the paramedic asked.

"Rory, you passed out during the team performance," Rajiv said to her over my shoulder. You're in Irvine. Don't worry, the paramedics are here and we're all going with you to the hospital."

"What? The paramedics?" she mumbled. She was definitely in a haze. I reached toward her again but the head paramedic grabbed my arm and held me away. "Sir, please. We've got to get her into the van."

"But I don't know where you're taking her," I said, a bit taken aback by his use of force.

"Come on, we'll follow them," Rajiv said, brushing my arm and pulling me toward the door. "It's okay. She's going to be okay," he said once we were outside, obviously seeing the worry in my eyes. I nodded, thanked him.

Rajiv knew where they were going, so I followed him in my car.

Rajiv, Samantha, and I all arrived at the same time. "I know how this works. You can let me do the talking. I mean, if you want," he said while we walked in together.

I nodded. He was a doctor, he was Rory's friend and therefore definitely trustworthy.

"What's up? How is she?" A voice behind me asked, as Rajiv approached the intake desk.

I turned to see Kendra, Rory's friend. Following her were Mitsi, Pepe, and several of Rory's teammates. The lobby was filling with Rory supporters.

Before I could answer, he walked in. The bastard ex. His mouth opened into a wide O as he took a slow survey of the room. *Yes, she has real friends now that she's rid of you, asshole*, I thought. The second our gazes met, he looked away, took a step back from the group of us, turned on his polished Oxford heel and walked quickly toward the front desk. I'd been so pissed at our confrontation before the paramedics, I hadn't even stopped to think. What the hell was he even doing here? How did he know Rory would be performing? Had they been in touch all this time? Why didn't she tell me? I watched him talk to the woman at the desk. Rajiv was no longer there. The ex seemed to be having more difficulty getting information out of her than Rajiv had. I was thinking how thankful I was for Rajiv's presence when he called out to us.

"Okay, here we go," he said, approaching us with a young woman with dark blonde hair held back with a clip. She was dressed in slacks and ballet flats with a medical jacket over her top. She was about twenty-five.

"We're with Rory," Rajiv said, extending his arm toward me.

She looked back and forth between the two of us. "She fainted," she began. She had a deep, stern voice that sounded much older than she looked. I heard footsteps shuffling up behind me. Without turning, I knew it was him.

"Is this about Aurora Laudner?" he called out over my head, sounding almost accusatory. "Because I'm a lawyer and...a very close friend of hers."

The doctor looked at us. Rajiv eyed me. I didn't know what to say. I badly wanted the fucker gone. I didn't know if Rory wanted him here—if she even knew he'd been in the ballroom. What did he want? "We would prefer you just tell us, for now," Rajiv said.

"You know what, it's okay," James said with a sarcastic laugh. "Her family's on their way. We'll catch you after you're done with...these guys."

I could tell without even seeing him he was giving us a condescending glare. *Me.* But his mention of her family made my heart stop. What was going on? Why were they here? Had she told them about her performance without telling me? I knew so little about her family. This was how I'd meet them. He walked away but not without another dramatic sigh.

"Okay," the doctor continued, now speaking in a low tone. "She passed out. I'm not sure at this point what from. We're trying to figure it out. Her blood pressure is low and her heartbeat is irregular, which could simply be an effect of the fainting, or it could signify something more serious."

"Something more serious? Like what, doctor?" I said, hearing the panic in my voice.

"I don't know that right now, sir. We're doing blood tests and an EKG for her heart, and some other tests. I will let you know as soon as I get the results." She gave me a firm nod, then Raj, and walked away.

"What do you think?" I asked him.

He shook his head. "Irregular heartbeat can definitely be from the fainting. From not getting enough oxygen. It could also be the result..." he spoke slowly.

"Of what?" I said.

"Of an eating disorder?" Samantha asked.

He nodded.

"Oh, jeez. I was afraid of that," Pepe said.

"How serious is it?" I asked Rajiv, trying hard not to raise my voice. What had I let happen to her? Her anorexia wasn't my fault, but it was on me for knowing about it and not doing anything. Or not doing enough.

"I don't know yet. She's not that bad, Sasha. She's only lost some weight. I mean, she doesn't weigh, like, ninety. She's probably a good twenty pounds from that. There's still enough time for her to get better," he said. But there was a tentativeness in his voice. And he saw the look in my eyes. He shook his head and looked off to the side and I could read his thoughts: *Don't delude yourself. This isn't going away on its own. Not without a lot of work.*

***

After what seemed like hours, a young man with curly hair came out. "Is there a Sasha here?" he said. I shot up.

"Yes," I said.

"Ms. Laudner is asking for you."

Asking. That meant she was awake and alert. And okay. Yes, okay. I followed him down a long hall and into a room.

My pulse beat hard and fast when I saw her

beautiful but frazzled face. She was lying in a hospital bed, sitting up. Her complexion immediately lit up when I walked in, and she bounced on the bed. Her face was wet with sweat and her cheeks and forehead were red, but she looked radiant. As always.

"Careful with the bouncing," the nurse barked. "I'll leave you alone until the doctor comes back." He gave a cursory nod and closed the door.

Ignoring his advice, Rory sprung up in the bed and I rushed toward her, taking her hand and squeezing tightly before raising it and pressing my lips to her knuckles. Then I bent over the bed and gave her a long but soft kiss on the lips.

"I was so worried," I said, moving my lips to her cheek, then forehead. I put both hands on the bed and knelt down until I was face-level with her. "I saw you having difficulty. You looked like you were sweating too much. You looked like you were having trouble breathing. My heart almost fell out of my body when you collapsed, Rory."

"I'm sorry," she said.

"No. Whatever it was, it's not your fault. My God, I just want you to be okay."

"I'm definitely feeling much better now that you're here." She smiled but held her head down, as if she was embarrassed.

"I'm so sorry they wouldn't let me ride in the ambulance with you. I'm so sorry they made me leave your side. I should have insisted. But I didn't want to cause a scene or anything." I didn't want to mention the asshole. I didn't want to upset her if she didn't know he was there.

"It wasn't your fault. But yeah, that was weird. It sounded chaotic, from what I heard. I heard people

35

saying you were my partner. I heard Rajiv. And it was weird but I thought I heard someone else saying the same thing. I mean, fighting you." She frowned. "But I was in a haze, so…I don't know what I know."

I couldn't let her think she'd hallucinated the whole thing. I nodded. "Yeah. There was. I mean, I don't think there would have been a problem with the ambulance situation if he hadn't been there." I was being pissy and competitive and trying to shift blame. There was no place for this now. What the hell was wrong with me?

"So, there was someone else?" Her eyes widened and I could see confusion and a bit of panic. Now I knew she didn't expect him there.

"Your old boyfriend. At first I didn't recognize him. He wanted to ride with you. He seemed very upset too."

"James? What? He was in the ballroom? I don't understand. That makes no sense. What was he doing there?"

"I don't know. He showed up here too. The medical people spoke with Rajiv and me first. He said—" I stopped. Glad as I was she obviously hadn't spoken with him, this was making her upset. I thought about leaving out what he'd said to the doctor, but decided I had to prepare her.

"What? He said what?" Her voice was laced with panic and I was more pissed than ever that the bastard had shown up like that out of the blue. What was he thinking? "Is my sister okay?" she asked.

I knew next to nothing about her sister. She, like me, hadn't talked much about her family, and I hadn't prodded her. I well understood not wanting to talk about such things, about the past. Especially if it caused any pain. And the way she was speaking, there was pain there.

"He said he was waiting for your family to arrive, then they'd all talk to her—the doctor—together."

Her eyes opened wider and she looked out the window as if to gather her thoughts. I could feel her heart race through her skin. I rubbed my thumb along the fleshy part of her palm, caressing it, not knowing what to say.

She shook her head. "Family has to mean my sister. I mean, my mom's never shown up all the way out here. And if my sister's coming that means…she's okay…" She shook herself out of her reverie and looked at me and shrugged. "I know I've never talked about them but they're close friends. I actually met James through her. So it's not that odd they'd be together. But it's just weird they'd be here."

"I don't know about her but he was at the hotel to watch the performance. Before you fell. He never told you he was coming?"

"No. But I haven't checked my cell phone in a while. A few hours. Maybe there's a message." She began looking around her.

"Oh, your bag's in the lobby with Pepe. I meant to bring it to you. I be right back. *I'll* be right back." My grammar had waned for the first time in a while. "Right back," I repeated, opening the door.

"How is she?" Pepe asked when I got to the lobby.

"Good. She needs her things, though," I said, grabbing her purse.

"Sure thing. Tell her we love her, man!"

I looked around. No James. I nodded and gave Pepe a solid pat on the back before returning to Rory.

"There are messages, sweet," I said, glancing at the phone's face.

As she listened to her voice mail her face paled, the edges of her mouth turned downward, and her eyes narrowed. My stomach took a nosedive. Anyone who upset my love, particularly at a time like this, was my clear enemy.

"They're both from my sister," she said, throwing the phone facedown on her bed. Her voice sounded more angry than upset.

"She's okay?" I sat down next to her and placed my hand atop hers.

She nodded. "She's always okay. Better than okay." I wondered what she meant but let her continue. "James was there. Watching me. He called her when I collapsed and now she's on her way to the hospital. With him. I guess she was in Santa Monica for the weekend. So, lucky me, she just happened to be in town." Rory's voice was full of sarcasm. And her face was growing paler by the second. She looked almost as sick as she did when the paramedics arrived.

"She doesn't live around here?" I didn't know what else to say. There were obviously issues between her sister and her.

"No, she lives in Northern California. She and James met at Stanford." Rory blinked then kept her eyelids half closed.

"Well, she cares," I said, treading lightly.

"She's coming to chew me out," she said, picking the phone up again and looking at it as if it were to blame.

"About what?"

"She doesn't think I should be dancing again. She…" Rory took a breath. "She thinks it will make me sick again. She thinks it's...stupid, and I should be happy being a lawyer, like her. She's a great lawyer. So, good for her, but it's not for everyone, you know?"

"Yes, of course. But...what do you mean by sick?" My stomach took another nosedive. *Anorexia.*

She took another breath and looked off toward the corner. "When I was a teenager and dancing ballet, I developed...an eating disorder. My mom pulled me from the program. It was a really prestigious program too. In New York. I was so upset. I wanted it so badly. My dad had just died and he wasn't there to be on my side."

She took another breath and I could tell she was holding back tears. I rubbed her shoulder. I remembered her broaching the subject of her former dance life once before, and she hadn't wanted to talk much about it. A sore spot. I hadn't pushed, and now wish I would have. At least a little bit.

"She insisted I was too vulnerable to be a dancer," she went on. "And that dancing was a waste of time and I'd never make a living. It was like being a prostitute, to her. She insisted I go to college and law school like my sister. Make a responsible, respectable living. And that's how I screwed up my life." She looked down again, placed her hands on her legs and ran them the length of her thighs, as if to test their size.

I should have known she'd had an eating disorder before. And that dance had brought it back. I saw the signs. I knew other ballet dancers who'd had it too. I was an idiot for not seeing it.

I brushed my fingers up and down her arm, then placed my hands over her hands, and traced her thighs along with her. She looked up at me and smiled weakly.

"Perhaps it won't be as bad as you think," I offered. "Seeing her, I mean."

She shook her head. "No, I could hear the absolute disgust in her voice when she said the word 'dance.'" I placed my finger on her cheek and traced the beautiful architecture of her face. She finally cracked a smile. "When they get here, you have to stay with me," she said.

"Of course I will."

Just then the door opened and a young Asian woman wearing a lab coat stepped in. She was reading some kind of printout, a concerned frown on her face.

"Hello, Ms. Laudner," she said, finally looking up at Rory. Then her eyes shot to me. I now saw her nametag. She was a doctor. She had a soft, round face but a severe look in her eyes, similar to the one the earlier doctor had.

Rory looked back and forth between the doctor and me.

"We need to talk," the doctor said, eyes fixing on me. "Would you please excuse us, sir?"

"Oh, he can stay," Rory said. "He's my partner."

The doctor looked at me again. "Okay," she said cautiously. She pulled up a chair, and sat. "The good news is that there's nothing wrong with your heart...yet."

"Yet?" Rory and I said in unison.

"Your blood work shows that you have mild hypoglycemia, which is low blood sugar. You've got to eat more often than you do to keep your blood sugar up. You've got to eat more than do you in general, Ms. Laudner. Your body mass index is well below what it should be for your age. Well below." She looked at Rory straight on. "Ms. Laudner, the paramedics detected an irregular heartbeat. From your EKG it looks like it's a murmur at this point. But I must tell you, Ms. Laudner, starving yourself of important nutrients can have a long-term effect on your heart."

"Starving myself?" Rory said.

"Have you lost a lot of weight recently?" Her tone was not yet accusatory but I was worried it could turn into that. That wasn't what Rory needed. But I knew I couldn't protect her from everything. And she needed to be confronted with this.

Rory laughed nervously. "I don't feel like it but it's funny because people are telling me I have, and my dance costume is fitting a little loosely."

"There's nothing funny about anorexia," the doctor quipped.

"Well, I didn't mean ha-ha funny," Rory said.

"She has, doctor. Lost a lot of weight, I mean," I interjected, trying to deflect the building annoyance between the two, and trying to help out by adding another perspective, hoping Rory would understand. "But just in the last two or three months," I added, picking up Rory's hand and caressing her palm.

The doctor nodded. "Thank you," she said to me before turning back to Rory. "When was the last time you ate? And what did you eat?"

"I, I had a glass of fresh-squeezed orange juice just this morning," Rory stuttered, lifting her chin. I could tell she felt on the defensive. And she was. Unfortunately, it was for her own good.

"How big?" the doctor said.

Rory released her hand from me to show the doctor the height of the glass.

"Is that how much liquid was in it?"

She showed her the amount of liquid with her fingers.

"Okay, what else?"

"A piece of cake that my teammate made for a celebration," Rory said.

"Really?" The doctor sounded dubious.

"Yes," Rory said, straightening her back.

"Anything else?"

"Some blueberries in the morning and ten walnuts on the bus."

The doctor wrote everything down. "Okay and yesterday?"

Rory glanced at me, I assumed because she needed help remembering. "Last night I had a glass of this kale-celery-apple juice Sasha makes and insists I drink," she said, motioning to me with a little laugh.

I smiled and nodded at the doctor. She made a note and turned her straight-lipped mouth back to Rory. "What else?"

"Um, I had a pretty bad day at work and actually, I think besides that, I had only half a banana in the morning, and a bottle of mineral water."

"Okay. And how large was the glass of juice?"

Rory shook her head and shrugged. "I mean, regular size."

"She did drink the whole thing, doctor," I added.

After Rory continued listing the contents of her meals for the last week, as well as she could remember, the doctor told her she was going to release her but only on the condition that when she got back to L.A. she saw a psychologist as well as a nutritionist. Rory's eyes widened. A psychologist did sound serious. But I was glad for the doctor's pushing; this could not be allowed to grow any worse. Any help she could get was a good thing. She gave Rory a list of referrals and said she was putting in a call to her current primary care doctor to make sure Rory followed her advice.

"You think I'm actually anorexic?" Rory asked, worry tingeing her voice. "I just thought that was so over."

"Not full-blown. Yet. You have anorexia spectrum disorder. You *are* eating. You're just under-eating and if you continue to do that, or you eat even less, you'll continue to weaken your heart. That could have very serious consequences, Ms. Laudner. And you're so physical, the next collapse could be from a heart attack. I'm not exaggerating."

My heart fell. I grabbed Rory's hand again and squeezed it firmly. Her pulse had increased as exponentially as mine. She took a breath, but looked away from both me and the doctor.

"I don't mean to frighten you," the doctor said. "But your heart is the last thing you want to damage. See your doctor first thing when you get back and she'll hook you up with good people."

"Thank you, doctor," I said.

After she left, I leaned over and wrapped my arms wholly around Rory, cocooning her small body into mine. She was shaking. Or maybe that was me, with anger at myself. "I'm so sorry. I knew something was wrong. I just didn't know it was so bad. I will do everything I can to help, my princess. Everything," I repeated, then kissed her forehead and her cheek. I'd begun trailing kisses down her neck when the door opened again.

We both looked up. It was the nurse.

"There are two people here requesting to see you, miss," he said.

"Okay, you can send them in," Rory said.

"We can't have more than two visitors at a time. I have to ask your friend to step out for a moment." He gestured to me.

"Oh, well then they can see me one at a time—"

"It's okay," I said, giving her forehead another peck before releasing her. "I want to go down to cafeteria and get juice anyway. I can let them have you. But only for a few seconds, of course," I joked.

"I'll miss you," she said, reaching out to me melodramatically as I walked to the door. I turned and blew her a kiss.

I was expecting to see Rajiv and Samantha or Pepe and Mitsi, but instead I locked eyes with a very dramatic-looking young woman, probably around thirty, with long, onyx hair and large, bright green cat eyes. Her face was perfectly made up and she wore a dark professional-looking dress and high, patent leather black pumps. She carried a Gucci bag, and her neck and earlobes were adorned with pearls. She gave me a once-over, then returned my gaze, and narrowed her eyes at me. Then I locked eyes with the man behind her—James. Of course. With the stress of the doctor's report, I'd forgotten about Rory's sister.

James glared for about half a second before turning his gaze to the back of the sister's shiny head. This guy was a supreme joke. He was ridiculously intimidated by me, and needed her for support. I looked back at her. She continued to glower.

"Excuse us," she said, her voice low and laden

with judgment. I hesitated before stepping away from the door. I'd told Rory I'd stay with her during their visit. "I said, excuse us," she repeated, speaking with more enunciation, as if she thought I might not know English. When I still didn't move, she harrumphed and circled around me, bumping my shoulder as she opened the door. "Ugh," she moaned, rubbing her arm as if I'd hurt her.

"Hi, sweetie," she said, opening the door. It occurred to me I didn't even know her name yet.

James tried to follow her in but he was larger and it was harder for him to circumvent me.

"So, how are we feeling?" the sister said, her voice syrupy sweet.

"Are you going to let me through?" James said loudly, as if to let the sister know he was being held back and needed her help.

I said nothing, leaving Rory to decide whether I should let the asshole by.

"Rory, please," the sister said with a laugh.

"Sasha, it's okay," she said. "You can go get the juice. But come right back, please." I turned to her. She had a worried, insecure look in her eye, but nodded. *I should do what she says, not what I think is best*, I told myself. I stepped aside all of an inch, let the asshole through.

"Jeez, is he in the Russian mafia or something? Talk about thuggish," I heard the sister say under her breath to James as the asshole pulled the door closed. Rory likely didn't hear; she said it more for my ears. I took a deep breath to calm myself. Now was not the time for a fight. I stayed at the door, listening through the crack. I wasn't about to leave until I knew it was okay.

"I'm feeling a lot better," Rory said, answering the sister's earlier question, wisely ignoring whatever else she might have heard. "Now that I have fluids in me, and after talking to the doctor. I know what I need to do and I already have a plan to set things in motion for when I get back to L.A." Rory's words were wonderfully assertive but her voice was shaky. Her sister really made her nervous.

There was a pause as the sister seemed to move away from the door, closer to the bed. "Oh honey, you do look incredibly thin. I, I feel so badly I haven't been around much for you. And I know you guys had that fight, but I just, I thought James was taking care…" She stopped without finishing that thought.

So, she believed her little sister needed to be taken care of? And by this pathetic excuse of a man?

No one said anything for a moment. Then the sister continued. "Anyway…what is this about all this dancing you've been doing? It seems to have gotten very serious."

Rory was completely right about the way her sister spoke about dance. She had nothing but disdain for our art.

"Yeah, I'm training with this Russian ballroom dancer, Sasha, for the largest competition in the world. He's currently ranked number two in the world in Latin dance, and we're trying hard to shoot for number one, so…I have my work cut out for me!" Rory nearly shouted.

She was met with silence.

"I mean, not today," she continued. "Today was just for fun. I joined a mambo team at the studio Sasha teaches at, just for fun. I thought being on a team would be fun, and competing before the big competition would be a good experience and a lot of fun." She was definitely full of nerves. She was, as she'd often put it, blabbering badly.

"Was passing out from anorexia fun?" the sister asked, using Rory's word against her.

I had to restrain myself from pushing open the door and going back in.

"Jacqueline, be careful," James said, coming to Rory's rescue, unbelievably.

"I'm sorry. That was a little too harsh, too soon," the sister—Jacqueline, apparently—said. She did have the air of a typical lawyer, able to crush you with words uttered ever so innocently.

"You don't need to worry about me. I don't even have anorexia," Rory said. "The doctor said it was only spectrum and she gave me a plan to follow. I'll be fine."

"Like last time?" Jacqueline said with an audible snicker.

"Yes, exactly like last time," Rory shot back, her voice now sounding less shaky. "I overcame it, remember?"

"Rory! You only overcame it after you left that stupid dance school and went to college!" This time Jacqueline yelled.

That was enough. I opened the door a smidgeon, peeking inside. Rory was grabbing the bed rail with one hand, using the other to gather up some of the bedding with her fist. She brightened when she saw me. "Are you okay?" I asked her.

"Sir, sir, please," came a voice behind me. "I told you, only two visitors at a time."

I didn't budge.

"Please, I need to help my sister," Jacqueline said

in my direction, not even fully turning to face me. Disgust tinged her voice.

"Don't you dare talk to him like that," Rory said.

"Rory, Rory, please, just talk to us a little while longer. Just hear us out." This was from James.

"I'm going to have to ask one of you to leave." The nurse opened the door wider.

I eyed James, giving him the nastiest don't-you-fucking-dare-go-near-her glare I think I'd ever issued in my life. James turned to me, caught my scowl, and this time actually physically backed away from me.

"It's okay, honey, I can handle them," Rory said to me, with a confident smile that suddenly looked genuine. "But thank you!"

"I'm right out here if you need me," I said to her, shooting James one last glower.

I smiled back at my lovely Rory, her face still radiating with assuredness, and slowly stepped away.

"Thank you," said the nurse, closing the door behind me.

"You called him 'honey.' Rory, is that your boyfriend?" Jacqueline practically screeched.

"Obviously. And he's a him, not a that," Rory said, her voice now forceful.

"Psssht," Jacqueline said. "Okay, so now I see it. You've become obsessed with this Russian guy and you're giving up your whole life for him and some pipe dream."

Rory said nothing. I could feel her fuming.

"I mean, if you're doing all this training and competing, you're obviously not working that hard at your job," Jacqueline continued. "When I was a first-year associate I was at the office eighty hours a week, at least, to prove myself. Rory, your bosses have to realize your lack of passion." There was a pause. Then, "Rory, stop glaring at me. I'm trying to help you. You're my sister and I can't watch you spiraling out of control so early in your career."

"I'm actually taking some time off from my job. I'm focusing on dance right now," Rory said matter-of-factly. I wondered if she'd actually made that decision or was just saying that to piss her sister off. I hoped the former.

"Oh my God, are you serious? After all that work you put into your career. The LSAT, law school, the bar exam. All that money? You're going to let it go, just like that?"

"Stop being so melodramatic," Rory said. "It's only a few months."

"She doesn't sound ridiculous at all," James piped in. "The market is so tight these days. The field is saturated with too many attorneys. Starting attorneys are taking temporary document review positions forever. It's crazy competitive."

"You know what? Why don't you stay out of it?" Rory snapped. "What are you even doing here? How did you even find me?"

"That's right. If you leave your career now, even for a short time, it will be obvious your passion isn't there." I couldn't believe how brazen Jacqueline was, completely ignoring her sister's question. "Especially if you leave for something as ridiculous as dance," she continued. "You'll never get another law job. I'm not exaggerating here, Rory. I've been around. I've seen it happen to other attorneys. I know what I'm talking about." Jacqueline's voice was so serious, so frantic. It made me shudder.

I certainly didn't want Rory not to be able to

return to her profession in the future, if she wanted to. As much as I wanted her to dance with me, for now and forever, I didn't want to limit her life choices.

There was a long pause. No one spoke for a while. Then James did.

"Rory, that actually hurts. Telling me to stay out of it. I still care about you. Deeply. In fact, I recently realized how much I still feel for you and how wrong I was to get angry with you over taking a single ballroom class. I feel like if I would have been supportive, you wouldn't have gotten so carried away with this, and we'd still be together."

I wanted to kill him. I really did. But I trusted that Rory could take care of him herself now.

"I missed you," he went on. "I tried to call but you didn't answer. So I went to the studio. I thought I'd find out which classes you were signed up for and take one…" There was another pause. Rory must have shot him a bemused look because then he chuckled. "I know, me taking a dance class. Hilarious. I just… Rory, I should have never let you go. I was going through a lot. I really missed my job at the firm, doing corporate litigation. I really didn't like entertainment law. I really didn't like working for celebrities. They're just such vapid…ugh. Anyway, when you started dancing, I just, I guess I started thinking of all the TV shows about dance and I just started thinking of you like all the obnoxious a-list, a-hole, so-called artists we represented. I just… I took it all out on you. And I'm sorry. I really am."

She was not going to go back to him. She was not. I knew she was not.

"Are you trying to get your old job back, then?"

Rory asked, her voice devoid of emotion.

"Already did!"

"Well, good. I'm glad to hear that," she said. "It's important to do what you want, to be happy. No point being miserable, is there?" Poor pathetic asshole; this so wasn't what he wanted to hear.

There was silence for a moment, and then he said, "Is that...I mean, are you really together?"

"Yes," Rory said firmly. "Sasha's both my dance partner and boyfriend now. And I'm really happy."

Jacqueline loudly harrumphed and stomped around the room in her high heels. But now Rory ignored her. "By the way, what happened to that girl you were seeing?" Rory said.

"What girl?" James asked.

"James!" Rory laughed. "That girl I caught you having sex with on the couch!"

News to me. *Major, major asshole.* I should have known it.

"Don't be ridiculous, Rory. We weren't..." He tried to laugh it off. She wasn't having it. "It was over, like, right after that. It was never serious. She was just... Anyways, so you're dancing in the world's biggest championship? Is that what you said? It sounds cool."

This guy was about fifty times worse than I thought. *Don't fess up to anything. Try to pretend you care about her. After you fucking cheated on her. You bastard.*

"It's the biggest and most prestigious ballroom competition in the world," she chirped, not caring too much, apparently, about what a shithead he was, instead excited to talk about Blackpool. "It's in England. The winners are like royalty. Sasha won in the junior division a few years ago and he's been second in the top pro division ever since. Second only to his old partner. You should see the offers he gets to perform all over the world, and choreograph for TV and movies and teach at big ballroom boot camps. He practically has another house in Tokyo, he's there so often performing."

I swallowed hard. She still didn't know what was going on in Tokyo. I'd have to tell her. *Someday.*

"We're going to do it this year. We're going to get there together. We're going to win."

This was worth standing at the door eavesdropping for, to hear this certainty, this expression of commitment, of absolute devotion to what was now not only my dream but hers as well. I knew she would overcome her problem. There was no way she was letting it get in our way. She was going to be perfectly fine. How could I have ever doubted?

But no one inside the room said anything. Not a word.

"Excuse me, sir," the nurse said, nudging me away from the door. I thought he was going to admonish me to keep farther away, but apparently he needed to see Rory.

"They're going to release you soon," he said, darting in. "In preparation, I have to take your blood pressure again. Your friends can stay for this, if they like."

"No, they were just about to leave," Rory said.

And I loved her for that. Making their decision.

"I really appreciate you coming, Jax, you guys. I promise we will keep in touch better and I'll keep you updated on my progress. And, yes, we can remain friends." The latter was obviously to James, as she emphasized the last word, which was still, in my opinion, being way the hell too nice to the guy.

"Of course," James said.

"I'll be checking in on you frequently. You can count on that," Jacqueline said, her voice drenched with supremely condescending bitchiness.

Poor Rory. The shit I had to deal with from my family was of an altogether different sort. Hers was pretty bad too.

***

"Are you a celebrity or something?" the nurse asked, sounding completely serious as he walked beside me while I wheeled Rory out to the lobby. The nurse had insisted she be wheeled out instead of walking, which Rory tried to contest, but neither of us would let her. She finally gave in when I promised I would be in control of the chair.

"Of course not!" Rory said, embarrassed. "Why?"

Her question was answered when we rounded the corner and she received a huge round of applause. All of her friends from the studio were still here, waiting, hours later.

"Oh my gaaawd," cried Samantha, running toward her.

They hugged, Rory still seated. "What? Oh my gosh, I can't believe you came!"

"By this point, I think you know me." Samantha laughed.

Rajiv stood next to her, and Rory hugged him, followed by Kendra, Pepe, Mitsi, and each of her teammates in turn. "Everyone's so nice to…to care…" Suddenly, she burst into tears.

"No, don't cry, *florecita*. You're okay. Sasha says you're going to be okay!" Pepe yelped.

"No, I'm just so sorry I let you all down. You guys are so great and, just compared to my fam— You guys are just great, that's all—"

"Nah, none of that," Pepe insisted. "I know what you're going to say and no worries. Believe me. We didn't place, meaning we didn't place last. So our record's still clean. And they felt sorry enough for us that the competition organizer's letting us compete without paying any fees at his next one. In Miami. In July. You see what I'm saying, *chiquita*? You ended up saving us a shit-ton of money! That competition is way the hell more expensive than this one!"

CHAPTER THREE

Rory returned to work on Monday, with a doctor's note that she'd spent Saturday in the ER. Of course she was still worried Gunther would be pissed she wasn't able to prepare for Jamar's case and, worse, that they'd lose important hearing issues because of her.

"It's not your fault, sweet," I insisted. "If he actually had left it all up to you last minute, it's his fault. But I'm sure you can get the court to give an extension. You were in the friggin' ER, Rory." I threw my hands up. This would make a mockery of the justice system here if they didn't give her a break. "Text me as soon as you have time. Let me know what happened."

She nodded.

The hearing didn't happen today! It's not for another week. He lied. Can you believe it? she texted an hour later.

Y E S, I wrote back. The man was a psycho, to put it mildly. How did this woman get these people in her life?

He said he already did the hearing papers since he knew I wouldn't. Now he's having me do all this stupid boring work.

He didn't even ask me how I was, she wrote. I was just about to write back when she texted again. *Can't talk. G's here. Talk 2nite.*

"If I didn't want to work on Jamar's case so badly, I'd have no problem leaving," she said that evening before Greta arrived. Tears lined her lower eyelids but she didn't allow herself to cry. "I know he's crazy. He said he'd never told me that the hearing was today. He claimed he'd just needed it done by then. He lies through his teeth. I'm working for a pathological liar. I don't know what to do. Maybe something to talk with my new shrink about, as soon as I see her."

"Definitely." I hugged her and held her in my arms, running my fingers gently down her back. I'd worked for plenty of crazy people. That was part of being a dancer, part of being Russian. You just took their crap and did it. But this was another place. And she had choices. But she had to make them herself. She knew what I wanted. An objective third party would be good.

Greta gave her an awesome lecture when she arrived later that night. Rory had agreed to let me tell her about the situation, especially when I told her Greta had already figured something was up.

"I can't believe everyone saw it," Rory said to me, sounding bewildered.

"Not everyone. Just people who care. And, I mean, I guess that's not uncommon with psychological stuff, you know. Others see it before the person suffering does. That's why it's a psychological thing. Logic doesn't always apply here." My turn to blabber. I had to admit I'd personally feel like an ass if I had a psychological problem that everyone saw but me. But it was different with her. Eating disorders among dancers were sneaky.

"That makes sense. You always make sense." She smiled, burrowing herself into my chest. I kissed the crown of her head.

"You don't win a competition for being thin," Greta boomed. "You don't win a competition for the way you look at all." I stood behind her, nodding in agreement. "At least not in Latin. Seriously, look at all the dancers who have won. Look at me. Look at this." She flexed her bicep, making Rory laugh. "I am serious. Look at my thighs. They are not skin and bone. I work out hard for these muscles. And look at Micaela and Xenia. We all have muscles, we all have curves. They look far better than skin and bone in Latin," she said with a sly smile.

Rory raised her eyebrows and nodded.

"And how do you get these shapely muscles?" Greta continued. "Protein plus working out. If you want to obsess about everything you put in your body, please be my guest. We all do that. You don't need white bread, you don't need potatoes. So eat spinach. It weighs nothing. You don't feel fat after you eat it. You feel like you eat nothing. You eat the green leaves, you eat the nuts, you eat the salmon. You're not going to get fat, I promise you," she finished, her English grammar becoming sloppier the more excited she became.

"With you around, I'm not going to need that nutritionist." Rory laughed.

I went to the kitchen and returned to the ballroom with a bottle of tasty carrot-celery-apple juice in one hand, and a champagne glass in the other. I looked at Rory with puppy dog eyes and held both out to her. She smiled and took them.

She'd agreed to drink all of the juices I prepared for her. Three a day, plus two balanced meals. She'd made it more than clear she was so focused on winning Blackpool that she'd never let something stupid like this—her words—ruin our chances. So we'd agreed I'd make it easy on her and at least prepare the juices, if not the meals. I was a half-decent cook, if I did say so myself.

We started our practicing slowly, as the doctor recommended. The first few nights, Rory simply regained her strength, watching Greta and me. While drinking my juice, of course.

We'd planned to ratchet everything up that weekend. But of course Friday night, Gunther's inner mental case reared its ugly soul. Although he'd told Rory he did Jamar's papers himself since he couldn't trust her, and wouldn't allow her to work on the case all week, an hour before she was to meet me Friday night, his story changed. Nothing was actually done; everything needed to be completed over the weekend. I wasn't surprised anymore by his antics. Sadly, Rory still expected differently.

"Sasha, I can work hard on the case tonight, tomorrow and Sunday night, and we can have Saturday night and Sunday morning. I'll make up the time right after this hearing is over, I promise."

"Don't worry about the time, sweetie. We'll make it up," I told her, trying hard to hide my frustration. The hearing was two days away. We could work extra hard next week. But deep down I knew it was going to be a real problem. If Gunther really was going to have her as second chair on the case, she'd be very busy for the next couple of months—prime rehearsal time for Blackpool. I had no idea how we were going to do this. But right now, while she was in the midst of panic over the hearing, I didn't voice any of that. I'd figure it out later.

I drove to her office and picked her up around midnight. She held this huge litigation bag in her little arms. One look at her told me how dead tired she was.

"You know what?" I said, walking her to her front door. "Let's take the weekend off and just kill it beginning Monday." I couldn't believe what I was saying. I just didn't want her eating problems to return, and I didn't want her reinjuring herself over stress and lack of sleep. Plus I knew we wouldn't accomplish much if her head was elsewhere. I didn't want to get mad at her and make it worse. This was her big case—the only one she cared about—and this important part of it would be over in two days.

"Sasha, we can't—"

"Why don't you call me tomorrow night, *if* you feel like taking a bit off, and you can come over for dinner and watch Greta and me again?" I said, realizing if she spent the whole weekend without me, she might not eat much. Plus, could I really be without her for all that time?

As I knew, her mind wasn't completely with us Saturday night. I could tell she was rehearsing notes for her argument. I could even see her lips move. Panic surged through me when I thought about Blackpool, about the time we were missing, but I forced myself to stop thinking. *Let it be, for now. Let her be.*

It was sweet how committed she was to this client she knew was innocent. She had a tough, very serious job. And she was eating. I'd prepared some delicious goat cheese tarts and a huge spinach, cranberry and walnut salad. It took her a while, but she finished it all.

"Call or text the second it's over and let me know how it went," I said when I dropped her off at work Monday morning. I wasn't letting her carry that giant litigation bag on the subway. "And sweetheart, *merde*."

"Oh Sasha, thank you!" She giggled.

***

It was horrible, she texted later that day.

What happened? I wrote back.

The police officers cllaimed they didnt know there was anythrhin wrong with his menwal capabilitity . They didn't think it was weird at all he couldnt write his name even though they thought he was 19 years old. They didn't think he spoke slowowly and thjouhg he was faking his severr headache. Judge sia d there wasn't enough evidewne he was corenced, or that he was mentally ill, not even enough to have him examined or his IQ tested b4 goint 2 trial. I hate the system. I HATE it.

Wow. Her writing was fast and furious and chock-full of misspellings, which was totally unlike her. I could tell how upset she was. But I got most of what she was trying to say. *I'm so sorry, sweetheart.*

Thank you. I'll be off at normal time tonight. Can be at your place by seven.

I love you.

Me too, gotta gbo, guntehr!

***

I picked her up at her apartment and drove her to my place. I knew she was still upset and I didn't want her driving. She laughed at my alpha male-ness but I insisted. And it was a good thing I drove because she had a mini-breakdown in the car.

"They're admitting his confession. The evidence is so stacked against him. I swear those boys planned the whole thing and scapegoated him. And his confession is totally coerced because the police totally suggested to him what to say. How could they not know he was mentally deficient? How could the judge not care even with the mother's admission he was epileptic and 'daft' and the trial testimony from his brother's trial that people actually called him a 'retard'? That's on record. How can the judge not order an examination before proceeding to trial if someone has been called retarded by his peers? I just don't get it. I don't."

I put my free hand on her knee and rubbed. I didn't know what to say. I felt as she did. The judge was an idiot. She apologized for crying. I told her to stop it; she could do whatever she wanted in front of me. It was me, for God's sakes.

It was hard for her to concentrate during practice, as we both knew it would be. She kept making mistakes. She kept apologizing. And I kept telling her to stop apologizing. I couldn't really tell her to try to concentrate better, because it wasn't really her fault she wasn't. And it didn't help for me to correct her. She already knew what she was doing wrong. Greta wasn't there this time to act as a go-between; it was only the two of us.

Finally I turned off the music. "I know you know all of these steps like the back of your hand. It's in your muscle memory now and I know you can do this. And you know it too. We're not making progress because your mind is elsewhere."

"I know, I'm sor—" she began.

But I stopped her. "No, you don't need to keep saying that." I took a deep breath. As much as I didn't want to cut our practice short again, it had to be. "Maybe we should just stop for now and you talk about what happened today. Get it out of your system. As much as you can, anyway."

"Oh! Sasha, we need to practice. Well…really? Thank you."

She felt the same way I did—we were missing valuable time, continuously. But there didn't seem to be a way around it right now. She needed to talk it out. The car wasn't enough. She needed more. She walked to me, let herself fall into me. I wrapped my arms tightly around her and held her up, rocking her, pressing my lips to the crown of her head.

"I just feel like this system is such a let-down to the people who need it. My first client, who was friggin' schizophrenic and didn't understand anything happening to him. And now Jamar. Judges won't look past facades and the case law to see the real human beings whose lives they're affecting. I just can't imagine not wanting to know whether a defendant is mentally handicapped or insane before you put them on trial or give them a prison sentence. Like that wouldn't in any way be relevant to what they're charged with, how they acted, their level of culpability. They're just bad people. Period."

I rubbed her back, trailed kisses down to her forehead. "You've gotten to know these people through interviews and reading their files and talking to their parents. They're your clients. You see them as individuals. The judges can't. They only see facts and laws." I walked with her to the couch where we snuggled, she in a fetal position, my body cradling hers. "Hopefully, the jury trial will be different," I continued. "You'll have actual people in the community, not just judges and their laws. You can show them the human being." I said this because I knew Gunther was an asshole but not stupid. He needed Rory at trial. She'd be there. She'd be running the show if he was really smart.

Of course I wanted more than anything to concentrate on Blackpool. But this case was going to be with her over the next several months, throughout the rest of our training period, and into the competition itself. I had no idea how we were going to handle the two together. But I knew now Rory needed this one case. She needed to do well at this one case. Her client's life may well depend on it. I couldn't interfere.

She scrunched herself up farther into a ball, seeming to bask in the sensation of being cocooned by me.

"Mmmm, this is my profession, not yours. And yet you're so right. So wise. I feel like nothing can hurt me in your arms. I haven't ever felt like this before with anyone, Sasha. Except my dad. And that was a long time ago."

I squeezed her harder. I wanted to know more about her dad. She had a wound that hadn't completely healed. But I seemed to be helping with that. "Your clients are so lucky to have you, Rory. You really care about them." I rocked her gently back and forth.

CHAPTER FOUR

My beautiful, brave Rory was resilient, and the very next evening she was back at it. She slugged down a glass of kale-apple juice, then declared she was ready to work her ass off.

"I feel soooo out of shape and I know I'm out of practice. I'm ready to make up all that time I lost. I'm ready to nail this!" she declared.

Greta shot me her customary one-raised-eyebrow look as if to say, *What's really going on?*

"Was work okay, Rory?" I finally asked.

She shrugged. "Gunther has me working on other stuff. Says he doesn't need me for the trial."

I scoffed. "Yes, he will."

"I know. He'll throw it at me right before and I won't be able to prepare in time and I'll stress out and it'll ruin our Blackpool and we won't win Jamar's case anyway because he'll sabotage us." She said this all in one breath, her words coming out in a rush. "So you know what? I'm just not going to care. I'm not in charge and there's nothing I can do about it. I have no control. The only thing I have control over is this. Doing well. Winning." She held her arm out to me.

"So come on. We can do this." She ended on a genuine smile, with another shrug.

I took her offer, took her arm. I didn't want her giving up on her client. And I knew she ultimately wouldn't. We had to work hard now, be as perfect as possible, for when she did get busy again.

Our rehearsal went the best it ever had. Rory knew what her problem areas were. I didn't even need to tell her what was off because she knew it already. And when she made a mistake, she wouldn't continue with the routine until she got it perfectly. She was reminding me of myself, for better or for worse.

And we continued like that for a good three weeks, improving by the day, by the minute. I attributed it at least partly to the psychologist. Of course I wanted badly to ask what decisions they were making about her job, but didn't. That was between her and the shrink.

Rory was also improving on the nutrition front. She consistently drank at least two of my juices per day, and made sure she had at least two meals that included vegetables and protein. I cooked one at night, and sometimes even packed her a little lunch for the next day.

"You're like my mommy," she'd said, laughing. "Well, the mom I never had."

She'd laughed but there was pain in her eyes and I wondered how often she spoke with anyone in her family. Jacqueline seemed more intent on bossing her around and judging than showing her she truly cared. I wondered if she ever followed up after the hospital. But I didn't ask. I figured Rory would take the initiative when she was ready. It wasn't like I'd opened up about my family either.

***

But when we drove up to my designer's office in Malibu to order our Blackpool costumes, I realized that even though Rory's eating had improved, her self-confidence regarding her body was not fully there yet. Perhaps. Or perhaps our fight was about something else.

"You're going to love Daiyu," I told her in the car, cruising our way up the beautiful Pacific Coast Highway along the beach.

"Pretty name. Is it Russian?" Rory asked.

"No, Chinese. She's young, and she has a great aesthetic sensibility. You're going to love her," I repeated.

She laughed and shook her head, and this time I knew what about: my use of English.

"She does have a great aesthetic sensibility." I laughed back. "Seriously, that's why I chose her as our sponsor for Blackpool. And probably the Worlds."

"Sponsor? What does that mean?"

I kept forgetting Rory didn't know the world of professional ballroom comps.

"It means she pays for us—our airfare, our meals, our room and board, our competition fees, fees for hair, makeup, and bronzing, massages, waxes—you name it. Well, along with our shoe designer—they pay a little as well. Daiyu will give us two costumes. Actually, three—"

"Whoa, that's a lot of money." Rory raised her eyebrows. "A lot."

I laughed. Rory was a sweet novice. She didn't

know just how vast the world of the ballroom-obsessed was. "It's nothing compared to what she'll make back."

"Really? How?"

"Because of all the adverts and PR we do for her. Every major ballroom store you go into for the next year and beyond, you'll see a big poster of us in her clothes, with her watermark etched over us. You know how many people competing in the student or amateur pro/ams want to be dressed by the costumer to the stars?" Rory burst out giggling. "Yes, okay it sounds cocky of me to say. But you gotta get used to it, Rore. You're a star dancer."

She sobered, took a breath.

"You're up to it, believe me," I said, giving her thigh a squeeze. "Come on, you wanted a pro ballet career."

"Exactly. I guess I'll see now what that would have been like."

I realized her sobering wasn't about her thinking she wasn't up to it, but her reflecting on the past. I gave her thigh another squeeze.

"Wait, so you said three costumes?" she asked, lifting herself out of her reverie.

"Yes, finalists—and we are definitely expected to final, of course—wear one costume for the first several rounds, then change at the semifinal point, into another costume."

Another deep breath. "Wow. That's very cool. I'm starting to feel like Cinderella."

I squeezed again. "No one deserves this more than you."

She giggled again. My favorite sound in the world. "So, what's the third costume for?"

"What? Oh, the team match."

"The team match?"

I kept forgetting how little Rory's exposure was, all that she didn't know. If I wasn't careful I was going to forget to tell her something major. "Yeah, that's just a little thing at the beginning. They invite the four countries with the most top-ranked dancers to compete in a little team match. It means nothing but it's fun for spectators and it's good for the dancers because it allows you to warm up and kind of see how the judges are judging, what they're thinking. And, for you, it will be important so you can dance on the big ballroom floor before it really counts. I wasn't sure we were going to be asked to participate since we are a new partnership, and thus without a ranking. But the new judges have changed the rules so that one very high-ranked partner would mean the partnership's inclusion on the team."

"Of course, I can't imagine a big competition of any sort and you not being asked to participate," she gushed.

"Well…true," I said, laughing. Maybe cocky of me to admit, but true.

***

"Wow, they're…expensive-looking," Rory said in a dreamlike tone, as we entered the store. She fingered the costumes on display, looking like a little girl in a candy store.

"Hello, hello," Daiyu said, emerging through the red velvet curtains that led to her back room. "So nice to meet you. I am Daiyu," she said to Rory, giving her a slight bow. "Welcome to my store, Daiyu Dance."

"So nice to meet you too," Rory said sweetly. "I just love your designs. The fabric's so plush and rich and the embroidering and the stones are so... Just divine." My girl was in heaven.

"Oh, you're so nice. Thank you so much," Daiyu said. "Sasha," she said, turning to me.

"How have you been?"

"Great, thank you. Very busy! Very, very busy! Thanks to you!"

"No, no, thanks to your immense skill," I said, nodding at Rory. She raised her eyebrows in return.

"Thank you," Daiyu said with another slight bow. "So, you have ideas? Or you want to see catalog?" Daiyu's tone was always so animated, her eyes so bright and wide. She actually reminded me of Rory. They both saw the world with an almost childlike wonder. Not childish, but innocent-like.

"A catalog would be gre—" Rory began, just as I said, "I think we know what we want."

Rory and I looked at each other.

Daiyu laughed.

"Okay, why don't you take a flip through some of the catalogs, then, and I'll point out anything that looks like what I'm thinking," I said. I didn't want to be there all day, but I saw how Rory was eyeing the large books. I was enjoying her girl-in-the-candy-store delight too much.

"Wow," Rory said, her eyes widening as she turned the first few pages. "I mean, oh my gosh, some of these are so...skimpy." She laughed nervously. "I think maybe, uh, I need, uh…"

"You okay?" I asked her. She looked on the verge of hyperventilating, making me realize those body issues were not completely gone. It had only been a few weeks.

"Um, yeah. I just need something a little more…"

"Subtle?" Daiyu said with a light laugh. "Yes, yes, I understand. We just put these up front because they are, how you say…flashiest."

"Oh, good," Rory said, exhaling.

Daiyu took about an inch of catalog pages between her fingers and flipped to nearer its middle. "These are a little more covering," she said.

"Thank you," Rory said, flipping slowly through the pages. "Yes, yes, these are definitely more my style. I like the fully covered, um, chest area, you know?"

Still the breast issues. All over again I wanted to wring the necks of the people who'd once put it in her mind that she was flawed there. The ballet mistress, fellow students, whoever the fuck it was.

"Yes, I can see you in some of these, like this one," Daiyu said pointing to the very one Rory was admiring. It had a sexy low-cut back, but was very covering in the front.

"Your name is so pretty," Rory said to Daiyu. "What does it mean?"

"Thank you. It means black jasmine."

"Oooh, very cool. I love it. It's like complex beauty, beauty with shading, with a strong sense of mystery. Like Sasha," Rory said with a little giggle.

Daiyu laughed. "Yes!"

"That's actually not too far from what I was thinking," I said. I didn't want Rory to get too attached to something before she saw my idea. "Can we go into the back and do a sketching?"

"Of course!" Daiyu said.

She led us to the far wall, parted a thick, red plush curtain with gold trim, and brought us into her back room, which I loved. It was spacious and had floor-to-ceiling windows on each side that opened out onto a grassy green lawn.

"Wow," Rory said. Always on the same page. Well, except when it came to her body.

We sat across from Daiyu at a large metal table covered with sketch paper, charcoal, pencils and drawings.

She opened a drawer and pulled out a drawing. "Here is the one I was working on, based on what you had told me." She began to hand the paper to me then looked back and forth between Rory and me. She placed the paper between us.

Rory glanced down at it, just as I picked it up to look more closely.

"Oh, I didn't realize you'd already talked," Rory said.

"Just briefly," I said, focusing on the design. Rory leaned toward me and looked over my shoulder.

Again, Daiyu had done an excellent job of sketching exactly what I'd described. The woman was a miracle. The top part was sleeveless with thin straps and a cute, tube-like top. It connected to the skirt through swaths of fabric on the sides, leaving the front and back midriff areas bare. The skirt was asymmetrical, slit on one side to the upper thigh, and on the other to just above the knee. It was hot without being too revealing. The tube top didn't show any cleavage and at least one side of the skirt wasn't slit high. Daiyu, as always, made it look way better than the image in my mind. I really thought Rory would go for it. But I was wrong.

"Sasha!" she shrieked. "That looks absolutely nothing like the design I just admired in the catalog. The bra is exactly what I was saying in the first costume I saw that was so not me." There was panic in her voice.

Bra? What bra? "What do you mean? This is perfectly covering."

"No. It's not at all, Sasha," she said, shaking her head, her voice getting shakier by the second. "I really like the one I saw in the catalog. Can we have her sketch one like that?"

"The other design was from a few years ago, Rory. This is more in the current style."

"But shouldn't we be original? Do we have to wear what everyone else is wearing?"

"Tired and old is not the same as original. And, yes, we do have to fit in, to an extent. We can't go with whatever we want." Rory didn't understand the politics of ballroom competitions. Nor should she. I kept having to remind myself she was new. "We have to wear a certain amount of bronzer, for example," I continued when she shot me a bewildered look. "You have to wear at least a three-inch heel, myself a one-inch. There are standards. I've seen good couples go down because they didn't obey the standards. They thought they were above them. That's how the judges look at it, Rory." I was getting defensive.

The more I spoke the more I realized how it sounded, like competitions were about a lot of things that didn't involve actual dancing. It was true. It was politics. It was what it was.

"The judges are looking for a creative take on something currently hot. We will be laughed at if we wear something several years old, believe me."

"Fine," Rory said after a lengthy exhale. "But can we modify it? I just won't be comfortable in that, Sasha, I won't. I won't be able to dance well—"

"Allow me to add please that all of our designs are costume-malfunction-worry-free," Daiyu piped in. "Believe me. We use triple layering and stitching, with many invisible straps. It won't expose anything you don't want it to."

"I understand. But…that's not the problem," Rory said.

"What is the problem, then?" I asked. "She said nothing's going to show."

"It'll expose my disproportions, Sasha."

"What disproportions?" I laughed, though her completely distorted body image was not the least bit funny. "Rory, you are a beautiful woman. Please be proud of your body." I tried hard not to sound irritated. I was getting really sick of this. I'd worked so hard to make her proud of her body. Her brain and her body. I wished she'd listen for once.

Rory breathed deeply. "Sasha, my goal is to be happy and comfortable with myself. But I'm not completely there yet, and pushing it is only going to hurt. Especially at such an important thing. This is huge. Please listen to me. I know."

I could feel her rapid pulse from across the table. I didn't want to fight. I didn't want to push her. But she seriously couldn't dance in a sack, like in the olden days. My design was simply not very revealing.

"Look, why can't we just keep the design but keep the whole thing attached? I mean, no bare midriff?" she said.

"But that would look so plain, Rory. It would just be like a sack or a frock or whatever it's called."

"It would not be like a sack," she insisted, nearly pounding the table with her fist. "It would still be form-fitting. Maybe it could be cinched at the waistline."

I shook my head. "That's similar to the catalog. And as I said, that look has been done. I've been at this a long time, Rory. I know the styles that have come and gone."

"Can't we somehow update it, then?"

I sighed. She wasn't going to give in. I looked at Daiyu for help.

"Sasha, is this seriously that huge of a problem? Isn't my comfort more important than whether a look has been done at some point in the past?" Rory's voice was raised and her fist was hitting the table with practically each word.

"Of course your comfort is important. But there's no point in doing this if we're going to do something weird and not...jump through all the hoops, so to speak."

She looked at me square on. "The judges honestly care about something as superficial as the costume? Isn't that majorly judging a book by its cover?"

I tried not to lose it. I couldn't help how Blackpool judges thought. I knew what I knew. You had to play certain games there. It was part of the package. "I'm not kidding, Rory."

Her face reddened. We were getting nowhere. One of us had to budge.

"Isn't there some kind of stupid rule against newcomers competing in the pro division or something like that anyway? I mean, you keep saying with the changes in the judging, having me as your partner should be okay. Or something like that."

She was searching. But she had a point. Perhaps with the change in the judging this year, with the committee not allowing coaches to judge, the new arbiters wouldn't have the same focus. But then again, maybe they would. I didn't know and I didn't want to take chances. Not now. "It's just..." I looked around the room, my frustration at my failure to get her to understand me growing by the second.

"It's just what?"

I threw my hands up. My costume was so much better than what she wanted. And she only wanted the more covering crappy one because of her self-esteem. "This design is so sexy and fun. Confidence comes from within, not from what you are wearing, Rory."

"Sexy and fun. That's all you care about. That I look sexy."

"I didn't say—"

"You care more about the way I look than the way I dance." Her face was now tomato red. She was fuming. And she was ridiculously wrong.

"Don't be ludicrous. Of course I—"

"If you didn't, you'd want me to be comfortable so I could dance as full-out as possible, not hold back."

"Might I make a suggestion?" Daiyu said, sitting upright and holding her hands up as if in surrender.

Her voice actually made both of us jump a bit. As if we'd both forgotten she was there.

"Yes, please," Rory said.

"I think that toga-style tops are soon going to be very in. I've seen them on the runway in Milan just last month and they looked very sharp. I mean at a regular fashion show. Trends in ballroom follow general trends. That kind of top would give you more support and cover. And then I could make the costume one piece, and it wouldn't be plain at all because of the remarkable cut. And we could still have the asymmetrical bottom. That way, it would not be rehashing a tired style. It would be, if anything, updating a classic."

"You mean, like a Greek toga?" Rory said.

"Yes, like that." Daiyu smiled.

Rory considered it for a moment.

"I could make a weaving-like motion with the fabric so that there are waves," Daiyu continued, sounding more excited the more she spoke. "And it would be form-fitting, not like a typical, loose toga. With the skirt, we could coordinate the higher cut side with the strapless top so that side would have the shorter leg line. Yes, that's unique." Daiyu's eyes were bright. She was definitely excited about her new concept. And with Daiyu's proven brilliance, it was hard not to trust her.

"That sounds fun. I think I'll be comfortable," Rory said, finally lightening.

"We can play around with the fabrics and colors too, for two different but similar looks for the regular competition and the finals. Don't worry, I'll throw together a sample and then you can try it and see what you think," Daiyu said.

"Sounds good to me!" Rory chirped. Daiyu's excitement was contagious.

They both looked at me. Daiyu was Wonder Woman. I was definitely in. But I was still disturbed by Rory's continuous lack of confidence. I could see her getting this costume, trying it on in the fitting and freaking out over something. Or over every little thing.

"Come on, we need to compromise, Sasha."

I shook my head. "That's not it. I just want…I just want you to be happy. Self-confidence comes from within. If you're not confident in general, you're not going to be comfortable in anything, Rory. Including this."

Rory looked down and I immediately felt badly that I'd ruined her excitement.

"Well, let's give this a try. Okay?" Rory said.

I nodded. "Yes, it sounds like a good design. Let's."

"Oh, good," Daiyu said, peering back up at us hesitantly, as if she was afraid to ask the next question—which was about which colors we wanted.

"Black," Rory said just as I said, "Gold." Gold was brilliant, radiant. The color of winners. Black? Was this a funeral?

Daiyu laughed but heartily this time, not nervously. "Colors are always an issue," she said, emphasizing the 'always.'

"Okay," Rory began. "How about I wear a dark tan/dark golden hue for the finals and you let me wear the black for the first several rounds. That way I'll have my confidence up when I wear the flashier color?"

I closed my eyes and exhaled. "Rory, I don't want to fight. But black is way too basic for this kind of dress. And depressing. We need a color that stands out a little more and says something."

We ended up with a deep rich magenta for the first dances—a color that wasn't basic but would still hide what Rory insisted were flaws on her perfect body. And I got my gold for the finals. But with a clever twist. Leave it to Daiyu. She'd gone into her back room and unearthed a gold pattern with an intricate black embroidery weaving through it. It resembled the dress the female lover in the Klimt painting *The Kiss* wore.

"It's like art," Rory squealed with delight. Finally, we were back on the same page.

I told Rory and Daiyu I'd have to get back to them on the color for the team match. That would be up to the team captain. Rory shot me a dubious look. "I'm serious," I said. "He decides. That part is out of my control."

***

"Skinny, skinny," Daiyu's assistant said as she took Rory's measurements. Rory looked at me, but I remained closed-lipped.

"I'm trying to lose weight. I mean gain. *Gain* weight," Rory told Daiyu with a nervous laugh. "Hopefully eight to ten pounds."

"Very good that you tell me," Daiyu said. "I'll make everything a size bigger. We can take the lines in if you don't gain what you expect. That's good?" She looked at Rory.

Rory took a breath and forced herself to nod.

Yes, a commitment! I winked at her, and blew her a kiss.

CHAPTER FIVE

Things were going well. Rory was seeing her psychologist and her nutritionist and she was eating much, much better. There were no crises at her job—Gunther was giving her little things, leaving us plenty of time to work hard. And work crazy hard we did. She was just as determined as I, and we were making serious progress.

"You actually look like a true Blackpool couple," Greta had told me in private. And she meant it.

But of course something had to go wrong, to put a dent in our progress.

It was Gunther again.

Rory called me at four o'clock, from her office. I was supposed to see her at seven. My heart sped up, as I initially worried Gunther was pulling last-minute shenanigans again, hystericizing over Rory's lack of preparation for a trial he'd completely forgotten to tell her about. We'd been doing well, but we couldn't stop now. We had to keep it up or we'd lose what we'd accomplished before Blackpool. If the trial was starting now, we were screwed.

"Hi, honey," I said, hoping the panic in my voice

wasn't obvious.

But there was no response.

"Rory?"

She breathed deeply. Something was very wrong. Worse than before if she couldn't even speak. "What's wrong, Rory?"

"I just, I just got fired," she stuttered, her voice nearly a whisper.

"What? What are you talking about?"

No answer.

"I'm coming downtown. Stay in the lobby and wait for me."

This being work hours, there was nowhere to park in front of her building, so I parked in the lot across the street. She stumbled out of the lobby when she saw me. She had five huge bags strapped around her shoulders. She really was leaving.

I simultaneously hugged her and took her bags. She gave me a weary smile and I could tell she was doing all she could to hold back tears.

She said nothing for most of the ride back to my place. She didn't cry. She just looked out the window. I could tell how devastated she was. This was her dream. Or at least had once been. I knew what it was like to feel like a dream had died. But she would be better off. Whatever the future held for her would be better. I was sure of that. But I didn't say anything. I held my hand over her knee, caressing it with my palm. I didn't ask questions. She'd talk when she was ready. She pressed her hand over mine, but continued to watch L.A. pass by.

Once we were settled in my kitchen, a tall glass of pomegranate-blood-red-orange juice in front of her, she started to tell me what happened.

"So, this woman named Melinda Berenson from a small firm called Berenson and Fredericks called me. I had no idea who she was. She said she was representing Patrick Warren on appeal. That was my first pro bono client, remember?"

I nodded. She'd spoken a lot about him. She'd been convinced he was schizophrenic and without treatment was decomposing. Gunther had insisted everyone pretended to be crazy to get out of going to trial and she was simply naïve for not knowing that.

"Well, this new lawyer called to tell me his conviction was overturned and a retrial was tentatively ordered, depending on the outcome of his mental competency examination. She said after her dealings with him and reading the trial proceedings, she couldn't agree with me more. He's totally schizophrenic. Can you believe it? They're finally going to have a psychiatrist evaluate him! I told her how hard I'd tried to get the judge to order that exam. All in vain. She said, yes, I'd preserved the issue on record so well and that's why she was able to prevail on appeal. And then she faxed me the court's decision. My name was mentioned by the presiding justice who authored the opinion!" Rory's face was aglow. She fumbled in her bag and pulled out a couple sheets of paper. "Here it is—*Aurora Laudner from Vanderson, Rickels, and Edelstein, the law firm representing Mr. Warren pro bono, made numerous, specific, detailed, and timely requests for a competency exam, each of which the court below denied. We find she well preserved the issue for appeal and that those requests should have been granted...* She was so nice to me, Sasha. She told me what a great job I did preserving the issue and trying so hard to get the judge to examine him. And, I mean, it's recorded right here, the court said so too."

"Intelligent people recognize your skills," I said, kissing her hand as I took the paper and read it. I now knew exactly what had happened. This had shown Gunther up. To be the ignorant asshole he was. Rory deserved so much better. She'd see soon how good it was that she was free of the bastard.

She took a deep breath and looked down. I continued pressing my lips to her knuckles.

"So, I was so happy. I skipped down to Gunther's office to tell him the good news. I mean, it was a victory not just for me but for the whole office. The firm's name was right there in black and white…" Her voice broke and she took a breath. "I mean, the second I saw his angry, frustrated face, I began to lose my nerve. But then he was like, 'What's in your hand,' almost accusingly, you know. He hates it when I bother him. His frown grew deeper and angrier, but I told him, 'No, it's good this time!' I told him the whole thing. I couldn't decipher the look on his face. It was a combination of shock, anger, confusion, and relief all at once. The mass of emotions so contorted his features, I actually took a step back from him. He held out his hand, and snapped his fingers when I didn't immediately hand him the decision. I just stood there shifting my weight nervously while he read the whole decision. I was hoping he'd perk up when he saw the firm's name mentioned. But…he didn't. Instead, he looked up, blinked hard, and said he'd been meaning to talk to me. He told me to sit down and shut the door. Then he smiled. I knew something was up at that point because I've never, ever seen that man crack anything even mildly approximating a smile. I always blabber, out of nerves. So I asked if I had a new pro bono assignment. He said no, unfortunately not. 'There will be no new assignments for you, Rory. I'm sorry.' That's what he said."

Now the tears came and she let them. I moved across the table and sat beside her, wrapping my arm completely around her.

"Two weeks ago I thought he was ready to fire me because I went to the competition instead of working all weekend. But then he had me help him with Jamar's hearing. I just had the biggest victory of my career so far. I mean, I made the firm look good, and it's in an official appellate decision. Why would he fire me now?"

"Because he's a jealous fucking dickless asshole," I answered.

She looked at me, wide-eyed and open-mouthed for several moments, then broke into laughter. She laughed for a couple of minutes. Then she sobered. "Thank you, Sasha. That felt good."

"I'm being completely serious," I said.

"I know you are." She bit her lip, in thought. "But what made me so, so mad was the reason he gave for firing me. He said my work has been under par and I've shown a clear lack of passion for the law. He said I wasn't taking my cases seriously, mainly with important cases like Jamar's. Which is so profoundly not true. He said I've only been working forty to fifty hours a week and he called them secretarial hours. 'You want to work those hours, you should have been a secretary.' To say I lacked passion? I worked so hard on Jamar's case and on the Warren case that I ended up in effect winning." She started to cry then stopped, as if it wasn't worth the effort anymore. She took a deep breath instead.

"He's jealous of you, Rory. He's jealous you have a life, and you're obviously able to balance your work and life well if you won this appeal. What a fucking, fucking asshole…" I murmured through tight lips, clenching my fists. I forced myself to calm down. She needed comfort, not anger bordering on violence. "He'll get what he deserves someday. He'll lose cases and clients. It'll come back to him and he'll be sorry." I wrapped my arms more tightly around her. I felt her muscles finally relax.

As I sat there cocooning her in my arms, I realized we'd now have a lot more time for practice. We'd have all day, every day.

I was immediately ashamed of myself for letting my thoughts go there, to *me*.

"Well, I guess in the end I didn't have to make my hard decision. I had it made for me," she said, completely on the same page as me, as always. "Now we can totally concentrate on Blackpool." Her muscles tensed again. "I mean, I think. I don't have a lot of money saved up. I can't take off very much—"

"Rory, no." I rocked her in my arms, trying to get rid of the tension. "The absolute last thing you should worry about right now is money. I will pay for everything for now, even your rent."

She shook her head. "I can't let you do that."

"Yes, listen," I insisted. "It will be payment for you spending all day every day training with me. You're a professional dancer now. The big pros are compensated by their sponsors. I am simply paying you your portion of our sponsorship payments. Think of it as a kind of advance. You are a professional dancer now," I repeated, trying to get it into her brain. She was; she needed to think that way. "You can go back to law in the future, but for right now, you have the dance career you've wanted."

She took a breath, swallowed.

I had to admit I didn't want her to return to her law career. I wanted her to dance with me. Permanently. But I knew there were those cases that impassioned her, despite what the asshole said. That she might not be whole without this aspect of her life. So I added something. "Not that I want you to, but if you decide to return to law, you can use your illness as a reason for taking a leave of absence. Your anorexia caused health problems—both physical and mental—you can say, and you needed a little break for your health."

Again, her muscles relaxed and her whole body went limp in my arms. In a good way. Like she wasn't on her guard. "Oh thank you so much for that, Sasha. I'm the lawyer, and you're the logical one who thinks of everything."

I pressed my lips to her forehead.

"I actually thought about what Gunther said on the way home, in your car. About my supposed lack of passion. And I realized that I did lack passion—when it came to helping the rich clients find loopholes in the tax laws so they could get out of paying their due. I didn't go to law school for that. So he wasn't entirely wrong. I'm definitely most passionate about helping the down-and-out, like Jamar, you know."

I nodded. "I do."

"So, if I go back, it's not going to be the same type of place, anyway. And that's another thing I'd tell a potential employer—that I left to do something I was more impassioned about. And that would make sense to a public interest employer. But I'll figure out the rest of my life after Blackpool. I need to focus on that now. So we win. Because we are going to win!" She squirmed out of my embrace to pump her fist in the air.

I kissed her again, this time a long, slow kiss, on the lips. That was what I so needed to hear from her. Her certainty. It was contagious. We were going to win.

CHAPTER SIX

Over the next few weeks, Rory and I practically lived together, she was over so often practicing. It felt good. It felt like it should be. Like I could definitely do this with her, permanently. But we didn't talk about that right now. We were too focused on training. Plus, she'd told me how much it meant to her to live on her own for the first time in her life. Before, she'd been in college or law school, with roommates, and then lived with James. She wanted to savor this time in her life, her independence. I wanted her to savor it as well, before she became mine forever. Plus, we needed some time apart and space of our own or our nerves would easily fray. So she spent most weeknights at her apartment.

While I was at Infectious Rhythm teaching, she'd use my home studio for her own practicing and the barre for stretching—sometimes with Greta, sometimes on her own. As I knew there would be, there were a bazillion applications for the many private lesson spots left vacant by Cheryl and Luna's departure. I'd managed to convince Alessia to agree to fill the majority of them once Blackpool was over; I compromised with her and let her fill two of them in the meantime. We'd told the remaining students desirous of one of the few slots that, come June, there would a lottery held. To put it mildly, despite Cheryl, I was very much in demand.

Rory returned to the studio, taking all of her regular classes while I was at work on my privates. The studio was a much nicer place for all of us now that Cheryl and Luna were gone. Rory still worried they had something "up their designer sleeves," as she called them. She was sure they were planning some way of sabotaging us at Blackpool. I told her to stop thinking such thoughts. I promised I wouldn't let anything happen. And I wouldn't. I had Sadie, along with lots of friends in the ballroom world on our side. Some from Russia, some from here. We didn't see each other a whole lot, but we often ran into difficulties like this in the competition world. We had an unspoken agreement that we'd look out for each other when requested. So several of my ballroom friends at the studio Luna and Cheryl had transferred to were keeping an eye on them. My friend Maurizio, a standard ballroom champ, told me they were both training like crazy with the top Latin dancer there, Nikolai, for the upcoming Vegas Pro Am, which she'd wanted to do with me. I knew of Nikolai. He hadn't made it to the general pros yet in the big comps but he'd placed very well in the Rising Star category at last year's Blackpool. Good for them. *Train with Nikolai and forget all about me, please, ladies.*

I didn't tell Rory this, because I'd thought it better just not to mention them at all, keep them far from her mind. But perhaps I should have, so she'd stop worrying. One night, as I pulled up to her apartment to pick her up, she pointed to a black sedan parked in front of her building.

"That car's been parked there, illegally, for several nights in a row."

"Illegally?" I asked.

"Yeah, I mean without a permit, which you need to park here after seven. Parking enforcement is so strict here."

"Probably just someone who doesn't have the money for a permit and is willing to take a chance," I said. "People do that all the time here. Until they get that first ticket."

"Yeah, but it almost did get a ticket. When I was waiting for you to pick me up the other night, I saw one of the parking enforcement Priuses pull up. But just before it reached the sedan, the sedan's lights came on and its tires screeched and it pulled away. It kind of freaked me out. I hadn't realized there was anyone inside the car. But then it was there again last night. The windows are so dark. I tried to peek in to see if someone was in there again, but I couldn't see. You don't think it's Cheryl, do you?"

"Rory, no, don't be ridiculous. She's happy at her new studio. She has far better things to do than stalk you."

"But why is it still there even after the police almost gave it a ticket? And don't you think it's weird it pulled away right as parking enforcement approached?"

I shook my head and shrugged my shoulders. "People park illegally in L.A. all the time. Especially in Hollywood. Yeah, it's nonsensical. But this can sometimes be idiot central when it comes to drivers."

Still, I looked at the car in my rearview mirror as we pulled away. She was right—you couldn't see a damn thing through those tinted windows.

"You're right. I'm being paranoid," she said with a nervous laugh.

"Well, I mean, keep an eye on it. It's always good to be aware," I said. "But I'm sure it's just someone who lives around here who doesn't yet have a permit and is trying to get away with it. Don't worry, sweet." I shot her my best boyish smile and caressed her knee between gear shifts.

That was the first and last time I'd ever blow off her worries. As I'd later find out, inside that car was not Cheryl, but someone far, far more sinister.

***

Training was going well. Rory was progressing much more rapidly now that she was dancing full-time. With her ballet training, rumba was by far her best dance. And samba ended up being her most challenging, which also made sense since ballet demanded such straightness in the upper body and that dance required the greatest ability to rotate hips and pelvis fully and quickly. We worked hard on her loosening up her lower body. It was happening, but she needed to gain speed and precision now. Still, she was really blowing me away with the progress she was making. I knew she could do it once she put her mind to it, and once she had adequate time.

But the fact that she couldn't move anywhere near as fast as I could meant we weren't entirely in sync. It meant that on the beautifully sexy shadow samba rolls we both so loved, where my arms were wrapped around hers from behind, either our footwork was off and she'd step on me repeatedly, or our hip rotations were off and she was bumping her ass into my crotch. Often both happened. Of course her first instinct was to giggle. And of course I was so hyper-serious, my first instinct was to get mad. But I tried hard to lighten up so she wouldn't be overwhelmed. Yelling and/or seething wasn't the way to get things done. I knew that now. It was only one dance we weren't stellar on, I told myself. And the more flubs we made, the more serious she became about getting it right. In other words, we were working together. We were becoming a true partnership. This was a first for me. Not even Micaela and I in our early days worked together so well.

"No couple is perfect in every dance," Greta assured us. "That doesn't mean you can't win the overall Latin if you are perfect—or near perfect since we know there's no such thing as perfect—in the others." I knew she was trying to assuage me. She knew me well.

"Nope. We're going to be the best in all five dances. Every single one of them," Rory asserted. "I'm going to nail it."

Greta worked with her on it. They decided that making her movements smaller was one way to solve her speed problems. They also simplified the footwork, since Greta made clear that excellent technique on basic movement was far better than fancy footwork that the dancer just couldn't execute properly. True. I, of course, badly wanted the more flavorful footwork but I recognized Greta was right. We could make things more complicated as Rory's strengths grew.

We also reworked some of the movement so it would look better on Rory's body. Greta was a genius at this. After trying different things with Rory, we decided she looked really beautiful doing a stretch upward with her long limbs and straight body. So, we substituted that for the Rio-esque hip rolls she'd choreographed. Those weren't part of ballroom samba anyway, but were some authentic Brazilian flavoring she'd decided to add. As much as Rory loved them and their cultural authenticity, she decided Greta was right and maybe they just weren't her. I was fine with it. I just wanted Rory to look and feel her best—the best route to success, I now knew.

But damn, I did like those crazy-fast Rio hip rolls. And I could execute them well.

"What if I do the stretch, while he does the rolls, and as he goes faster and faster he gets closer to the ground, like a real samba dancer, all the time gazing up at me stretching up to the sky?" Rory suggested, reading my mind. "We'd still be dancing as partners, connecting with each other's movement, without doing the same step in tandem. And it would maybe look like his looking up at me while madly shaking his pelvis is expressing his feeling of being awestruck by my statuesque beauty." She cracked up and waved her arm about, making it clear the statuesque beauty thing was a joke.

But I thought about her suggestion. It actually made damn good sense. I looked at Greta. She had the same thought. "I love it!" we said simultaneously.

"Let's see it," Greta said.

We did it, everything working it out exactly as Rory had planned.

"Yes, yes, yes!" Greta declared, throwing her arms up. "The dance now shows off both of your strengths, minimizes weaknesses, and tells a sassy little story to boot," she hooted. "Rory, I'm so proud of you for coming up with that. That's quite good. Maybe someday you'll have a career as a choreographer!"

Rory laughed, but I had the same thought. It was amazing that she came up with that, when she was still pretty much a novice. She really could be a choreographer someday. Yeah, my girl had serious talents.

While I was at the studio, she and Greta worked together to make more tweaks that simultaneously hid Rory's flaws and made both her body and our partnership look more special and unique. Every day when I got home, they'd teach me the new additions and alterations. I truly thought they were genius.

"I can't believe it but that was near perfection. It looks absolutely splendid, you two," Greta enthused after we performed the whole dance for her.

Rory had done the routine without any flubs. She was nothing short of euphoric, her euphoria caused by surprise. I wasn't at all surprised. I knew all along she could do it.

After Greta left for the evening, Rory wanted to practice our samba again. "I want it to stick so much in my muscle memory it's impossible to get it out of there," she said. "And, okay, I just want to dance my favorite crazy-mad dance with my favorite crazy-mad beat with my absolute favorite crazy madman over and over! Seriously, Sasha, I'm proud of myself."

"Yeah, well don't let it go to your head," I joked, shooting her my sly, lopsided smile.

So we went at it again. Of course I shouldn't have said the thing about letting it go to her head because her confidence did kind of get the better of her. We were doing her favorite step—the samba rolls with me standing behind her like a shadow, and, instead of keeping the hip action smaller like we'd practiced, she got too excited and made hers a tad too large. Resulting in her ass smacking straight into my groin. A sharp pain shot through my balls, and I couldn't help but tense, very briefly.

"Ooooh, I hurt you," she said, trying to turn around.

"I am leading smaller steps now. We agreed—? Let's just finish. We are almost done," I said, trying to ignore the discomfort and not get worked up over a now-unusual flub.

We resumed, doing our series of rolling-outs, when she rolled out and back into me several times in a row. We were supposed to end with her curled in toward me in a sexy little hug. We ended up right, upper body-wise, but for some reason, probably because it was past our regular practice time and we were both getting tired, she bent her knee. This resulted in another of her lovely body parts ending up in my groin. And that knee, being more bony, was more painful than her ass.

"You trying to tell me something?" I said, untangling myself from her.

"I'm so sorry. I don't know what happened. I d-don't know…" she stuttered.

I straightened up, the pain gone. We were done practicing for the night. We'd had a good day and now it was time to end it before things got bad. Now was time for fun, in other words. I tried to make myself look as annoyed as possible. "Seriously, that was twice, at once." I started to walk away, pretending to be annoyed.

"Sasha!" she called out behind me. "I didn't mean it! Either time. I was just…letting excitement get the better of me."

I maintained the charade, refusing to turn back. She ran up behind me, reached around me, grabbed my hand, and whipped me around, fast, exactly like I would her during a rumba routine. Giving me a taste of my own medicine, I supposed. I spun around lightning fast, right into her, my defeated groin ending up smacking straight into her hip bone.

"I don't know…honestly—oh my God, I don't know how that happened three—"

"See, this is why you cannot ever lead. You will kill me," I said.

"No. No. It's not that I can never, ever be a leader. Not in any circumstance whatsoever," she insisted, shaking her head.

"Okay fine, then. You want to lead so badly? You're the leader." I said the last sentence slowly. Tantalizingly slowly. She wanted so badly to be a leader, both on the floor and in bed. Let her try. I could let her. I could follow.

She giggled nervously, knowing full well we weren't talking about ballroom anymore. "What do you want me to do?"

"As I said, R-r-rory, you're the leader." The rolling r's were obviously intentional.

She looked around, thinking, her cheeks reddening by the second, her eyes widening, her thoughts growing wild. "Okay!" she squealed, placing her hand on the back of my head and pulling it down toward her beautiful face, forcing my lips to press into hers.

After several long, deliciously deep kisses, she

transferred her lips to my cheekbone then moved on, tracing kisses to my jawline, my neck, as she ran her fingertips from my shoulders, along down my front side, ending at my waistline, which she fingered the same way I'd fingered the tops of her tights on my ballroom floor not all that long ago. She knew exactly what she wanted from my body.

"I can make it all better," she whispered, her voice drenched with sex, which made my cock pulse.

I responded with a strong exhale, heavy with expectation. She bent her knees and continued running her hands along the front of my shirt, unbuttoning it as she went along. She traced her tongue from my clavicle down my torso to my navel. She opened my shirt all the way and took my pants down, finally freeing my now rock-hard cock. She licked the tip and traced her fingernails around my hips. *Oh my God.* I rocked my head back and just breathed as she wrapped those delicious lips around my shaft and took nearly all of me inside her mouth.

Then in an instant she took her mouth away. *What?* I waited. One second, two seconds, three. I was just about to explode. Then she returned her beautiful full lips to my shaft, swirling her tongue around to trace my balls. Again she took her mouth away completely, making me almost hurt with want, before returning to my head, grabbing my flexed ass and kneading her fingers into my glute muscles. She pulled me toward her and took all of me inside her. The tip of my dick touched the back of her throat. Fuck, that was so amazing, I was becoming unable to control myself. I moaned a deep, guttural groan.

She pulled her mouth away and tore her leotard down to her waist. She grabbed my cock and rubbed its wet tip over her face and neck, then lifted herself up and rubbed it down her chest, lingering over her heavenly nipples. She pushed her breasts together and stroked me with the insides of her breasts. I knew what this meant. She was so self-conscious about her breast size. For her to use that to make me feel so damn amazing was huge.

I whispered her name and rocked my hips. She took me in her mouth again, sucking and licking, until my body twitched with ecstasy and we both collapsed on the floor.

"Definitely worth the pain," I whispered after we'd both recovered, reaching over and stroking her lips with my thumb.

After catching her breath, she looked down and laughed. I followed her gaze. We were a sight. Her leotard was halfway down but all her other clothes were on. My pants were at my ankles and my shirt torn open. She rocked herself up and took her shoes off, then the leotard and tights. She then buckled her feet back into her shoes.

"What are you doing?" I laughed.

She untied my shoes and took my pants off. "Get up. We need to finish with our rumba."

"We need to dance now?"

"Absolutely," she said. "It's our best dance, and we need to end the night feeling as positive as possible after the, you know, foibles."

"That's just an excuse to dance naked." I laughed, sitting up and taking my shirt off. "We are both naked this time?"

She nodded, a deliciously wicked grin on her lips that made me start to get hard again.

"Don't look at me like that if you want to

dance," I ordered, brushing my finger down her lips.

But with us both naked, it was impossible to finish the dance. I turned on an über sexy, throaty version of "*Bésame Mucho.*" I slowed the beat so we'd have additional time on some of our tricks, if we so needed. On the first backbend, I couldn't help but trace her navel with my finger. She giggled and pulled herself up enough to lightly slap my hand. We were already off the slow-motion beat.

I pulled her toward me with strength I'd managed to refrain from using for some time now. I didn't mean to overpower her but to pull her body into mine with enough force that her nipples and her pelvic region would engage with mine. Of course I didn't pull too hard. It worked perfectly. As she began to lift her leg up along my backside, tickling the back of my thigh with her pointed toe, I felt her beautifully opening sex wet my hip. My hard dick was practically plowing into her abdomen. My entire body was pulsating and I knew she could feel it. She fully extended her leg behind me and began to arch that amazingly flexible back, curving her torso toward the floor, her breasts breathtakingly full. I lowered her into our favorite dip. As her fingertips graced the floor when she was down as far as she could go, the music stopped. We were so behind the beat it was laughable.

"Screw it," we said simultaneously as I pulled her upright and lifted her up onto me, abandoning the routine. She straddled me and wrapped both legs around my back, her sex now creating a deliciously hot pool on my stomach as I carried her up the winding staircase.

And so it became our custom to end our practice

with samba, followed by naked rumba, which we never finished.

***

Things were going superbly well. Rory kept exclaiming that we were looking like a true partnership more and more, our bodies fitting together so perfectly like two proverbial puzzle pieces. And I agreed with her. For once, I really had a true partner. We weren't fighting each other or trying to outdo each other. And it was due to the fact that unlike all my prior partners, Rory was a profoundly different dancer than I was. Together we were the lightning-fast Latin man combined with the soft, lithe, beautiful ballerina. And though I'd first struggled to train Rory to be more like me, thinking that was the only way she'd keep up and we'd win, I was supremely glad she and Greta had made me see that wasn't the way at all. We worked because of our different strengths, not in spite of them. Our partnership was truly unique.

I hoped the Blackpool judges saw it the same way. But in all honesty, I was so happy with the way we looked together, I dare say I was actually beginning not to care. Far from fighting each other, our passion and our love for each other clearly showed. Greta said so. Everyone who saw us practice in my studio said so. But we didn't need their validation. We knew it because we felt it.

CHAPTER SEVEN

But then, on one seemingly very ordinary evening, our partnership, our very lives, took a huge turn. Rory and I were both at Infectious Rhythm. Her advanced Latin class with Bronislava would end two hours before my last private, so she'd decided to walk home, eat a little something, then either drive up to my place herself or call me if she decided she'd rather me pick her up. We'd decided to play it by ear. Greta had the night off and Rory and I had agreed to take it easy tonight, take a break from practice. So if she felt like it, she could go for a swim or a hot bath or use my gym, or we could just snuggle and watch TV. It was unusually cold for spring in L.A. and she was tired. So I told her if she got home and just wanted to stay in, that would be more than fine with me. After all, we needed breaks from each other once in a while to keep our partnership healthy.

But not this kind of break.

I finished my two lessons and spoke briefly with Alessia, going over my group class schedule for the next month. I wasn't in a hurry to get home since we didn't have solid plans. I drove up the Sunset Strip to my favorite pizza place and ordered a pizza. When I got home, Rory wasn't there. I checked my phone but there were no messages or texts. That was fine, I thought; she'd decided to stay in. Because she was tired, I figured she might have fallen asleep, and decided not to call and wake her.

I turned on the TV to HBO's "Boardwalk Empire." It was a gangster show set in New Jersey in the twenties that I found to be dramatic, entertaining, escapist fun. I fixed myself a tall glass of Guinness, sank into my favorite leather chair, put my feet up on the ottoman and dug into the pizza. Of course the hours of practice we were missing tonight crossed my mind, but I forced the thought away and laughed at myself for having to struggle to relax.

After back-to-back episodes of the show, I checked my phone again. There really was no reason to check, of course, since the thing was sitting right next to me and I would have heard if Rory called or texted. But I checked anyway. No word from her. It was almost midnight. I felt a pang of worry, then assured myself she was okay. She wasn't downtown; her neighborhood and her building were safe. She was simply tired. She'd definitely gone to bed by now. As should I. Tomorrow we would be back to usual, back to the grueling practice schedule.

I cleaned up in the kitchen, went upstairs, undressed and slipped under the covers. I'd lived alone for some time, but now I was lonely not having Rory next to me. Even if she didn't stay over at night, it was weird not having her around at all. I resisted the urge to call or text and thereby wake her up. She needed her sleep. I set my phone on the bedside table, feeling like I was close to her anyway that way.

Suddenly I heard my phone buzz. I woke up, looked at the alarm clock. It was a little past two in the morning. I swiped the phone off the table, looked at the face. It had no name but I recognized the odd area code as a number my uncle and cousin used when they needed to get in touch with me. Had they found Tatiana?

"What happened?" I said on answering.

"Sasha," was all he said. It was Uncle Oleg. The stiffness and worry in his voice were palpable. They'd found her and she either wasn't alive or was very badly off.

"Where is she?" I shot up and ran to the closet to get my clothes on.

He didn't answer me.

"Tell me now," I shouted so loudly my next door neighbors might well have heard, far away as they were.

Deep breath. Then, "I don't know."

"What do you mean you don't know? Why are you calling me? It's two o'clock in the morning."

Another pause. *What the hell is going on?*

"We're in front of your house. We need you to come downstairs."

"What?"

"Just do it. We'll talk to you inside."

What the major fuck? I hit "end" and threw my phone on the bed, jumped into my jeans, slipped into my sneakers and pulled on the closest shirt in my closet. I ran downstairs, grabbed my keys off the table in the foyer and threw open the door. It was black, except for the light from my porch, and from the moon. I flipped on the bright patio lights. I could barely see him outside the gate. His fingers were wrapped tightly around the black metal.

"Sasha, we're out here. Let us in."

I walked toward the gate. "What's going on? What—" Then I saw it. There was a black sedan that looked very much like the one that had been parked in front of Rory's apartment building several nights ago. The one she'd pointed out to me. And that I'd told her to ignore. "What are you doing? What is this?"

I unlocked the gate and opened it enough to let him in. But just then the back car door opened. My cousin slowly emerged. Oleg turned and nodded at him. My cousin, Pasha, turned back around toward the car and bent over the seat. He was a large, heavyset man and each movement took considerable time. Oleg placed his hand on the gate and forcibly opened it wider.

Before I could ask what he was doing, Pasha turned back toward me. He was now holding Rory in his arms. Her body was limp. Her torso lay over one of his big arms, her legs over the other. He was huge, making her look all the tinier and more fragile in comparison.

I slammed the gate open, knocking Oleg out of my way, and rushed toward Pasha.

"What the fuck!" I yelled.

"Shhh," he said, motioning to the neighbors. I wanted to kill him. "She'll be okay, but let's get her inside, not make a scene."

She was wearing her dance clothes. Both her jacket and the leotard underneath were ripped open. "Give her to me!" I took her from his arms. "Rory!"

She was breathing, but seemed to be in a very deep sleep, almost comatose.

"What the fuck did you do to her?" I yelled.

"Please, please, inside," Oleg said, pushing me through the gate and shutting it behind them.

"Baby, baby," I called out. I ran her inside, past the foyer into the living room, and carefully laid her on the sofa. I took her wrist and felt for her pulse. It was there but slow. I cupped my hand on her forehead. She felt a little warm but not much. I placed my hand by her nose. She was breathing. Her chest rose and fell with each tiny breath.

She looked more like Tatiana than ever. I felt tears well. This should be Tatiana, brought back to me. Rory should be upstairs sleeping in my bed. *Where she should always be.* I wanted to cry for both of my women, as well as beat my uncle to a bloody pulp.

I could feel him hovering over me from behind. "What did you do to her?" I said without taking my eyes off my love, trying hard to contain my anger and keep my fists from balling. If I turned to look at him I might not be able to keep control.

"We thought she was Tanya. We're very sorry. She is okay. Completely unharmed. We only gave her a drug to make her sleep. She will wake up in a few hours."

They thought she was Tatiana? So, instead of asking me, they just took her? "What do you mean?" I whipped around toward him, bunched the material of his collar with my fists and pulled hard on his neckline, bringing his face within millimeters of mine.

"Okay, calm down now," Pasha said.

I eyed him. Instead of appearing tough, like he at all meant his words, he had a sad, removed look in his droopy eyes. *Fucking loser. Fucking psycho.* I hated these people. I let go of Oleg and rushed toward my cousin.

I grabbed his arms, and shook him.

"What the fuck? What did you do?" I shook and shook, hoping I'd shake his pathetic stupidity right out of him.

"I said calm down and we will tell you everything. If you don't calm down, we can't talk. You want to know what happened. You want to calm down, Sasha." As much as I shook his large body, his words were completely steady.

"Sasha, she is unharmed. Sit down." This came from Oleg. He placed a firm hand on my shoulder. "Back off Pasha. This is my fault. He only followed my orders." I turned back to Oleg. "Sit down, son," he repeated.

They told me they'd been following us for some time. They thought Rory was Tatiana, they looked so much alike. They'd found more information than I did, not surprisingly. Information they didn't bother to share with me, since I'd become their suspect in kidnapping my sister, or harboring her from them, rather. They'd been told through "affiliates of the agency" that she'd met a man in Tokyo who was from the U.S. From California. He was the one who'd paid off her debt to the agency and he'd brought her back to California with him. Of course they inferred that man was me. That I was the one who'd paid off her debts, and had moved her out here.

They'd told my mother as much, and she'd cried. She wanted her daughter back more than anything. She pleaded with them to go back to L.A. and take Tatiana away from me, bring her back home, where she belonged. They knew they'd have to use force, that I'd never release her into their hands willingly.

I listened to their story, growing angrier and

angrier by the second. So angry I thought I might kill them with my bare hands. When we'd met at Musso & Frank, I'd had such a strong vibe they were they were testing me by asking me to go to Tokyo to look for her. Now I knew at least the last trip had been a ruse, since they thought I already knew where she was. I had to admit though, I understood why they'd thought I would keep her with me without telling them. I'd never make my sister return to Russia against her will. Ever. That's the last thing I'd do. And though I hadn't told anyone, I'd rented the apartment for Rory expressly for that purpose—to keep Tanya safe and sound. They would have been right. Had Rory been Tatiana.

"We weren't going to take her back without talking to her first. That's why we took her to the storage room, to talk to her," Oleg said.

"Convince her to come back, willingly. We just wanted to talk," echoed Pasha.

"When she spoke, we realized her English was too good for having been here such a short time. Something wasn't right. When we looked for her scar," he said, pointing to his breast, "we couldn't find it. We knew then it wasn't her."

"How could you seriously mistake them?" I said, still inwardly raging, though my voice was now more controlled.

"We haven't seen Tanya in years," my uncle said, shrugging, as if what he'd done was nothing big. "They do look very much alike."

They did. Of course they did. A fact that had haunted me since I'd met Rory.

"And you couldn't possibly have just asked me if Tatiana had come to me?" But I knew the answer to this. If I thought they'd snatch her up, I would have hidden her; I would have lied to them. No one should ever have to go back there, to that horrible town, to my mother and her emotional abuse, and my father and his physical abuse. I would definitely have protected her from them.

"I think you know the answer to that," my uncle said.

I took several deep breaths, then turned back to the sleeping Rory. She looked unbelievably peaceful now, despite her torn clothing. I couldn't imagine what she'd been through. How scared she must have been of these...these Russian mobsters. *My family of thugs.* "Get out," I said to them.

"Sasha—"

"Now. Get out." I stood and turned to them, forcing myself to keep my hands at my sides. "Don't you ever come near Rory again. Don't you ever go near Tatiana again. Don't you ever come near me again."

"But of course you want to know when we find her."

I closed my eyes. Of course I did. Tatiana was alive. Now I knew she was. And she was apparently somewhere in the U.S., in California. But who was this man she was with? Was he good to her? Had she gone with him willingly or had he used his money to force her to go? Was she a sex slave? God forbid. Why hadn't she trusted me enough to contact me? He must have been preventing her from doing so.

All these thoughts flooded my head. I knew my uncle was far better at digging up information than I was. He'd find her. And when he did, I wanted to make sure he didn't take her back to Russia.

"Okay, listen to me," I said, trying to force my anger aside and be rational, trying to come up with a plan to get them to work with me, not against me. "Rory is a lawyer. She's an upstanding citizen here. She's completely innocent. You screwed with the wrong person. She'll want to know what happened to her when she wakes up. What am I going to tell her? She'll definitely want to turn you in. And I would never stand in her way."

"Come now, Sasha. You would never turn a family member in? We're family. Your mother—"

"Shut up and let me finish," I barked. "In exchange for us not turning you in, for me refraining from telling her all about this—for a while, anyway—you must agree to bring Tatiana to me once you find her. You will not take her to Russia. If you take her to Russia, I promise you I will hunt you down. You will pay. I promise you. Rory is a very, very smart girl. She and I will find you, and you will be in a great deal of trouble. You will never be allowed in the U.S. again, and if you are captured, you will rot in prison."

Saying my sweet love's name made me seethe all over again. I was practically foaming at the mouth, like a rabid animal. I'd never been more serious about anything in my life. Not winning Blackpool. Nothing. *Nothing* meant more to me now than protecting Rory, and preventing my uncle from snatching my sister and carting her back to a place I knew she didn't want to go.

"You promise me you will bring her to me. And we'll all talk it out. You give me your word. And I'll give you my word that your criminality, the assault, kidnapping and drugging of an American citizen, which can result in thirty years in an American prison, will not be spoken of." I had no idea what sentence these convictions carried. Oleg would be a very old man in thirty years. It sounded sufficiently threatening.

My uncle thought, then slowly nodded. "It is a deal," he said.

"Give me your word, on my mother."

"Sasha…" He took off his sunglasses. A first.

"Give me your word, Oleg. I can't believe I'm doing this, but I'm letting you go. I'm making myself into a criminal for you. You give me your word or I'll come after you, with the American criminal justice system behind me. And I'll get her back if you take her. Believe me. You'll never see me or your niece again."

"Sasha, Sasha, please stop with these threats. They are unnecessary. We are family. I give you my word I will bring Tatiana to you once we find her."

I looked deep into his immense pupils. They appeared purplish, as if they were bruised by life, by all he'd seen. We stared each other down for a few seconds. Then he looked at Rory. He blinked. He knew I meant business. He knew I was being very gracious, after what he'd done to the woman I loved more than anything. He knew he was avoiding very serious trouble. The U.S. was not exactly a Third World country with a weak government. And I think he might even have felt badly about abducting an innocent girl whose only transgression was getting involved with me. But to say he had feelings might have been giving him too much credit. Maybe. I didn't know this man at all. I didn't know my family at all.

With a final nod, he and Pasha left.

As I heard the sedan pull away, I got mad at myself all over again for not trusting Rory's instincts. She knew there was something sinister about that car. And I hadn't listened to her. First and last time that would ever happen.

I picked her up, carried her upstairs, and laid her down on the bed. I removed all of her clothes. Those fuckers, they'd tied her wrists and ankles together with rope. She had rope burns. I ran into the bathroom and collected a bottle of hydrogen peroxide, cotton balls, and aloe vera cream. After I doctored her up, I placed her under the soft, warm covers, pulling them all the way up to her chin.

I went back downstairs, grabbed a picnic basket from the pantry, walked outside, into the garden, over to the rose bed in full spring bloom. My rose bed that Sadie had insisted I keep up. *Sweet Sadie.* It was largely because of her that I had Rory in my life now, after all, since she'd made sure James was the winner of the private lesson package, ultimately leading Rory to the studio.

I pulled off red petal after petal, placed them in the basket. After I had half a basketful, I walked back inside, upstairs. And I laid the rose petals all around Rory, outlining her beautiful body. I scattered some remaining petals over the top of her, ensconced in the blanket. She looked so beyond beautiful, so angelic, so innocent.

I got blisteringly angry all over again at my family. My horrible, awful, pathetic family whom I would never be free of.

***

"Mmmmmm," Rory moaned, hours later. She was coming to.

I hadn't slept a wink. I lay next to her, in bed, waiting for her to wake up like her namesake, Aurora, in "Sleeping Beauty." How absurdist this whole situation was, I thought. I'd been thinking all night what I would say to her, and I still had no idea. I really wanted not to tell her anything until we knew something definitive about Tatiana. Until I knew she was safe. I was so humiliated by my family. I just wanted them to go away. I hailed from a family of brutes, who completely fulfilled the American stereotype of Russian mafia.

I had to stop thinking about them and focus on the wonderful woman in front of me. They were my past, or would be as soon as I had Tatiana. Rory was my future. Her beautiful, long eyelashes began to flutter, and her lids slowly opened to reveal her beatific, dreamy green irises. She blinked hard. I'd had the velvet curtains parted slightly to let in some early morning sunlight.

"Mmmm, hello," she said, seeing me next to her. "Ooooh," she moaned, looking down at the covers. "So warm. So cozy. And so, mmmm, what's that aroma... Oh wow, rose petals!"

But then she suddenly shot up as if waking from a nightmare. She held the blanket around her chest, but removed an arm from underneath the comforter to touch one of the petals. Feeling it, rubbing it between her fingers, she looked confused. Then, though she'd seen me, she seemed suddenly to realize I was in bed beside her. She turned fully to look at me, a frown now crossing her face. She shook her head as if shaking off a bad thought, and wrapped her arms around her chest, rocking herself under the covers.

I sat up with her.

"Oh my God. You won't believe…I had the most awful—"

I wrapped my arms around her and pressed my lips deeply into her soft, creamy cheek. Holding her more tightly so that she was completely encompassed in my arms, I transferred my lips to her forehead, then traced kisses all around her face and neck. She moaned and giggled, her body relaxing, but just momentarily. As her muscles tensed again, I knew she realized something wasn't right.

She struggled out of my grasp and turned to face me. She opened her mouth but I was the one who spoke first. I had to talk. I had to beg for forgiveness, above all else. "I'm so, so, so sorry, my love. My beautiful, sweet love. It will never happen again. I promise. I promise I will never doubt you again. Never. And I promise you those men are gone. They will never harm you again. No one will harm you again. I swear it. I swear on my life." I spoke fast but each word was pronounced clearly and weighted.

Her beatific smile evaporated. Her beautiful hazy jade eyes widened, her pupils growing, piercing mine. "Sasha, what—"

I brushed my index finger lightly over her lips and caressed her chin with my thumb. "Please, I can't talk now. I will. I promise. I will tell you everything. Just not now." I needed to wait until I had word on Tatiana. And I couldn't tell her about Tatiana now. I just couldn't. Something told me if I did, everything could go horribly awry. She'd let out to someone what had happened to her and my family of brutes would come back after her, and would break our deal about Tatiana. But more seriously, they could hurt her. And I would never, ever let anything happen to her again. I promised myself that. I promised her.

She shook her head. "No, Sasha. You know about those horrid men. You know. You have to tell me. I have to know what just happened to me." Her voice was shaky but she wasn't crying. She was shaking with anger and fear.

I closed my eyes and swallowed. "I promise I will tell you. I can't now. I can't. For now, please just trust me, Rory. Please."

"I do trust you. But that doesn't mean I don't need to know what happened. I could have been raped. I could have been killed! Who were those men, Sasha? Are you in some kind of trouble? You are, aren't you? Those men were pure evil!"

"No." I shook my head firmly. She thought I had dealings with the mafia. "They never would have killed you. Nor rape you. They never would have hurt you at all. They would never hurt anyone. That was not their intent."

"Sasha!" She backed away from me, squirming to the far side of the bed. "How do you know that? How do you know those horrible men? What are you involved in?"

"Nothing. They are not mafia, Rory. They aren't. I am involved in nothing. I just...know them. I just...do." I shook my head and looked away, unable to face her. "I cannot tell you right now," I said, looking out the window through the parted curtain, where I could glimpse the rose garden, mostly shorn of petals. "I promise you, I will tell you as soon as I can. When I know it's safe. But right now they will not hurt you again. They will not hurt anyone. At least not anyone who does not deserve…" My voice trailed off and I closed my eyes and pinched my temples.

If she knew about Tatiana, if she knew how much she looked like her, if she knew that she might be in trouble because of that—something I didn't even know for sure—it would take over her entire day-to-day consciousness. She'd constantly be panicked, scared. I wouldn't let anyone touch her again. I wouldn't. And for some reason, I trusted Oleg to honor our bargain. But I didn't know if she'd trust me enough not to be frightened all the time.

"Anyone who does not deserve what? Sasha!" Fear radiated outward from her eyes, encompassing her entire face.

I turned to her again, looked her straight in the eye. "Please, Rory. I need you to trust me. I promise you they will never, ever harm you again in any way. But you have to trust me. I can't talk about this now. I need your trust." Again my words were fast but I pronounced every syllable with razor-sharp precision and immense weight.

"Sasha, are they mafia? They're mafia, aren't they?"

"No. Absolutely not." I shook my head for emphasis. "Don't even…please don't even… I promise you they are not mafia. They are not related to mafia. I know this for a fact. Rory, this is not about me and it's not about you. It's…I can't…please. I'm not making light of this by not telling you right now. It's totally the opposite. I need your trust." I scooted to her and placed my hands on her arms, running my palms up and down them from her shoulders to her wrists. Then I wrapped my arms around her body and rocked her back and forth.

The friction from my hands and the heat from my body and its proximity to hers created warmth. I tried to envelop her, let her disappear into me. She was an innocent, middle-class girl. She knew nothing of the bad things that happened to certain people, innocent though they were. I had to protect her from it all. Not just the reality of it, but the thought of it all. I had to banish this whole thing from her mind. How?

"Sasha, I'm a lawyer. I do criminal law, for crying out loud. At least I did. A crime was committed. A kidnapping. Do you realize how this goes against every fiber of my being not to report—"

"Yes," I said, whispering in her ear, now even closer, as close as I could get, my arms engulfing her even more. "I do. I do," I continued whispering. I wrapped one arm around her back and one around her knees, now cradling her, my body cocooning hers. "I do," I said once again. I held her like that for several moments before continuing. "You are so brilliant. My brilliant lawyer. I love you so much. I love your good soul. You are everything to me. Everything."

It wasn't that I didn't trust her not to report my uncle and cousin until they found Tatiana. I knew she loved me and would do what I wanted. But I also knew it would create such a contradiction in character for her that it would harm her soul not to report a crime. I didn't want to do that to her. And I feared if she knew anything, at this point anyway, it just wouldn't lead to anything good. It would make her a target for my uncle, or perhaps for the people who actually had Tatiana. It would at least make Oleg want to keep her quiet. Who knew what he'd do to that end?

I needed to keep her innocent. I needed to keep her ignorant. For now. After I'd had a chance to see Tatiana, after this was all over, everything would be different. I prayed.

She took several deep breaths. I could feel her heart pumping, and her brain working. Slowly, she lifted her chin toward me. Her lips, her face, were so moist. I placed my lips on hers, my tongue coaxing them apart, filling her mouth. Soon we were both lying down, my body covering hers protectively, our limbs entwined.

"You are mine. If anyone ever tries to touch you again, they will answer to me. And they will be very sorry," I whispered into her ear, kissing her earlobe, neck and face.

She said nothing, but nodded. I soon felt her muscles relax and heard the steady rhythm of her breathing as she slept.

She was agreeing to trust me, allowing herself to forget about those horrible men, at least for now.

CHAPTER EIGHT

I knew Rory couldn't truly forget, though. I'd never be able to either. I'd promised her I would tell her, eventually. And I would. She deserved to know. It was the most frightening thing that had ever happened to her. I knew that.

For now, we threw ourselves into practicing for Blackpool—our singular challenge at this point. Probably the only challenge we could actually control. Somehow, after what had happened, we were dancing better than ever. She was eating better than ever. The first thing she'd do when she got to my place was down one of my juices. I prepared snacks for her when I went to work and she stayed in to work with Greta. I enjoyed preparing food. Maybe when I retired from competitive dance, I'd open a restaurant. Daily I filled little containers with baby carrots, peppers of all colors, radishes, artichoke hearts, sliced avocado, beets, bananas and apples, a variety of nuts and cheeses, and slices of smoked salmon, and most of them would often be near gone when I got home.

One evening, after we'd ended practice and were enjoying a bottle of champagne in the hot tub, she said something that momentarily made me go cold. "I'm so glad you're so healthy," I said to her, wrapping my arms around her from behind and lightly sucking the delicate skin of her neck.

"I guess that's one not-horrid thing that came out of the ordeal. I realized how much I loved my life. How I'd miss it if it was taken from me. Eating is an affirmation of that, I guess." Her voice was so soft and sweet. She said this with no anger whatsoever.

"I love your life too," I whispered, and continued tasting her, taking in her beautiful scent, her deliciously soft, creamy skin.

Despite the fact that this ordeal would hang over our heads at least until Tatiana was found and I could tell her, Rory worked harder than ever on her dancing. She put everything she had into winning Blackpool. Maybe it was also that I was likewise overwhelmed, and that finding Tatiana was more in the forefront of my mind than it had been, but there was simply nothing now to criticize about our partnership, not a single thing to harp on. A first for me. We were simply at our best. We were, I hoped and actually thought, the best.

"We're getting there," I said at one point during practice.

Rory cracked up. It always warmed my soul now whenever she laughed.

I shot her a bemused frown.

"That's your way of saying we're actually looking good. We're actually ready. Or, like, semi-ready. I mean, you can never be one hundred percent ready. Good lord—I'm starting to think like you! I'm developing your perfectionist ways! You're becoming optimistic like me and I'm becoming a perfectionist like you!"

"No, no, you'll never be as bad as me," I said with a smile and a peck to her cheek.

Then she sobered. "Yeah, I've never worked so hard on anything, Sasha. Not college, not law school. Even the bar exam. I don't think I worked this hard even for that. I don't know, it's like I have a new lease on life, and there isn't a single aspect of it I'm not going to live to the fullest." She shrugged, and I wanted nothing more than to take those shoulders and pull them into me closely, wrap my body around hers, never let her go.

***

We returned to Daiyu's two weeks before the competition. Rory had gained enough weight that her dresses fit her perfectly. I was so proud of her. She was proud of herself. The costumes looked absolutely breathtaking on her. Daiyu had embroidered all the rhinestones on and they glimmered in the bright Los Angeles sunlight gleaming through the opened window.

"I can't believe how...glamorous I look!" Rory squealed. "Like never before. Certainly not in any of my ballet costumes. I look like a real ballroom dancer." She blushed.

I hugged her. I was quite unable to keep my hands off her these days. "I'm so happy you think so."

"Don't you?"

"Rory, are you kidding? I have never *not* thought you were absolutely gorgeous."

She giggled.

***

We recorded ourselves practicing in the costumes.

"I love them so much, Sasha," Rory squealed, watching the video and running her fingertips over her costume yet again. She was truly happy with Daiyu's work. I'd feared she'd be too fixated on her weight to see how beautiful she was. But I'd been wrong. Of course, a lot had happened since we went to see Daiyu. "She's put in all these little hidden skin-toned straps, so there's virtually no chance of a costume malfunction! Oh, but what am I saying. I'm totally going to jinx myself!"

"No you're not." I laughed. "Daiyu is a pro. You can trust her to know what she's doing."

"I do." Rory's eyes were aglow. "They're all so elegant and sleek. Sexy without looking gauche or trashy. And, we just…well, I'm just in awe by how much we look like real partners, just like all the dancers on the videos I've watched ad nauseam."

"Of course we look like real dancers. That's because we *are* real dancers." Again, I had to remind myself how new this all was to her. It was endearing how excited she was. And relieving to see how focused she was on this, something beautiful, and not on the ugly thing that had happened.

"You were wrong. Wrong, wrong, wrong," she teased me, pressing her index finger into my chest after we'd finished practicing our final dance.

I frowned, although I knew exactly what she meant. "What are you talking about?"

"On our first day at Daiyu's, you thought I wouldn't be happy with my costume. With whatever costume she made for me. That I'd never be happy with my body." She put her arms behind her back, clasped her hands, and swung her body back and forth, smiling up at me sweetly like a happy schoolgirl.

I smiled and nodded. "That's true. I do remember saying that."

"And you were wrong. This costume is hot, hot, hot!" She swung about more fully, now swirling her arms about too. "I actually look…good." She blushed, looking suddenly embarrassed at her new, improved self-esteem.

I shook my head and laughed. "No."

"No? Did you just say—"

"I mean to say that the costume looks very, very good on you. But it is not the costume that is hot. It's the wearer." I grabbed both of her hands to stop her from swinging. I tightened my lips, made a faux serious expression.

I stepped slowly toward her and, still holding her hands, pressed my lips to hers, where they remained for a good many minutes. Then I began brushing my lips against her sweet, creamy cheek, then down to her chin, to her neck, and to her clavicle before running my tongue along the top of her right breast, out toward her right shoulder—the one left bare by the toga top.

I stopped and looked at her with my best puppy dog eyes. I ran my finger along the top line of the costume. "I would like to see more hotness, please. Less costume, more wearer."

She emitted an embarrassed laugh. "Yeah, probably not a good idea to do anything in these anyway. We don't want to, you know, soil anything."

That was true. Of course I knew Daiyu could fix anything, but it was a good excuse to get out of our clothes.

I unfastened the hook atop her zipper, which was located directly under her armpit. I trailed my fingers down her side and she giggled.

"Oh wait," she cried out as I finally got the zipper down. "My shoes." She looked down at her feet. "I don't want to snag any stones or anything on the way off."

I mock-harrumphed and bent down. "What I won't do to get you naked," I muttered as I slowly unbuckled her shoes, then delicately removed each foot from its high heel.

She giggled again. "I feel a bit like Cinderella, except my prince is freeing my foot rather than fitting it into the glass slipper."

Every time she said something cute like that I had to kiss the nearest body part, which now happened to be her right ankle.

After her shoes were off, I gingerly pulled the top of the toga down, over her left shoulder, down past her breasts to her waist, then on down her thighs. I went deliciously slowly, ostensibly to avoid snagging any part of the costume, but really so that I could run my nose and lips over every inch of her breathtaking body, every pore of her skin as the material revealed it. At points, I ran my tongue over her bareness, but more often, I just breathed in deeply, stopping every few inches, taking in every bit of her beautiful body, so happy she finally agreed with my assessment of it.

When I finally had the damn thing off, I sauntered to the chair near the window and draped it over the back. Then I turned to her, looking her up and down with hooded lids.

"Let me see your rrrumba walks," I commanded with my r's.

"Oh stop it! No way!" she shouted. "Take off your costume, put your pants and top on the other chair, and get over here."

I tapped my foot and widened my eyes, making it clear I was waiting for her to do what I said, that I wasn't taking no for an answer. She took a deep breath, shifted her weight to her left foot, pointed her right toe to make her trademark gorgeous leg line, and, tracing her toe along the floor, began doing those breathtaking walks toward me.

My plan was to watch her all the way, but when she was about halfway to me, I couldn't help it. I began walking toward her. At first slowly, seductively, then faster and faster until I practically rushed her. When I reached her, I pulled her to me.

"Perfect," I whispered before kissing her deeply, wrapping my arms around her, one on her back shoulder blade, one around her waist, pulling her closer.

"Sasha," she said, after catching her breath. I looked at her with my same heavily lidded eyes. I could tell she wanted me to take her. "No. Come on. We don't want to mess up anything," she said, emphasis on the last word. She rolled her eyes in a downward direction and crossed one leg slightly over the other, indicating that she didn't want the wetness between her legs to meet the material of my pants.

I took a breath and stepped back, releasing her. Then I got another idea. I pivoted around and darted toward the chair, grabbed the iPod remote from the side stand and set the speakers to play Tom Jones's "You Can Leave Your Hat On," then pivoted sharply back toward her. By the time I was facing her, the music came on. We'd used it to practice a slow cha-cha and she'd said she thought it was so sexy.

As Jones crooned the first line, telling his baby to take off her coat, I began to run my fingers down the deep v-neck of my shirt. The shirt had no buttons, so I had to mime undoing them, which made her giggle. Then I fingered the solid black lining of my top, slowly, before moving my fingers to the top of my pants to finger the thick waistline. She gasped. I'd never done a striptease before. It was fun! At least doing it for Rory was.

And when I slowly undid my zipper then lowered my pants, I could tell from the way she was breathing that she was pretty much on fire. I kicked off my shoes, tossed off my socks, and whipped off the shirt all in one fell swoop, leaving my black dance briefs the only particle of clothing covering any part of my body.

I began doing these very slow, pelvic-swaying *cucarachas*, but then threw in some lightning-fast steps to the side, dancing about four steps to every beat of music. I just couldn't do all slow and seductive. I had to fly at some point. I had too much energy. And fly I could with the dance briefs, you know, holding everything in. But then I suddenly stopped, right when Jones tells his paramour she's the reason he lives, and I drilled my penetrating gaze right into hers.

Her breath caught again. Then, as suddenly as I'd stopped, I started again, this time cha-cha-ing toward her, moving like a flame. She gasped as I reached her, whipped her into a close hold, and cha-cha'd with her around in a circle. I pulled her in closer and closer with each step. She wasn't spotting, her eyes remaining on me the entire time we whirled around, so those steps had to be dizzying. We were going faster and faster and her glorious breasts were bouncing straight into my pecs, nipple brushing nipple.

"Stop!" she cried out.

I did as she asked and she pushed me back, into the barre, and closed her eyes for a second, likely to regain her balance. She opened her mouth to take in a deep breath. I couldn't resist—I immediately covered her mouth with mine. While I kissed her deeply, she reached around my backside, grabbed my ass, bunched the only material remaining on my body in her hand and pulled down. Then she moved back toward me, my hardening cock pressing against her silky skin. She pulled her mouth away from mine and backed up, so as to look at me. She eyed me up and down, focusing on my cock, now beyond hard, and pushed me down farther onto the barre, pulling herself up as high as she could, standing on her tiptoes, ballerina-like, spread her beautiful creamy thighs, and slid me into her delicious body. *Damn. Glorious.*

My back was against the mirror and she placed a palm on either side of me, onto the glass. She arched back and lifted her chin. I took advantage of the position to lick the sweet hollow of her neck.

As much as I relished being inside her soft wetness, my ass pounding into the wood of the barre was not ideal. I moved forward off it, lifting her completely off the floor.

"Muscle power!" she giggled.

"You're a feather, Rory. But yes, I am very strrrong," I said, flashing my wicked grin. I walked forward, still carrying her. She wrapped her legs around my waist and her arms around my back more tightly as I carried her all the way across the floor and up the winding staircase to the bedroom.

CHAPTER NINE

Blackpool time was here in a flash. Rory was full of nervous excitement the day of our flight. I splurged on a nice UberLUX to LAX to calm her down a bit. We sipped chardonnay and I caressed her now perfect knee and kissed her cheek as we wended down through Beverly Hills onto La Cienega Boulevard. When we checked our baggage and the extra luggage weight—due to the heaviness of the stone-ridden costumes—cost an additional two hundred dollars, Rory gasped. I had to keep reminding her it was all okay, it was all paid for. And this was all normal. Everyone's luggage cost a ton for the costumes and shoes alone. She obviously grew up without a lot of money, like I did.

After we checked in for our flight, I recommended we get shoulder and back massages from the terminal's salon before the long flights ahead. We'd be in business class but I was such an active person I still found it hard on my back to sit or lie down for long periods of time. Rory had never taken a flight over five hours, so she didn't know what to expect. And she'd never been abroad. Even showing her new passport to the check-in agent filled her with glee. She was the sweetest thing. Just watching her eyes full of wonder filled me with happiness. I was thrilled to show her the world. The world as I knew it, anyway.

She'd never taken business class before and delighted in the expanded leg and elbow room, and the way the seats reclined to almost lying position. And that they gave us unlimited cocktails. I ordered a scotch for myself and another chardonnay for her.

"It's eleven in the morning and this is already my second!" she squealed.

"It'll relax you," I said with a kiss to her cheek.

Rory was equally thrilled with the expanded entertainment system. We were set up to watch "Dark Knight Rises" but she ended up spending the flight to New York peering outside at the passing clouds.

Despite the squeals and the giggles, I could tell she was anxious about what was to come. "There's no point in stressing out now, sweet," I said. "Everything's in our muscle memory. It is what it is in terms of how the judges will like it. We can't control that any more. Stressing out now will only give us the potential to screw up."

She nodded, sobering. "I know."

"What are you thinking?" I asked her after the movie ended and she was still gazing outside.

"What all is down there. The farms, the plains, the mountain ranges, the cities, the lakes, just everything. I've only flown cross-country twice. Well, between California and North Carolina. And it's been a while."

It had been a long time since I'd seen the world with those eyes. I missed it, in a way. I rubbed my thumb on the inside of her thigh, and she giggled softly, still lost in her thoughts.

After we landed at JFK for our connecting flight and were settled in the lounge, her eyes began to fill with tears as she stared down at the bubbles of her glass of champagne. There was so much going on behind those eyes that I couldn't decipher and it was killing me. One minute she was giddy, the next nervous, then pensive, and sometimes sad.

"Oh sweet, another penny for your thoughts," I said, trying to amuse her with another of my "Americanisms" that she so loved.

But she didn't laugh. She'd finally gotten used to me, apparently. "It's just weird being back here. I mean, I wish we had time to go to Lincoln Center and catch a New York City Ballet performance. It would be nice to see how the area's changed, or stayed the same, since my try-out for the summer intensive."

I'd been so wrapped up in the drama with my family and the stress of Blackpool, I'd totally forgotten how she'd almost become a student at the School of American Ballet, before her father passed and her life changed. Of course she was going through a lot right now. It probably brought back a cornucopia of memories, both good and bittersweet. "I'm so sorry. I forgot about your experiences here. I should have arranged for a longer stay-over," I said.

"I didn't think of it either," she said. "I didn't feel this until now that I'm here. I mean, I'm just thinking how much life can change. Twelve years ago I came here with the intention of becoming a ballerina. It didn't work out and I was heartbroken. And now here I am with a law degree and an entirely different dance dream. Not to mention"—now she giggled—"a gorgeous Russian boyfriend and professional dance partner!"

I kissed her long and soft. "We'll come back and explore together. I was here for a year as well. You can show me your old places, and I'll show you mine."

"I'd like that," she whispered.

Once we were on the plane, Rory was all squeals and giggles. For dinner, she ordered Shepherd's pie with Caesar salad and chocolate mousse for dessert. And yet more chardonnay. I started to worry she'd get a headache. But I had aspirin. She'd be okay.

"I'm a bit drunk already but screw it. It's my first flight abroad!"

After dinner, I reclined and dozed off, still holding Rory's hand. When I woke up hours later, she was looking out the window, now more excited than sad and pensive. I looked over her shoulder. We were still over Ireland. She couldn't have seen much but clouds. I knew she hadn't slept. Good thing I'd scheduled us to arrive a day early. She'd need it to catch up on rest and adjust to the time difference.

The flight attendants soon came by with another meal—English breakfast. She gobbled it right up, delighting in every flavor, though the meal was loaded with lard: sausage pudding, fried bread, fried tomato, beans. I was glad to see her enjoying food so, without even thinking about it.

We had to go through separate lines at customs since I still had a Russian passport and she an American one. I hoped to hold an American one someday. Someday soon.

"It's weird being separated on our way from and to the same place," she remarked. We kissed and hugged goodbye like we wouldn't be seeing each other again for a long time.

"I'll see you on the other side," I said with a faux sinister tone before planting a long, solid kiss on her lips and dipping her dramatically. She lifted one leg up high, pointing her toe, giggling. People looked at us like the crazed in-love paramours that we were. *Let them look!* I was so over my PDA-phobia.

It took forever for her to get through the non-European line, there were so many Americans. I waited outside for her for nearly an hour.

"I was worried they suspected you of being a terrorist, and put you through the third degree," I said when I finally saw her approaching.

"Do I look like a terrorist?" she said, play-slugging me in the arm.

"Sure, why not? Yellow-blonde hair, big jade doe eyes, soft, milky skin, good enough to drink. Mmmm," I said, licking her neck.

"Uh huh. Still waiting for the terrorist part?" She laughed.

"Oh yes. Well, terrorists come in all shapes and sizes, no? Wasn't there an American newspaper heiress who was perhaps a terrorist? Something like that?" I wore a cocked smile to let her know I was kind of serious, but not completely.

"I don't know if terrorist is the right word for her, but Patty Hearst," she said. Just as she said the name, she suddenly sobered, as if she'd seen something, or remembered something.

"What's wrong?" I said, pulling back to look at her while cupping her chin in my hand.

"Nothing," she said flatly. It was clear she was trying to cover something up.

"No, seriously. You suddenly are upset by

something. Please tell me."

"No. I'm just feeling a little upset stomach over all that I ate on the plane," she insisted.

I decided I'd let her off the hook. If she wanted to talk about it later, she would. I wasn't one to make anyone talk about something they didn't want to talk about. And after my silence regarding what had happened, I'd be a huge hypocrite if I was. "It will wear off. If it doesn't we will get something at the pharmacy," I said, kissing her forehead.

***

We passed the train station connected to the airport on our way to the taxi stand. The station's Blackpool-bound platform was filled to capacity with competitors, also making their trek to the mecca of the ballroom world, also pulling heavy luggage. I didn't see anyone I knew personally, but many of them looked at me and smiled in recognition, then looked away. I smiled and nodded in return.

When we arrived at the taxi stand, Rory had another fit of giggles. I was glad she was over her blue funk. I looked at her, eyebrows raised.

"These are for real? I always assumed these old-style cars were only used in movies, and that English taxis were yellow and newer, like the ones in New York."

"Nope, this is England. These are for real," I said, and kissed her cheek. It was quite impossible not to kiss her after every sweet, wonder-filled thing she said.

I spotted a man holding up a large sign that read "Zakharov." I led Rory toward him. As he took our bags, I opened the back door for her. She giggled again when she got in. I was just about to lean in for another kiss when I realized there were a plethora of cell phones aimed at us. I stood back and smiled out at the crowd. But they startled Rory. I heard her audibly gasp inside the car.

"It's okay," I said, patting her arm as chattering erupted from the opposite side of the taxi line.

"That's her. His new partner!"

"Who is she?"

"I don't know!" said the voices.

"Oh, I keep forgetting you're a star," she said.

"You'll get used to it," I said.

"Sasha! Obnoxious a bit!"

I laughed. Not really. Just realistic. "I'm serious. Next year, everyone will be saying, 'Look, there's Rory Laudner! Quick, take a picture! Who's that guy she's with?'"

"Stop!" She laughed.

Of course she didn't take her eyes off the passing landscape through the window for the entire forty-five minute ride from Manchester to Blackpool. I put my arm around her and closed my eyes, resting my chin in the crook of her neck. "Mmmm, try to get some sleep at some point, love."

"Are you kidding? This is fascinating!"

I laughed as I looked out the window at the rolling hills, the grazing cows, sheep, a few horses.

"You don't have horses and cows and green fields anywhere in America? Well, maybe not Los Angeles. But not in North Carolina?"

"Not English cows and horses and green fields! Look at those gray buildings!" she squealed, bouncing in her seat, when we came to a town center. She pointed at them as if they were the Eiffel Tower. "It's like something straight out of Dickens! Look at the cobblestoned streets!" She took her cell phone out of her bag and snapped at everything. "Look, a sign for Liverpool! That's where the Beatles are from!"

Her excitement was contagious. When we arrived in Blackpool, I felt like I was seeing it anew myself. The little seaside city, with its winding, narrow brick roads lined with pubs, fish and chip places, Indian restaurants, billboards and double-decker buses bearing advertisements on their sides for casinos, its boardwalk and, off in the distance, its little theme park with its Ferris wheel, did have its charm.

"The beach looks beautiful," she said. "Too bad it's so chilly."

"This weekend's a bank holiday here. You'd be surprised how many people go out there," I said.

"Mmmm, I dunno. I'm used to California weather."

"Me too," I said proudly. "That's it. That's where the competition will be held," I said as we wended around the large round civic-center-type building that was the Winter Gardens. I was holding her hand, and I could feel her heart pulsing.

We continued circling around the rotunda, turned off, and took another smaller street bearing a series of small hotels, including ours. Again, she giggled.

I looked at her.

"That one's called the Ruskin Hotel. Just brings back memories of college English classes!"

I was embarrassed to say I knew nothing of Ruskin. A writer I'd definitely have to look up. But I was delighted she was so delighted with England.

The check-in line at our hotel extended out the lobby and practically outside, making me kick myself for not having arrived a day earlier. The second we entered, all eyes were on us. As I expected. What I didn't expect was that Rory would be so overwhelmed with the attention.

"Hey, Sasha, hey man, how are you?"

"Sasha!"

"Oh my God, look!"

"Where's Xenia? Are you competing? Is she competing?"

We were suddenly surrounded by so many people, I couldn't respond to everyone fast enough. Many were friends and fellow dancers from Russia, who I saw two or three times a year, at this competition, the Worlds, and sometimes another large one in Germany or Austria, if I chose to do those. Some were fellow top-tier competitors who I saw at the show dance performances.

"Sergei, I'm good, how's it going?" I said, in Russian to a friend from the Ukraine.

"Xenia and I broke up. I have a new partner—" I said in answer to Yulia, his girlfriend. Before I could introduce her, I saw an old, familiar face, my good buddy, Valentin.

"Sasha!"

"Hey, man!" We hugged and gave each other solid back pats. Val was a good friend from St. Petersburg whom I'd met at my first Blackpool with Micaela. He was a friend of hers and a champion standard ballroom dancer. We'd become better friends when we both lived in New York and taught at the same small studio. We had our first experiences at Blackpool, and then in America together. He now divided his time between New York and Russia and danced for Russia, but we'd remained friends. I felt badly for having been so horrible about keeping up with people in the months between competitions and show dance performances. I'd been a shit friend. But we were all busy. I wanted to talk more with him but there was a sea of arms swinging about my head.

"You're just arriving. I'll let you check in." He laughed. "We will definitely catch up later."

"Absolutely," I said. I turned to introduce him to Rory, but I felt another slap on my back coming from the other direction, and when I turned to look for Valentin, he'd already gone.

"How are you? What happened with Xenia?" a woman I recognized but couldn't place asked me.

"Ah, we broke up. This is my new partn—"

But I couldn't answer everyone simultaneously. There were so many slaps to my back and shoulder, I knew I'd be bruised if this continued. I realized all the cacophony was exacerbated by the fact that I was with a new woman. Everyone was confused and intrigued.

Then I heard people speaking Japanese. A group of Japanese men and women, all wearing Taka jackets—the main Japanese sponsor—were fast approaching, waving about Blackpool programs and taking pens out of pockets. They were going to ask for my autograph. I definitely wasn't opposed to signing, but I didn't want Rory to get overwhelmed. Hell, I was overwhelmed enough for both of us.

"Hello, I am Max, from New York," I heard a familiar voice say. I turned to see an old friend from Russia via New York introducing himself to Rory, in broken English. She smiled nervously at him, but I could tell she was very freaked out by all the hands and arms being thrust about, now her way as well as mine.

"Yes, Rory, this is my friend, Max. He teaches in New York." Max was a nice guy but more than a bit of a horndog when it came to women. I'd have to make it clear she was mine.

Max wore a wolfish grin, and asked me in Russian who she was. I told him she was my new partner, and cut him off before he was able to ask, with raised eyebrows, what kind of partner.

As I heard the Japanese voices now at my side, I said to him, "Yes, girlfriend." I'd meant to whisper but in my haste, it came out rather loudly. At least I'd spoken in Russian. But everyone had heard my answer, and they all—at least the Russians—ooohed and aaahed, and turned to gawk at Rory. *Poor girl.* She'd never had this much attention all at once before. I couldn't tell how she felt about it, if it would be good or bad for her still recovering self-image issues, and I didn't have much time to ponder it now because the autograph requests began, big time.

"Excuse me, excuse me," the head of the Japanese team said as another tugged on the bottom of my jacket, handing me a program to sign.

I graciously smiled and nodded, as per my usual, taking the booklet and the pen the man was holding. I opened it to the first page and signed my name. The group then formed a line—in a very organized manner; they were definitely a formation team—and, one by one, handed me their booklets to autograph. Before I knew it, another group had headed over. This one was composed of people of different nationalities. They clearly weren't a team and weren't organized. Nor did they all have booklets, and many were handing me paraphernalia: a ticket to today's pre-comp competition for qualifiers; a greasy receipt from the fish and chips shop next door. And then suddenly everyone had a pamphlet showcasing the hotel we were in. It was turning into a mad romp, and I found all manner of items thrust in my face. This was fairly normal, but every year I seemed to forget how crazy it could get.

I usually soaked it all up. As did Xenia. But this year, I had Rory. This was all new to her, and she had to be tired from getting no sleep during the whole trip. I needed to check us in and get her up to the hotel room.

"Ah, wait, wait, please," I heard the desk attendant calling out, apparently unhappy about people taking the hotel's pamphlets.

"Okay, just a few more. Just a few…" I signed as fast as I could, looking at Rory every so often to make sure she was still with me, not about to kill me. She looked around wide-eyed, taking it all in. Okay, she wasn't about to fall over with exhaustion yet.

About two hours later, we were finally checked in and on our way to our third floor room.

"I'm really sorry. I hope that wasn't too much," I said, pushing the lift button.

"Not at all. That was fun." She yawned, her words an amusing contrast to her tone. The lack of sleep was starting to get to her.

But she was awake enough to find the elevators amusing. They were basically wooden boxes that went up and down in an open shaft, and you had to jump on and off as they slowly rose and descended in the open wall.

"I love how the English word for them is 'lift'

because that's literally what they are." She laughed.

I was going to book us at a fancier hotel farther away, but now I was glad I'd opted for the local one. Not only could we easily get to the Winter Gardens without having to rely on the sometimes unreliable cabs, but she was enthralled with these small hotel things.

***

I emerged from the shower, expecting to find Rory asleep. But she was wide awake, having gotten a second wind apparently from the charm of the lift, along with our view of a cobblestoned side street bearing a ubiquitous fish and chips and a couple of other hotels. This street, like the others in the area, was crowded with dancers. I hoped she'd settle down soon and could get some rest.

"My turn," she said, jumping up and taking a pair of red lacy underwear and a silky bra into the bathroom. I raised my eyebrows, but then thought better of saying or doing anything. We'd agreed to focus completely on dancing, and refrain from any sexual escapades until after Wednesday's competition. It was going to be killer hard, but we were on the same wavelength, both of us afraid nerves would just ruin it, make us bitter and all the more anxious. It gave us all the more reason to be single-minded until Wednesday, and look forward to Wednesday night.

She took a nice, long shower while I dressed and blew dry my hair, leaving it wavy and wild. It was the last day I could do so, and sometimes people didn't recognize me without it being gelled back. If we were going out to dinner, it might give us some privacy, I thought.

She was still in the shower when Valentin called, asking me to meet him at the bar downstairs. I figured I'd let Rory take her time. She needed that long, hot shower. I left her a text and walked downstairs. We found a secluded area in the back so we could catch up in private. It was so good to see him. He was a top competitor in standard ballroom, having placed second last year. He was hoping to win this year since the top competitors had retired and there were new judges. We'd kind of come up together. He was on the rise at the same time as Micaela and I but since we concentrated in different dances, we weren't competitive with each other. I always liked seeing him and of course I didn't run into him at the Latin-only comps. So we didn't see each other often enough. But when we did, it was like we were the best of friends.

Soon several other friends from that time in New York showed up, including Max the horndog, who was now a top amateur competitor in Latin, and Sergei, who'd retired and was now coaching. Of course they all wanted to know what had happened with Xenia, and how things were going with Rory. I had to tell the story anew with each new friend who arrived. We needed to get a Facebook group or something to keep in touch. I got so involved in catching up that I soon realized it had been a while and I hadn't heard from Rory. I checked my phone. No message. I texted her again. No response.

Just when I was about to go up and check on her, there she was, entering the bar. I practically fell off my stool, she looked so damn gorgeous. She'd really done herself up. She wore a short miniskirt, a form-fitting red sweater, and very hot over-the-knee black boots. She didn't see me.

"Rory, Rory!" I called out.

"Whoa," Max said.

"Woot," echoed Val and Sergei at once.

"Okay calm down, guys," I said to them in Russian.

I raised my arm and held my hand out to her. She smiled and indicated she'd make her way over. Wow, it had become pretty crowded in here. It might take her some time to get through the crowd. Sergei was talking about changes in the judging rules and I turned toward him, wanting to hear what he had to say since it very much affected us too. I kept my hand up, but soon realized it had been a while since I'd made eye contact with her. I looked around, asking him to hold off on continuing until I found her. I didn't see her. But right then, she grabbed my still-raised hand, bumping into two people who I now realized were blocking her. It had gotten insanely crowded. Insanely crowded right around us, that is.

"Sorry," she said to them with a nervous laugh as they were forced to part and allow her through.

"Thank you," I said to them. It was a man and woman, both blond and fair-skinned, both Danish-team-looking, though I didn't recognize them. They seemed confused, but calmed down and smiled when they realized she was with me.

"Mmmm, you look delicious," I whispered to Rory, eyeing her up and down, licking my lips.

She didn't laugh. "I didn't know where to look for you. I'm glad I found you."

"I left you a text. I came down to catch up with some old friends. I wanted you to take as long in the hot shower as you needed," I said, pulling her closer to me, unable to do anything other than ignore everyone else around me.

She smiled. "Well, I'm rarin' to go. I thought we could go out and explore the town. And believe it or not, I'm hungry again. It's like now that I'm eating regularly again, I can't stop."

"It's been a while since breakfast on the plane," I said. "I'm very glad your appetite's back." I kissed her right on the lips, everyone watching. I took out some English bills and put them on the bar, then turned toward Sergei and told him I wanted to hear the whole story but had to go eat with my girlfriend. I said it in Russian, so Rory didn't understand, but of course they all raised their eyes at my use of the term "girlfriend." I excused myself, patted Valentin on the shoulder and told him we'd talk again very soon.

"Yes, of course," he said.

"Have fun, kids," Max said in English, raising his eyebrows at Rory.

"You look so good," I said, taking her hand in mine and walking to the exit. "I'm just afraid you might get a little cold. The weather here is not like L.A."

"I'll be fine," she asserted.

But once we were outside, she immediately huddled against me.

"You sure you don't want to change?"

She shook her head adamantly. Something was odd in her demeanor, her attitude. Like she needed to look hot even if it meant freezing.

"We'll go to the Italian bistro. It's the best place here and it's just around the corner." I pulled her to me and wrapped her in my arms as much as I could while walking.

We became the center of attention in the completely packed restaurant the second we walked in. So many old, familiar faces.

A woman holding menus approached us. "I see Leo, a guy I know from London," I said to Rory. "I'm going to go say hi. Get us a table in the back, in a quiet area." I gave her shoulder a squeeze and her cheek a gentle peck.

"Will try," she said.

I hadn't seen Leo in a few years. Though I'd known him from London, he was Russian as well. I'd heard he'd had an injury and I wondered if he was back to competing.

"Hey, man," I said as he rose. We hugged, man-patted each other on the back. "How are you? How's the leg?"

He began telling me about his injury, a torn calf muscle that sounded horrible. No wonder he was out for so long. Those were a bitch to heal.

"Sit down," he said, pulling out a chair. We spoke in Russian.

"I have my girlfriend and partner with me," I said.

"There's room for her," said Gleb, another dancer I knew not from Russia but from England as well, from what was beginning to seem like a past life now that I had Rory.

"Hey!" I said, hand-slapping him in greeting.

Gleb pulled out a chair from across the table. "Put this one over there," he directed me.

"Thanks, man. But we kind of wanted a little privacy. It's her first night here. Her first night abroad—"

"Look around you!" He laughed. "Where else

you going to sit?"

Holy crap. There was now a huge line at the door, wrapping all the way around the block.

"Rory! Rory!" I called out, looking for her. I couldn't see her anywhere. I put my hand in the air again and waved madly, feeling like I was at a rock concert. Finally, I caught her eye. I waved her over, relieved. "Come on!"

She made her way through the bodies blocking us. I couldn't see her through them, but I sensed when she was near and stuck my arm straight through the bodies to part them this time. I stood, reached out, and grasped her hand, interlacing her fingers with mine, guiding her the rest of the way toward me.

She laughed when she got inside the crowd and eyed the small wooden chair reserved for her. I knew it wasn't exactly what either of us had in mind. I should have known this restaurant would be packed. Truth was, I'd never cared before. I hadn't wanted to spend any intimate, romantic time with Xenia in a while now, and she was the person who'd accompanied me here for the past several years. I'd forgotten how crazy it got.

I laughed with Rory and shrugged my shoulders. "Sorry, honey," I mouthed. "It appears that's all there is." I caressed her arm and gently guided her down onto the hard wood seat. I introduced her in Russian as my girlfriend and partner to everyone.

"Yes, very, very good to meet you," Gleb said in English but with his very thick Russian accent.

Most Russians had thick accents when they spoke English. I was quite proud of myself for standing out from the masses. He extended his hand to her. She took it and told him it was wonderful to meet him too.

She nodded and smiled at the others as well. I told her about Leo's injury, but until everyone around the table laughed at me, I hadn't realized I was talking to her in Russian. She gamely laughed with them and held up her hand.

"That's totally okay. You catch up with your friends. We have more than enough time together." She smiled graciously. I took both of her hands in mine and pressed them to my lips.

"Thank you so much," I said.

I returned to Leo, wanting to hear more about his recovery. Poor guy had to survive not only multiple surgeries but the anger and bitterness of his coach, which reminded me how horrible Russians could be to each other. If you got hurt as a dancer, it was your fault. You had to make amends to them for any time you lost, which hopefully was no time at all. You danced through the pain or you were a loser, a weakling. It all made me sick, made me so happy I was gone from there. That I'd never go back. I was glad Rory couldn't understand anything. There were certain things about my homeland I just didn't want her to know.

I was listening so intently, I hadn't realized we'd been sitting there a while and the waitress hadn't come. Until Rory stood.

"I'm sorry, it's just that I'm actually getting really hungry," she said, when I looked up at her.

"Yes, we need to order—"

I began to get up, but she gently pushed my arm back down.

"No, no," she said. "You stay and chat and I'll just go to the bar to order. It looks like that's what you have to do for food around here right now. You want me to get you anything?"

"Ohhh," I said in contemplation. "You know, just whatever looks good. I'm not really that hungry. I'll trust you, honey."

"Will do." She smiled and was off.

I returned my attention to Leo and his story of woe. Soon, we were joined by Valentin, Max and Sergei, who all sympathized with Leo and agreed the coaching system sucked badly. Again, I got so involved in catching up, I didn't notice the passage of time. Everyone had so much going on, so much that had happened since I last saw them. I felt horrible for being so out of touch, so into my own drama, fighting with Xenia, looking in vain for Tatiana. And the reminder of Tanya was what made me realize Rory had been gone for some time.

I got up and looked at the bar. I couldn't see her anywhere. It was actually starting to clear out a bit. I excused myself and walked to the bar. I looked everywhere. She was nowhere. I went to the ladies restroom and waited outside. I checked my phone. No text. I texted, asking her where she was. I waited several minutes, but there was no answer. I walked outside, looked around. Where the hell was she? I went back in, asked the guys if they'd seen her. They all shook their heads. I then realized Rory had no English money. I'd assured her I'd take care of all the money. I should have given her some. I didn't foresee we'd get separated. What the hell was wrong with me? I should have given her money to be on the safe side. I told the guys I had to go search for her and we'd talk more later.

"Good luck," Sergei called out.

"Wait, I'll go with you," Valentin said.

Thinking she'd gone to change money, we walked to the closest exchange kiosk. But she wasn't there. Thinking maybe the wait at the Italian place was just too long and she decided to run into another place, we stopped in at the other restaurants in the area, looking around, asking around. Like I had with Tatiana. I felt a hole in my core. Where was she? Why hadn't I paid more attention in the restaurant? Not that she couldn't take care of herself. And this was England, and not a crime-ridden area. But neither was our L.A. neighborhood. If anything ever happened to her again, it would destroy me. I'd never forgive myself.

I texted her again. *Where are you?* No response. I was thankful for Val's help, but I was getting more worried by the minute, and I kind of wanted to be alone with my frustration and self-directed anger. But I said nothing, and just walked around some more with him.

"We'll find her," he said, reading my emotions.

Finally, thank God, my phone beeped. I had a message. It was from her. She went to the fish and chips place because, as I'd suspected, at the Italian place they said it would take too long. She said she didn't want to disturb me with my friends and that I didn't seem that hungry anyway.

I practically sprinted to the fish and chips place, Valentin running along at my side. But she wasn't there. *Is she at another one? Did she get lost?* Even though I now knew she was okay, I just wanted her back in my arms.

"Let's just go back to the hotel," I said to him. He checked the bar while I went to the lobby. There was still a line at the front desk, though not nearly as long as earlier today. I excused myself and walked past the crowd to the check-in clerk. Good thing about being a celebrity was that everyone forgave you. I asked the clerk where there was another fish and chips place besides the one around the corner. But he said that one was the only one in the immediate area. The next closest was about half a kilometer beyond the Winter Garden. She wouldn't have gotten that lost, certainly.

My worry grew. Then I realized there might be a time lag. She hadn't received my text earlier that I'd gone down to the hotel bar. I texted her again.

Where r u? I just got this. There might be time delay. Looking 4 u everywhere. Lost track of time. I'm so sorry. Worried.

She didn't respond right away. Maybe by now she was actually back in the room. I went to the bar to tell Val I was going upstairs. Max had joined him.

"Oh man, you don't look good," Max said, grasping my arm. I knew he meant well, but I was annoyed.

"I don't know where she is. This is a foreign country to her and we had an…incident earlier—"

"What?" Val said. "Incident?"

Shit, I so didn't want to go there. He looked truly concerned.

"No, it was nothing. It was in L.A. But it freaked… I just have to find her."

"Okay, let's go," Val said.

Max put his beer mug down. "I will help. Should we split up and text each other if we find her?"

"Good idea," I said. "But first let me just check the room. I think our texts are getting lost or there's some kind of time lag or something. She might already be up there."

We made our way up.

"Sasha," she nearly screamed as I unlocked the door.

"You *are* here," I said, sighing deeply.

"I just texted you. I didn't know there was a lap—"

She was in bed. Her face was covered in sweat and she looked sickly pale.

"Rory, you are white as ghost," I said.

"I don't feel well. I got sick on greasy fish and chips. I need privacy. I need to get well before…everything starts." She didn't want to say the word competition. "Please!" she muttered, nearly in tears. "I know you haven't seen your friends in a while but…I need you." Her eyes flickered to my right and left before her tears really came on. I'd momentarily forgotten Val and Max were behind me.

"Of course, of course, sweetheart." I nodded and backed up, closing the door.

I started to thank them, but they got it.

"Just happy she's okay. See you tomorrow, man," Val said.

I shook their hands and returned to Rory.

"I'm sorry, Sasha. I feel like an ass in front of your friends. I just really don't want to be sick for the competition. It's too import—"

"Shhh," I said, brushing her head with my palm, which was considerably colder than her head. "Just get some sleep. It will all be better."

I began giving her a head and shoulder massage, and covering her in the blankets. I retrieved another from the closet, worried one wasn't enough. I turned up the heat. When I returned to the bed, she was asleep.

I took the envelope containing our Blackpool information out of our luggage and wrote a paper message on its back, telling her I was going out to the drugstore to pick up some medicine for her. I wasn't going to trust the cell phones again. Not right now anyway.

When I returned, she was tossing and turning but still seemed asleep. I readjusted the covers, which woke her. "I didn't want to wake you," I said. "You feel hot. I went to market and bought water and nuts and crackers. And Pepto Bismol and Excedrin. Whatever will help. I will get more if you need."

"What time is it?" She groaned.

"It's nine o'clock English time. It's only afternoon in California. We're going to be jet-lagged for a couple days. That's why we arrived early. Can you take this medicine?"

She sat up. I gave her a large bottle of Evian and filled the top cap of the Pepto Bismol to the indicator. She took both and drank.

"Here, this should help," I said, handing her a box of saltines. She ate two. I also handed her two Excedrin, which she swallowed as well. She ate a few more crackers before lying back down.

"I'm so sorry, sweet. I spent far too much time with old friends and fans today. I got carried away." I patted her forehead with a cold washcloth. "The first day is our day to catch up and do autographs and all that. Because everyone knows not to bother me when rehearsals really begin. The rest of the trip is all about you. All about us. I promise. Sleep and get well." I trailed kisses across her cheeks then down her neck before shutting off the lights.

***

"Rory, sweetheart. How are you feeling now?" I asked when I felt her move in bed.

She slowly opened her eyes, looking confused. Her skin looked much less pale and her eyes looked alert. She didn't look sick.

"Mmmmm, your breath smells like mint," she moaned, then smiled. "Where—" But then her eyes focused on the costumes hanging in the open closet. I felt her pulse quicken.

"Yes, we're in Blackpool," I said, brushing my lips to her forehead, which now felt normal temperature.

"What time is it?" She rubbed her eyes.

"It's nine. You slept almost twelve hours straight. You needed it, darling. How are you feeling? You look so much better than last night."

Her eyes darted around the room, as if she was remembering. "Mmmm, better, I think," she said, now covering her mouth with her hand. "I need the restroom." I moved away and she rose and made her way to the bathroom. "Ugh," I heard her say.

"You look beautiful," I hollered.

"I threw up last night. Gross," she mumbled, returning to the bedroom, covering her face with her arm. She bent down into her suitcase and retrieved her cosmetic bag.

When she went back to the bathroom, I heard her brushing her teeth and swishing mouthwash around.

"Wow, I am feeling better. Much," she said,

returning.

Yes! "You look so much better. The paleness is gone."

"Weird. I feel almost like it never happened. I even want to eat, unbelievably."

"They have a very good breakfast here. Much like the one on the airplane. Full English breakfast. I didn't know if you wanted me to have it ordered up, if you were up to eating," I said.

"Yes, definitely."

***

"Mmmm. I could really get used to these English breakfasts," she said, devouring her meal. "Especially the baked beans and fried tomato and this heavenly toasty-hushpuppy-doughy thing!"

I laughed. It was pure lard, but I was just so happy she was eating and enjoying.

But she stopped halfway through the deep-fried toast, held her stomach.

"Oh no, what's wrong?" I said.

"Okay, maybe not. It's starting to feel the same as the greasy fish and chips from last night. I don't want to go there again." She forked the toast aside and took a big spoonful of beans instead. When she finished those, she polished off the fruit bowl. "Okay, that soaked up the grease. I feel better."

***

She took a long shower, and this time I waited for her in the room. Then we headed out to the Winter Garden to meet our fellow U.S. teammates for our first practice. I'd scheduled a private practice in the back room for us before the team meet, but I canceled this morning, deciding it was better to let her sleep in.

"Thanks so much for letting me take my time this morning," she said to me as we walked toward the hotel's lift.

"It's most essential that you are feeling well," I said, kissing her forehead as we waited for the wooden box to arrive in our empty shaft. "Far more important than getting one more practice session in. We know our routines. It is what it is now." I kissed her again, now on the lips.

Despite my words and soft kisses, I could feel her nerve endings practically vibrating with energy through the pores of her skin. As were mine.

We exited the hotel and walked, hand in hand, toward the opera house. I heard my name called from behind. It was Valentin, with several other familiar faces I hadn't yet seen here.

"Everything okay now?" Val asked, looking back and forth between Rory and me.

"Yes, it is. Hey, thanks for last night, man," I said. "I really appreciate it."

"Hey, any time, any time," he said, patting me on the back and giving Rory a nod and a smile. "Just glad you're okay," he said to her.

"Thank you," she said, blushing. "Nice friends," she said to me under her breath.

She was right about Val. He'd always been a good guy. We'd definitely have to keep in better touch between comps this time.

Daniil, another Russian I knew from New York, always the joker, gave me a big bear hug from behind, wrapping his arms tightly around my waist. I laughed, though I wasn't really in the mood for his hyperactivity right now. He tapped Rory on the shoulder, making her turn suddenly. Russians were a bit more harsh than Americans with movement and physical touching. I could tell the tap was harder than she was used to and that he'd startled her. He asked her if I was giving her a hard time, like I did all my "poor women," but he asked in Russian.

"No!" I said to him, laughing. "I'm not giving her a hard time, and…what do you mean, my poor women? Xenia? What about poor me?" I was so caught up in my response, I'd forgotten to tell him she didn't speak any Russian. She looked back and forth between the two of us, wide-eyed and questioning.

All my friends burst out laughing.

"You are a known pain in the ass, to all of your partners," Max said.

"You're infamous for it!" Sergei added. More wild Russian laughter.

I had to join in. Okay, they were right. I had been a pain in the ass. But no longer.

"Anyway, we should hear it from her," Daniil said, turning to Rory. "Sasha's hardly one to be objective." He looked at her and raised his eyebrows dramatically. "So, is he treating you well?" Rory's eyes widened at his raised brows.

"She doesn't speak Russian, D-Man," Val said. "She's American."

I thought it was funny anyone had even assumed she was Russian. Rory looked one hundred percent American to me.

"Ooooooooh, American!" Daniil said, making

the word sound ridiculously sexual.

"How did you get an American to take all your shit? You've got to be kidding me!" Lucas, Daniil's friend, joked, in Russian. More laughter.

Rory shot me a look I could read well: *What the hell are you telling them?* I grinned and rolled my eyes.

"Okay, guys, you're embarrassing her," I said. "Seriously, we'll talk later and I'll catch you all up. Right now, we've got to get to team practice. "It's a big day, her first time here and all." I raised my hand in the air, as if asking them, please, let us go for now.

"Okay, yeah, yeah, we'll get off your case. But only out of respect to your new lady," Lucas said, imitating Daniil's raised eyebrows.

"You treat her nice, now," Daniil joked then patted Rory again. She was ready for it this time and smiled sweetly at him, her eyes still filled with question marks.

"Mind telling me what that was about?" she asked after they took off, bounding ahead of us.

"I just told them we needed to get mentally prepared and needed to get going."

She stopped and put her hands on her hips, shooting me a dubious look. "Seriously. That's all you're going to tell me?"

I shrugged. My adrenaline was starting to surge and I didn't want to go through the whole *You're a miserable partner* jabbing.

"Sasha! They were talking about me? What did you say about *me*?"

"Just that you are my new partner. And then I added that you're American when it was clear Daniil didn't get it," I said.

"Well, it sounded like you said something sexual,

by their reactions."

I knew she was going to think that, the way they acted. "No, not me. The one who made it sound sexual was Daniil."

"How is my Americanness sexual? Does he think we're all Pamela Anderson or something?" She laughed but I could tell she was annoyed. And her reference to Pamela Anderson made me think she was back to the body issues thing again.

"Rory, no." I stopped and looked her straight in the eye, my mouth a solid line. "Rory, don't be ridiculous. They think nothing of the sort. I haven't seen Daniil in a while, but that's just the way he is. I'd forgotten. He and Lucas and the others, they are just very…they are just very happy for me. That I have an American partner and that I seem happy. For once. Because they know I'm…I'm usually not. Especially at this point in the game." And then I realized how much being with Rory had changed me. My partners and I were usually on the verge of killing each other by competition time.

She softened and her lips curled. "Aw, how could I be annoyed with that?" she said, pulling my arm around her and wrapping herself in my embrace, snuggling next to me as we walked. I squeezed her arm and kissed her cheek.

***

We entered the Winter Garden and I checked us in at the registration desk. When I returned to Rory, she was holding her cell phone, a huge grin lighting up her face.

"What is it?" I laughed. Her beautiful smile was

infectious.

"Just a funny text from Samantha," she said, putting the phone in her bag.

I looked at her quizzically, prompting her for more information.

"She just said she knows we'll rock it and I'm a goddess and all," Rory obliged, with a giggle.

"And she's so right. On both fronts." I was unable to refrain from kissing her soft, sweet cheek again. I loved seeing her at ease. She tasted like honey.

"She also says I should try some Japanese restaurant in the basement that's set up just for Blackpool? She said they have great curries, and it's the best place for food around here."

"Oh yes, it's the Japanese costumer who puts it up every year. She's right. Probably the healthiest alternative. We'll go later today."

***

I laced my arm through hers and took her down the long hall that led to the ballroom.

"Sasha!" someone shouted.

I turned to look. It was someone I didn't know. A twenty-something woman with short blonde hair, holding a Blackpool program.

"I was wondering if you'd be so kind as to sign my booklet?" she said, holding it out to me along with a pen. She was British, by the sound of her accent.

"Of course." I took the program and pen and signed, as I had last night. She giggled when I returned them to her.

"Thank you so much! I can't wait to see you dance! You're just, so amazing!"

"Thank you very much."

"And you're on tonight too, right?"

"Yes, for the team match," I said, then heard another voice.

"Hey, he's signing!" I looked beyond the woman and saw in the distance, many, many more people coming toward me, likewise holding programs.

"We're such fans," said a voice behind me. I turned to see two more women, one with long dark hair, one with a platinum bob. The one with the bob, who spoke, was also British. "We heard you had a new partner. Can't wait to see the two of you out there!" She didn't at all acknowledge Rory standing beside me. She only spoke to me. Her bob bounced with every syllable.

I smiled and took their programs. They giggled in unison as I signed.

"Really, we can't wait," the other one echoed, pawing my bicep. I smiled at them and handed their programs back.

"Thank you so much," I said in the polite, professional tone I always used at competitions when speaking with fans.

The masses that had been in the distance caught up to us. I didn't have time to be signing for long. We had to practice. But it wouldn't hurt to take ten minutes. We were early, as usual. I smiled and reached for the first program, then the second, then a third. Soon, I found myself trying to balance a stack of the booklets in the crook of my arm.

"No, no, you're not doing that," I said when Rory offered to help hold some of them. Altogether, they were heavy.

"It's Sasha Zakharov!" said another voice,

followed by the sound of a cell phone cameras being clicked.

More cameras clicked, and more programs were thrust toward me. I was used to this, but Rory wasn't. We needed to practice now. I looked at my watch to see half an hour had already passed. Funny, but when I'd been with Xenia in years past, I was so excited for the fans, to be taken away from her clutches, her jealousy and competitiveness, and just plain bitchiness. Now, I felt like my fans were keeping me from my Rory. She was happy to help me appease them, but I soon began to feel her nervous energy, that Samantha had briefly quashed, returning. We had work to do.

"I'm very sorry but I must go practice," I said. An Asian man tried to add his program to the pile I already held and I shook my head. "No more. I'm sorry. After the competition, I promise. After," I repeated to the man. I recognized him. I'd seen him at many competitions and I knew his English was limited.

But the crowd only grew.

"This is it. After this stack, I must go." I eyed Rory. She looked bemused, happy for the attention but concerned as to how I'd extricate us from it, not the least bit pissy and jealous, like Xenia. "Thank you for your support. Really, thank you so much. You don't know what it means to me," I said to the crowd again, trying hard to be as polite as I could. My pen was going at the speed of light, and the programs were flying out of my arms, yet more were somehow arriving.

"Hey that's mine," a man's voice called out.

"No, it's not! I gave him that one!" said a female

voice.

"Seriously, you just took my program. It has my name on the front," the man insisted.

Oh jeez, people were fighting over this.

The woman turned the cover over.

"See!" he said.

"Then where's mine?"

But I was done. "That's all for now. I'm sorry. But please do come to the Daiyu tent in the Pavilion on Thursday and I will sign anything you want. And there will be photos. And champagne."

"Anything I want?" a female voice called out, followed by an outburst of giggles.

"Ah, now, now, now," I said in a mock-reprimanding tone. "Thank you, everyone. Thank you so much. I'll see you Thursday."

"But what about my book?" asked the woman who'd apparently lost hers.

I shook my head, hearing her voice but unable to make out her face. "I don't know. I'm sorry. I have to go. See you all Thursday."

"We'll see you before then! Under the lights! Like tomorrow night!" a woman said. This was followed by more giggles.

"Well, yes, I guess you will, won't you?" I said, brows rising, cocky smile growing.

I hadn't meant to do that. I was so used to making that face in the past, that seductive expression. Now the giggling turned to mini-squeals of delight. I needed to get Rory and myself out of this.

"Thank you again, everyone." I forced my expression back to a polite, professional one. I waved, and took Rory's hand, leading her briskly down the hall.

Chants of "We love you, Sasha" and "Go, Sasha" echoed down the hall.

"You're pretty suave when keeping your hordes of fans at bay." Rory giggled.

We continued on at a brisk pace. I focused straight ahead, making sure not to make eye contact with onlookers off to the side. I could tell Rory tried to keep her gaze with mine, but she kept turning her head, apparently distracted by all the rooms and eateries, and the tangled maze of halls leading off from the main one. This place *was* immense, I reminded myself. It was fun to see her so intrigued and I was excited to show her around. Later.

We passed the large entryway branching off the main hall that led to the shopping Pavilion. "That's where we'll be signing on Thursday. It's where Daiyu's tent, and all the other sponsors are," I said, pointing.

"Wow, I can't even see down all the way," she said. "It's a bit bigger than the one in O.C."

I laughed. "Yes, quite a bit."

On the other side of the hall we passed the huge arcade of video game machines and retro pinball machines, the darkly lit pub with red brick façade, the deli with black and white checkered floors, and, around the corner, the massive candy stand. Nothing ever changed here. It was always the same. Which was nice, reassuring. Rory took it all in with the wonder of a child. At the end of the hall, the room forked into two other halls marked "Grand Ballroom" and "Opera House." Rory walked toward the first one, but I pulled her in the other direction.

"This one leads to several rooms we can use to

have private conferences and practice," I said. "We're supposed to meet the team here."

"This place is a maze. You could totally get lost in here," she said, her voice a mixture of trepidation and excitement.

I looked around. I didn't see anyone. I heard more people walking down the hall, and I didn't want to be accosted again so I took her hand and led us into the smaller, darkened hall.

"It's like a cave in here." Now I heard her attempt to keep her fear at bay. Blackpool was so not dangerous. But of course after what had happened in L.A. I could never blame her for being scared.

Suddenly one of the doors swung open and Bob, the American team coach, peeked out. He was a large, perpetually happy man with curly red hair who reminded me of a heavyset version of Ronald McDonald.

"Sasha, I thought I heard you," he said, smiling widely.

"Good to see you again, Bob." I shook his hand.

"Likewise. It's been a while. How's California treating you?"

"Well, very well." I smiled at Rory. She was a huge part of why I was doing so well these days.

"And you must be Rory." Bob extended his hand to her.

"This is Bob Maxwell," I told her. "He owns a large studio in New York and he's the team manager."

"Very pleased to meet you," she said.

"And likewise, my dear. Sasha's new partner! Am I excited to see you dance!"

She laughed nervously. "Um, yeah?" she said.

"You sure about that? Is there an imposter in the room?" Bob said, laughing.

His immense excitement, maybe along with his clownishness, was bringing back that awful self-doubt of hers. Or, maybe it was just her way of remaining humble. She was never the type to brag, even if she was expected to win, after all. And that's part of what I loved about her.

"I hope not," she said. "I'm just, kind of in a state of disbelief right now that I'm here and dancing with Sasha and all." She held her head down, bashfully. I squeezed her and kissed her cheek. "Yes, I'm sure," she said more firmly, holding her head up to meet my gaze.

The door behind us opened again and in walked the rest of the team. I guess we weren't late.

"Mariana, Dmitri, Alexandra, Oleg..." I shook hands, one by one.

"Oooooh, Xenia, you look just gorgeous, as usual, my dear," Bob waxed.

I turned to her and offered her a polite nod, which she returned, looking smug as could be.

"Piotr," I said, shaking her new partner's hand.

"Sasha," he said in return with his own polite nod.

"And beautiful, so beautiful Arabelle. Bella Arabella!" Bob sang.

Rory's eating disorder having been related to her feelings about Arabelle's ballerina body made me automatically wrap my arm around Rory's waist. Arabelle eyed me then set her gaze on Rory. Her lips curved into a slight, shy smile and she nodded, probably in appreciation that someone else had to deal with me now. She backed slightly away from me, subconsciously I thought, as if she wanted nothing from me but distance. Which, after the way I'd treated her, she deserved. Arabelle was a good person, and I'd been too hard on her. Her new partner was Andrew, a young man I recognized as being a recent champion in the junior division, now transitioning to regular pro. *Good for her*, I thought. Now at a mental distance from each other, with our eyes we wished each other the best.

Not so for Xenia. I reached out to her with my right hand to shake hers. But I kept my left arm wrapped around Rory's waist. Without taking my hand, she shot us each a brief smile, a look I knew well. I knew this meant she was angry and fiercely competitive. She wanted to beat us and thought she had a shot.

"Does everyone know Andrew?" Arabelle asked.

"Very pleased to meet you," he said, giving Rory and me a firm handshake. He had blond hair and light blue eyes that made him seem genuine. He was good for Arabelle.

"And this is my new partner, Rory Laudner," I said.

"Yes, of course. I've heard a lot about you," Andrew said, now wrapping his other hand over the one holding her hand, giving her a double shake. I liked him already.

She giggled.

After introductions, Bob explained how it all worked, which I'd already described to Rory. But it was good for her to hear it again, from the captain. The two ballroom couples would go first; she and I and Xenia and Piotr would be the Latin pair of dancers who took the floor. The other two couples would be alternates in case of injury.

They'd hired formation dancers for the opening presentation, during which the team would be announced. We'd be driven on stage in a caravan, exiting one couple at a time, beginning with Xenia and Piotr, then the other two ballroom couples. Rory and I would exit last, since we were the stars. Both Xenia and Rory flinched when he said this. *Women.* This was going to be an experience, to put it mildly.

The standard ballroom dancers would go first. A bell would indicate the first couple would leave the floor and the next take it. Same with the Latin dancers. Xenia and Piotr were first, and we'd take over at the sound of the bell.

"You okay, hon? You look like you're about to toss your cookies," Bob said to Rory.

I wrapped my arm around her again and gave her a little squeeze.

"Oh I'm fine. I'll just follow Sasha," she said, a little squeaky-voiced.

"That's good, dear. That's the way it's supposed to be, after all," Bob said, laughing. "Now for the actual dances," he continued, "don't worry if you don't have a special routine. We fully expect you to use the ones you've prepared for the individual nights. So don't—"

"We choreographed a special routine," Xenia interrupted, smiling sweetly at Bob.

"Oh, wow. More than expected. That's great, then!" He flapped his arms about like wings. The man did like to gesticulate. "Did you guys?" he asked me, a hopeful tone in his voice.

"No, sorry, we didn't." I saw Xenia's smug glare out of the corner of my eye. This was by far the least important part of Blackpool. She was more competitive, and more of an idiot, than I'd thought.

"That's quite all right, not at all expected. Especially with Rory being so new and all," Bob said.

Xenia transferred her smug smile to Rory, making me want to kill her.

Bob led us into the main ballroom so he could set the stage and tell us where to make our entrances.

"Wow," Rory whispered, her eyes glossing over. It was the first time she'd seen the floor. I squeezed her hand. "It's beautiful. And huge." Her eyes wandered up to the multi-tiered balconies. "What are they setting up for?" She pointed to maintenance crew as they checked chandeliers, spotlights, and worked.

"The Rising Star competition—the competition for newcomers. It's tonight."

"The one I should actually be in." She laughed.

"I don't think so," I answered.

I felt adrenaline surging through her veins. I squeezed her palm again.

"Don't worry," she said, reading my mind. Or my actions, rather. "It's good adrenaline, the kind that will make me do my best, not the type of nervous energy that sometimes paralyzes me."

This caused me to kiss her sweet little cheek again.

After we marked our own entrances out and watched a run-through of the Rockettes-like introductory number danced by the formation team, we left the ballroom and walked back to the Pavilion so I could talk to Daiyu about the details of the autographing. She hadn't yet arrived but some of her employees had. I told Rory to browse around while I talked to the company's publicist and that I'd text her when I was done. Our phones were working much better. We'd tested them several times that morning. But just in case something was again delayed, we agreed to meet back at Daiyu's large red tent in forty-five minutes.

Rory walked off toward the table closest to us, which bore glittering bejeweled accessories. She looked like a little girl in a fairy tale.

I walked back inside the tent and waited for Daiyu's publicist to get off the phone. By the time I got all the details I needed—when and where we were signing and doing the photo shoot, and, far more importantly, what time we were to arrive to have Rory's hair and makeup done—forty-five minutes had passed.

I found Rory right outside the tent, admiring some of Daiyu's fabrics, running her hands along the texture. When I walked closer to her, I saw that she was kind of crouching behind the swaths, peering out and around them. She was looking at someone.

I followed her gaze and saw Micaela examining the fabrics across the way. Her long ebony hair, her razor-high cheekbones, her flawlessly made-up face, her regal stance—she looked perfectly serene, glancing at Rory, shooting her that same magnanimous smile she gave all her fans. Her eyes shifted to me, then back to Rory, and she made the connection. She pressed her lips together, and waved at me.

"Micaela, hello," I called out to her.

"Sasha," she said with a pleasant smile and nod, first to me, then to Rory.

That's all we said to each other. We really had

nothing more to say at this point except pleasantries. She wasn't the least bit fazed I had a new partner. She looked perfectly serene and confident.

"Oh good. I was just going to text you," I said to Rory, trying to deflect Micaela's seemingly discomfiting presence. "We're all done. Ready to practice?" I wrapped my arm around her and pulled her to me. We walked toward the back exit of the Pavilion, she in the nook of my shoulder. I could feel her nerves. "You okay? Don't let Micaela intimidate you. Of course she's here. Of course she's good. Of course she's the champion. But not for much longer." I squeezed her.

She nodded, holding her head down. "That's all very true. But it's not her."

"What?"

She took a breath and stopped walking. "You're not going to believe this, but Cheryl and Luna and all of their friends are here."

I shook my head. I'd told Rory when she worried before they might try to sabotage us that they never came to competitions they couldn't perform in—in other words, the international ones that didn't have pro/am components. *What in the world are they doing here?*

"It seems like they're here to cheer on Xenia and Piotr," she said, answering my unspoken question. "She was walking through the Pavilion and they ran up to her. They were telling her they couldn't wait to see her tonight and she was going to kill all her competition and definitely win it all. And they were cackling." Rory's voice petered out until it was nearly a whisper. She was clearly worried.

As was I, after what Cheryl had done to her at

the studio. She wouldn't get near her again. I'd take care of it.

"Well, good for them," I said with a shrug. I didn't want to let Rory know I was the least bit worried. I had to remain solid, strong. "I haven't known them to go to competitions they had no stake in. But good for them to travel and cheer on their friend, see a bit of the world, broaden their horizons."

"Yeah, I know you said that," she said. "And they *don't* have any stake, right?"

"What? No, Rory." I laughed. "This is on a completely different level from the American pro/am comps. They're nobodies here. Don't worry about them, okay? They are the last people you should be concerned with. They can't hurt you even if they wanted to. I promise."

She looked me hard in the eye and nodded. She trusted me. I was not going to let her down. Ever again.

With all my friends here, I had the resources to ensure she'd do nothing to us. I'd text Valentin. I'd kind of come to his rescue in the past, without really knowing it, back when we were newbies in the U.S. at our first small studio. It was a tiny studio and they hadn't given us any lockers to put our things in as we taught; we had to keep them in cubbyholes in the lobby. I was teaching a private lesson in the space closest to the front door, and I spotted a beady-eyed little man looking around. He just looked like he was up to no good. I kept an eye on him, and minutes later, saw him walk up to the cubbyholes and pull out Val's nice black leather satchel.

"Hey!" I yelled just as he ran off.

I ran after him, downstairs—three flights—

outside, up Eleventh Avenue toward Hell's Kitchen. He wasn't too swift on his feet and I had him tackled within a block and a half. Bastard. I jumped him and took him down easily.

"Man, that had my passport in it," Val said when I returned, holding his bag. It was two weeks before Blackpool. If it was stolen, he would have had to return to Russia to get a new one before going abroad. "I'd have missed the competition. I owe you big time, man."

I never thought of it as us owing each other anything. And I knew he didn't either. It was just a saying. We were friends. Friends helped each other when in need. Just like he'd offered to help find Rory when I was clearly distraught over losing her the first night here.

Anyway, Val's competition was on a completely different night than mine, as were most of my friends'. We all had totally different schedules. I knew they'd help me out now. What I was far more concerned about was Rory's predisposition to let her anxiety take over. That's what would really sabotage us. I had to find a way to conquer that. Fortunately, Greta was due in town this afternoon.

CHAPTER TEN

Before practice, Rory used the ladies room to freshen up. I used the time to call Valentin. We'd verified the first night here we had the same numbers as before.

"Hey, what's up?" he answered.

"Yeah, man, I need a big favor," I said.

"Sure, shoot,"

I told him about Cheryl and Luna, describing them down to the last detail, and said I needed a lookout to make sure they were in someone's sight all the time. He promised he'd be on it. I found some photos on my phone Luna had sent me of us at the O.C. competition and shot them over.

Got your back, man, he texted back.

Rory emerged and I led her through the ballroom again, to a black door built into the wall, which opened into a hall with several doors on each side. I opened the one on my left, which led to a small practice room, and extended my arm, inviting her to enter. She laughed again, and I realized what a maze this place really was.

As soon as she was in, I closed the door and whisked her around toward me, pulling her close and kissing her deeply. It was the first time, outside of the hotel, that we were actually alone and had some privacy. I wanted to get her mind off Cheryl and her cronies, and I also needed my Rory.

"Mmmm," she moaned. "I could do this the rest of the day."

I released her and took a long inhale, then slowly and seductively unzipped her jacket, my fingertips trailing down her clavicle, to her nipples, to her belly, where they unfortunately had to stop. The jacket unzipped completely, I whipped it open and tore it off her shoulders, revealing her cute dance clothes. We both laughed. She knew what this was—an homage to her insistence on dancing naked together. Which we were going to pretend to do here. I kissed her again, deeply, my tongue massaging hers, exploring her mouth, plunging toward her throat, before letting her go and backing off. Another deep inhale.

"Okay, prrrrractice," I said, holding up a finger as if she were the one misbehaving.

"Don't you shake your finger at me. You're the one being naughty." She narrowed her eyes and gave me a sexy pout.

I kept a straight face. "Rrrrrumba!"

We went through all five dances, beginning with our favorite. She was nervous at the start of the rumba. I could tell. I understood. This was for real. She was really here and we were really doing this. I felt her confidence literally slide from her head to her toes, and leave her body.

"I'm sorry," she started.

"Don't talk. Don't think. Just dance. Only dance." My voice was strong and commanding. She didn't dare disobey. I was serious but not frustrated.

Not yet, anyway.

We kept going. She made a few more flubs but she did as I said, didn't apologize and kept going.

"Don't think. Just move. Just dance," I repeated whenever I felt her confidence begin to falter again. "Feel only my body, think only about my body, leading yours."

Slowly, I felt her nervous energy begin to dissipate. And she made no more mistakes, at least none of consequence that would show to an audience.

At the end of the first full run-through, I released her hand and walked briskly around the small floor, holding my head back and running my fingers through my hair. It helped me to do this to release my pent-up nervous energy. The routine wasn't perfect, but it was there. It was good for a first time, I had to admit, although I'd always been one to get crazed about lack of perfection. Especially so close to the actual competition.

"See how much better it is when you just focus on the movement and don't allow yourself to think?" I said to her, forcing my tone to remain soft.

"Yes, yes, definitely," she answered, voice slightly shaking, though I could tell she was trying to control it.

"Yes, there were mistakes. But this is the time to make them. To get them out of our system. Most of them were minor, anyway," I continued, partly as self-assurance.

"You know what they say," she said. "That an imperfect practice leads to an excellent performance. And vice versa. So we're good." She smiled sweetly at me and raised her eyebrows.

"Is that what they say?"

"Yes," she said, walking toward me. She could tell I was struggling with my patience. It was now her turn to be the calm, strong one. "Sasha, we're going to be fine. More than fine. Far, far more than fine. Our dancing is excellent. We're winners. We both know that. It's only ourselves we have to overcome. And we're going to do that."

She reached out and held my hands in hers. I closed my eyes for a few moments, then opened them and pulled her to me, kissing her forehead.

"You're right. As always. You're right," I whispered.

"Damn right, I am." She laughed.

***

"I'm famished. Are you?" I asked after practice, hoping the sight of Arabelle or Cheryl hadn't brought back any of Rory's body negativity.

"I am!" she said with a sweet smile, letting me know she could read my thoughts—and that her anorexia spectrum disorder wasn't returning.

"Good, good," I said, wrapping my arm around her waist.

She rubbed up against my side, lacing her arm through mine. I really liked walking around Blackpool arm in arm, or body in arm, like this.

"Samantha texted again and asked me if I'd tried the Japanese place yet. I told her we'd go there for lunch."

"Great idea. Let's go."

We walked back through the ballroom, where the Rising Star competition had just begun.

"It's not very crowded," she said.

"A lot of people aren't here yet. This place will be packed tomorrow and Wednesday. You'll see." I felt the adrenaline course through her veins.

"Davay, Sveta! Let's go!" The voice was familiar; someone from the studio.

My former student, Sveta? I looked around the ballroom floor, trying to find her.

"Can we just stand here and watch a moment?" Rory asked, that look of being totally transfixed that I so loved in her eyes again.

"Of course." I led her toward the floor, and ushered her into a row up close. She closed her eyes and breathed in deeply. I could tell she was getting prepared for tomorrow, letting the fire in the atmosphere penetrate her pores, picturing us out there. I could even feel her muscles move, dancing in her seat. Her eyes were still closed. *That's my girl*, I thought. Feel, not think. She'd finally gotten it.

The music ended.

"Woo hoo, Sveta! Yes!" shouted that same voice. Rory recognized it too and began looking to her left, where the voice had come from.

The dancers were taking bows. I spotted her. It was my Sveta. She'd told me she wanted to go pro. Good for her; she'd found herself a pro partner. I waved to her. She spotted me and waved back.

"Oh, there's Svetlana," Rory said.

"Yeah, I just noticed her. She'd wanted to go pro. She was going to wait till she won a pro/am, but I'm glad she didn't keep waiting. She was way too good to get held back by politics."

"I always thought she was awesome," Rory agreed.

"I know you did. I remember."

"No way! Girlfriend! Girlfriend! Woo hoo!" We both recognized that voice.

"Oh my gosh, 'no way' is right!" Rory squealed with delight. I turned and saw the mane of fiery red hair, the large palm waving at us. It was her good friend, Paulina, from the studio.

Rory opened her mouth and reached toward her. They were too far apart to touch. Paulina did the same and they air bear-hugged, then cracked up over it.

"I am so happy to see you," Rory yelled. The cha-cha music blasted on.

Paulina nodded exuberantly and pointed toward the back.

"Let's go say hi," Rory squealed.

"Of course." I was thrilled she now had someone here to support her. Paulina had always been a good friend to her, and I'd just realized how badly she needed that. I had all of my friends here; she'd had none of hers. She must have felt profoundly out of place. Paulina was the confidence booster she needed.

"Oh my gosh, I'm so happy you're here," Rory said when we met her in the back row. "I don't know anyone. And you're my favorite person in the studio!" Rory hugged Paulina for real this time.

I jokingly cleared my throat.

"Besides you!" Rory play-slugged me. "We're competing on Wednesday!" she told Paulina.

"Oh really? You don't say. I didn't know that," Paulina said, rolling her eyes.

"You knew?"

"Girlfriend! Why do you think I'm here?"

Rory shook her head, confused, and motioned to

the ballroom floor.

"I'm interested in seeing what Svetlana can do." Paulina shrugged. "But she no longer goes to my studio, so I'm not really here to be her cheer-party. I'm here mainly for Maurizio, my pro/am partner. To watch him compete professionally, and cheer him on. And for *you*, dearie. I'm not kidding."

Rory's mouth hung open.

"Seriously," Paulina continued. "You're a legend back in the studio now, my dear."

"Oh my gosh, I can't believe…well…I'm just so flattered," Rory said, a blush spreading over her face.

"Honestly, I used to come to this every year. I love the place. The retro pinball machines, the cheesy Vegas-style shows, the Ferris wheel, Liverpool. It's all a hoot. And I used to come see the top ballroom dancers I admire. I haven't been in the past few years because it kind of got old. The same couples winning all the time and all. And the place just hasn't changed in ages. But when I heard you were going to dance with hiiiimmmm!" She said the last word under her breath, pointing at me like a silly schoolgirl. "Honey, I figured it was time for me to give Blackpool one more look-see."

"Well, I can't tell you how happy I am you're here. I really can't." Rory's stomach rumbled loudly. "We're headed down to a little Japanese place in the basement. Wanna come with?"

"Actually, I just came from there. Food's always excellent. Best in Blackpool."

"That's what Samantha told me!"

"You two go on and eat. But first, honey, let me get your number so we can text."

The two exchanged numbers and bear-hugged

again.

The restaurant looked the same as last year. It was set up in a long, rectangular room, with a counter displaying the meals. Picnic tables and benches were in the middle.

"Japanese curry is their specialty," I said. "Some people think Indian is better. I think this is just as good."

Rory ordered vegetable curry and I got chicken. When she took her wallet from her bag I realized I still had the credit card for her that Daiyu had given me.

"No, here's your credit card," I said, handing it to her. "But we'll charge this to mine since we ordered together. It really doesn't matter because it's the same account. But in case you're alone, you have one too."

"Our own account! Decadent!" She giggled, making me laugh and kiss her sweet forehead.

The clerk handed me a large plastic number on a stick and told us to choose a table. It was pretty dark in the seating area. There were a couple of people up front, sitting next to each other in a booth, who seemed to be eyeing us. Fans, I assumed. Fortunately, they seemed as if they were going to leave us alone. Not that I disliked meeting fans. But at this point, I just wanted to wait until we'd competed.

But as we got closer to the table, the man motioned us over, which a fan would never do. Then I recognized him. It was Rajiv, with Samantha. More of Rory's friends were here to cheer her on. I think I was just as relieved to see them as she was. More, in fact, at first. She initially thought they were my people, and shot me a desperate look, hoping I wouldn't stop to talk. Instead I gave her a loopy smile.

"Took you long enough to get here!" Samantha shouted. Rory's mouth opened when she heard her friend's voice. Samantha jumped up and rushed her, arms extended.

"Yeah, we thought you'd never get here!" Rajiv said.

Rory squealed. She and Samantha hugged and bounced up and down in embrace. "I thought you couldn't—"

"Raj found a radiologist conference nearby in the Lake District. So, good excuse for him to get off work. And he got a big discount on the airfare and hotel—for two! So here we are!"

"Oh, oh whoa!" Rory was adorably speechless. Everything was going to be okay. Luna and Cheryl were a distant memory. "You don't know what this means to me," she said, blinking back tears.

"Yes, we do," Samantha said. "I put myself in your shoes. And realized you needed people here for you. What are friends for, Rore? Plus, I mean, if you can afford it, who can seriously resist Blackpool? Hello!"

After we ate, we all walked back to the ballroom, Rory and I arm in arm, and Rajiv and Sam hand in hand. Rory gave her friend a raised eyebrow, and Samantha returned with a silent giggle. I hadn't seen they were becoming a pair either.

We found unoccupied seats in the back and watched the end of the Rising Star Latin competition. Sveta and her partner made the quarterfinals. But they didn't get past that. It was very good for a first time, though. She had a fine career ahead of her.

CHAPTER ELEVEN

I could tell Rory was a nervous wreck when we woke up the next morning. She said nothing but I felt it. I didn't even need to touch her. I was so in sync with her body, her mind.

"Everything's going to be good," I said, spooning her before we got up.

"I know." She nodded.

We ordered breakfast—this time I told the restaurant to hold the fried toast and sausage pudding—and showered. I told Rory not to wear any makeup or do anything to her hair. When she frowned, I told her Daiyu's people would take care of all that in the tent before tonight's team comp.

"I'm not used to being treated like a princess." She giggled.

"You will need to. Because you are." I hugged her from behind.

Before practice, I took her to a local market that had an array of fresh fruits and vegetables and other snack items like nuts, dried fruit, granola, power bars, and kale chips. We filled two baskets.

Greta met us for practice. She gave Rory a great pep talk, which I knew I could count on her to do. I'd told her how Rory had reacted to seeing Cheryl and Luna here. Greta was also surprised and curious about their showing up but agreed not to let Rory on to our concern.

"Believe me, you wouldn't be anywhere near here if you weren't capable of winning. Doubting yourself at this point is borderline offensive to everyone who made it possible for you to get this far," Greta said.

Rory raised her eyebrows and thought, then nodded.

"And you don't dare get upset because these women show up. Who are they anyway, this Cher and Loony?"

Rory giggled at her mispronunciation. I don't think Greta meant to call them names. It was just her accent.

"So you are going to let Cher and Loony ruin this for you and Sasha? Finally you are here, and this is your chance."

Rory shook her head. "I wouldn't do anything to hurt Sasha." Her eyes grew watery.

"Or yourself," Greta said.

"Or myself," Rory echoed, smiling through the light tears.

We went through each routine, first marking, then dancing full-out. I felt Rory's jitters, but Greta insisted they didn't show.

"When the movement is so entrenched in your muscle memory it has to take a great deal of jitters to cause any harm. You did your work, and now it is paying off." Greta lifted her chin and raised one eyebrow.

Rory swallowed and nodded.

***

Before getting ready for the team competition, we went back to the Japanese restaurant for an early dinner.

"Eat well," I said. "After this we will only have time to snack the rest of the evening."

The place was dark as a cave and we sat at a back table. Good, we needed privacy. But about halfway through our meal Cheryl and Luna came in. *Fuck.* I pretended I didn't notice. But I could see out of the corner of my eye Cheryl's beady eyes found us right away. She raised her chin, stood tall and began walking toward us, Luna following. I immediately took out my cell phone and texted Val.

They continued strutting until they were right at our table. When they got up to us, they stopped, then did nothing but stare down at us. *Seriously?* Rory's eyes widened and she took a deep breath. I could sense her rapid pulse from across the table. I should have warned her.

I addressed them with a sneer. "Ladies."

They said nothing. Luna crossed her arms in front of her, shifted her weight to one leg and glared down at us, not averting her gaze. Cheryl looked at us like she might spit in our food.

I felt my phone buzz and looked down.

B right there, Valentin wrote. Thankfully, our phones were working completely normally and there were no more delays.

I decided to ignore them, and continue where we'd left off in our conversation but, honestly, we hadn't been talking. We'd been concentrating only on eating. Plus, I didn't really want them to overhear even our small talk. So I continued piling food into my mouth as if nothing was happening. But it was. Cheryl was really hovering over Rory now. Rory didn't seem to be able to eat. Cheryl's shadow on the back wall made her look like a witch casting a spell. *What a fucking psycho.*

"Could you please act like mature human beings and leave us alone?" Rory finally said, to my distress. I knew that would only egg them on.

"Excuse me, I am quite a mature human, and I can't leave you alone no matter how I try, Rory, sweetheart," I said, shooting her my sly, cocked smile, obviously pretending they weren't there and she'd been talking to me. And I knew she got it, but she had no patience for games.

"No, this is ridiculous," she said, rolling her eyes. "They're bothering us. We can't even—"

"Who's bothering us, sweet? I don't see anybody." I looked around, above, through them as if to check. "No, seriously, there's absolutely no one here. No one of any substance, anyway."

Rory shook her head and laughed nervously.

Suddenly a veritable fleet of people entered the room. They were talking and laughing in Russian.

"Hey, hey," Val said, extending his arm toward us.

"Thank you, man," I said under my breath.

"Sasha! Man of the night. Man of Blackpool! Just MAN!" Sergei shouted in strongly accented English. "And of course, lady of night too!" he added, extending his arm to Rory. "Beautiful lady!"

Rory giggled.

Sergei patted me on the shoulder, and started speaking in Russian. "Are these the two witches?

Yeah, they look like fucking monsters!"

The others laughed and echoed him, all in Russian of course.

Soon, they were completely surrounding the table. Rory tried to look between and around their bodies. Cheryl and Luna had miraculously disappeared.

"Go on and eat, sweetheart," I said to her. "You need to finish. Don't let them bother you while they talk to me. I am done." I pushed my empty plate aside. "Thank you so much, man," I said to Valentin and Sergei, in Russian.

"Are you serious, dude? Anything!"

My Russians were not all bad. Not at all.

***

We walked back to Daiyu's tent where all of our things were now stored. Daiyu's assistants had come to our hotel room and taken the costumes to the tent, another thing that wowed sweet Rory. Three other couples who were sponsored by Daiyu were in the tent as well. They were amateur, junior division, and exhibition/cabaret champions. I explained to Rory that it was customary for a sponsor to have champs from several different categories to build a solid following.

"Your world is so amazingly cool," she said.

"Your world now too," I responded with a kiss.

Daiyu's assistant introduced herself, and sat us in adjacent seats before brightly lit mirrors to have our makeup done. Of course mine took much less time since all I needed was a bit of bronzer on my face, neck and chest, and powder to keep me from looking too sweaty.

I paced around the tent, concentrating, mentally preparing myself while Rory's cosmetologist, an obviously gay, very excited British man with spiky blond hair, finished her.

"Whoa," she soon squealed, walking toward me. "I look nothing like myself. My eyes are like Cleopatra and my lips look like I just had a Botox injection on the spot, and my cheekbones look switchblade sharp. And my eyelashes—can you say Betty Boop!"

"I'm glad you are happy," I said, smiling, and not kissing her this time so as not to ruin her makeup in any way.

"I'm transformed!"

"Wait, wait, where'd ya go? Now we get to work with this gorgeous mane!" The cosmetologist walked up behind her and removed the bobby pins from her pulled-back hair.

"Oh yeah, forgot!" She laughed and returned to the chair. I followed. "Any preferences?" he asked, running his fingers through her beautiful blonde locks.

She shrugged and laughed. "I'm from the ballet world. We all wear our hair in boring buns. We never had a choice."

"There's nothing boring about ballroom, honey! I can do anything your little heart desires."

She looked at me wide-eyed again. "Wow," she whispered.

I shook my head and took the chair opposite her. "Your decision entirely.

"Um, an elegant French twist?" she suggested. "Or a French braid? No, maybe the twist would look more classy?"

He smiled. "Perfecto."

"Can you make it look like Audrey Hepburn in 'Breakfast at Tiffany's'? You know, elegant and classy?"

"Holly Golightly it is!"

Again, my hair was quite a bit easier. My stylist was done in minutes, giving me more time to pace about the tent and think while my Rory glorified in her new world. I texted Valentin.

Anything happening with the witches?

Not much. They're at the Italian restaurant's bar, boozing it up with pink martinis. The worst one—Cheryl—seems pretty drunk. Xenia stopped by but didn't say much. Good luck, and stuff like that. Clear for now.

Cool. Thanks. I owe you, my man.

Na. We'll keep owing each other. We're friends.

We are.

When I walked back into the tent, Rory was behind a Chinese dressing screen, getting bronzed by Daiyu's female costume assistant. I could tell she was naked. Her eyes were wide. She looked mortified.

"Sorry," I mouthed, before disappearing behind my own screen. I guess since she was getting dressed, I should as well.

Again, it took me a small fraction of the time it took her.

"How are you doing?" I strolled over to her screen after finishing.

She placed her hands over her breasts, though she was still covered by the screen. "Sasha!"

She was behind the screen so I didn't think it was a big deal. But it was her first time here. And she was American. Americans were used to more modesty, more privacy.

"Okay, I think the bronzer is dry and we're ready," Daiyu's assistant said, waving me away while she went behind the screen with Rory. I sauntered to the far end of the tent and checked email and phone messages back home. Not much was going on. Sadie and Alessandra called to wish me luck, and the latter had some scheduling changes for the following week. Couldn't be bothered with that now.

"Sasha!" Rory squealed. Finally dressed, she emerged. She looked even more astounding than I'd imagined possible. The toga-esque cut definitely gave the dress a classic look. She was a bronzed goddess, the epitome of elegance.

The way her eyes traced her reflection in the mirror made it clear she thought the same. "Okay, your world officially rocks," she said.

Daiyu's assistant led us outside the tent toward the elevated runway, where several couples were posing for a photographer. Rory took her place at the end of the line. Sweet Rory. We didn't have to wait. We were stars. We couldn't wait, actually. We had to be on in not too long. I placed her hand in mine and gently pulled her forward.

"We go ahead, Rory." I laughed. "We're on the team. We need to get going for our practice," I added when it was clear she didn't know we were expected to cut the line.

"Oh look, it's them!" someone shouted.

I turned to see the crowd of onlookers, completely filling the long hallway that led from the runway to the other tents and vendors and out to the main hall of the Winter Garden.

"There are people as far back as you can see. It's like the red carpet at the Oscars!" she squealed.

"Oh look how gorgeous she looks!" a female voice said.

An embarrassed smile crept across Rory's lips and she stared out at the crowd, fascinated but also somewhat bewildered.

"Rory, we don't have a lot of time," I said, trying to pull her out of her stupor, placing my hand around her waist and gently turning her body back toward the photographer. As we took the final step up the runway and walked toward the camera, the hall exploded with applause.

"Go Sasha!"

"Yes, Sasha!"

"Davay, *Sasha!"*

"Sashaaaaa!"

People screamed. Then, *"Sasha and Rory!"*

"Go Sasha, go Rory!"

I smiled out at the crowd and squeezed Rory's hand.

After the photographers finished taking pictures, we exited the runway and walked to the back practice room. We went through each of our routines once more, costumed. I could tell it took everything Rory had to put her nerves aside. Mine were gone. My adrenaline had taken over. I was on fire, unable to wait much longer to take that stage. We were going to kill it.

"I'm ready. What about you?" I asked, bouncing on my heels.

"Totally! Just touching you, just looking at you in that tight black costume makes me feel sexy!" No squeakiness in her voice whatsoever.

"Good, that's the way it should always be," I said, kissing the back of her neck, right underneath her hairline, the last place a little smudged bronzer would show.

As we neared the end of our practice, our team members began to file into the room. Of course that's when it happened. Our one flub. It was a jive kick, in a side-by-side step. So, very noticeable. I knew it happened because Rory was now on display. It couldn't happen out there. It couldn't. Of course I heard Xenia snicker.

You idiot, if Rory screws up it'll hurt you too, since we're on a team, I thought but of course didn't say. Then I reminded myself this was just the team comp. If a flub was going to happen, it needed to happen here. Not when it counted.

"I'm sorry," Rory mouthed.

I shook my head and whispered, "Don't think about it. Don't think."

"Okay, looks like we're on, folks!" Bob said with a clap. He told us to get in our proper dance order. I positioned Rory and myself in the back since we'd emerge from the caravan last.

We walked down a long, barely lit hallway. The cheers of the crowd grew the closer we got to the stage. A spasm of adrenaline shot through my veins and into Rory's where we were connected by the arm. Bob led us out of the hallway and into a small room. A door opened out onto a covered caravan on wheels, with a short step. Bob apologized and told us he'd made a mistake; we needed to reverse our order. Rory and I were to enter first so we'd be getting out last. I felt Xenia's rotten glare as I escorted Rory past her and up the steps. Rory didn't look at her. *Good.* She was learning how to deal with jealous, pissy competitors.

The roar of the crowd became stronger as the caravan inched its way along.

"Welcome, ladies and gentlemen," the emcee said. "Blackpool is a small holiday seaside town on the coast of Britain. And look what you've done to it. Every year from late May through early June it becomes the world's most international city. We have registered in our hotels right now people from a total of one hundred and two different countries. The most common first language spoken in this small English town right now is Russian, followed by Mandarin, then English. Also spoken widely here right now are Japanese, Dutch, Polish, German, Italian, Hungarian..."

The list went on and the applause grew with each new language announced. Everyone was proud to be a part of this most international scene, including my love. Rory giggled. I kissed the same spot as before at the nape of her neck and squeezed her hand.

We were the second-to-last team introduced. First was Japan, followed by Italy, then the U.S. As we exited the caravan and descended the steps to the main ballroom floor, the applause went wild, as it always did. I was practically jumping out of my skin.

As always, Great Britain was the final team introduced, and received the greatest ovation. They were the home team after all, and always won the country competition. It wasn't because this was their turf, but because they'd always boasted the most dancers who placed in the finals. England's standard ballroom pairs placed first and second in last year's competition, plus they had the top Latin couple— Micaela and Jonathan. Micaela was Russian but was now a resident of England with her longtime partner

Jonathan. I'd told Rory not to be disappointed if the U.S. didn't win; we weren't expected to. We should be very disappointed, of course, if we didn't win the individuals on Wednesday night, though. Very, very disappointed.

We took our seats around the dance floor. First was a waltz. From our side, Maurizio whisked his lovely pro partner, Alexandra, out onto the ballroom. They shared the floor with the first competing ballroom team from each country.

I could feel Rory's heart pounding so hard it felt like it might leave her body. I hoped it was the good kind of adrenaline, that made you hyperaware, hyper on fire, not the kind that made you worry to the point of defeat. This was her first time in the heat of competition, of performance. I realized just now that neither of us had any idea how she'd react.

We had two dances before we went on, since we were the last couple to go and each couple danced half a dance.

"I just want to get this over with," she whispered.

"Don't think that way." I felt my stomach sinking. This was the bad kind of energy.

"Once we start I'll feel better, I know I will. I just need it to be soon. It's the waiting that's killing me."

This sounded much better. Waiting sucked. She bounced, about to skyrocket out of her seat. I put my hand on her shoulder blade. She stopped but then her knees began to wobble. I laughed under my breath. "Glad you are so excited to move," I whispered.

Bob approached and tapped Oleg, the leader of our second ballroom couple, on the shoulder. He stood elegantly and held out his hand for his partner, and they began waltzing. Maurizio caught Oleg's eye and returned with his partner to their seats. It was almost time for Xenia and Piotr, then Bob would tap me.

"I feel like I have spiders crawling down my legs and I need to shake them off," Rory whispered.

"Good. You will be able to shake very soon," I said with another squeeze of her hand.

"Oh, my eyes are adjusting to the light. There's Greta in the middle of the first row. She's wearing this long, absolutely drop-dead gorgeous scarlet-colored dress. Oh my, she stands out so far and above anyone else!" Rory's energy was making her babble. I hoped it didn't mean she was losing focus.

I spotted Greta as well. She held up a finger pointed right at Rory. Then she held her index finger vertically, as if to say number one—*You're number one. You can do it.*

I returned my hand to Rory's shoulder blade, my fingers now gently massaging the muscle beneath it. I could feel her confidence surging. *Thank you, Greta.*

The music changed to a cha-cha and Piotr and Xenia rose. After a few seconds, I felt Rory's nervous energy surge straight through her fingertips.

"Oh my…I just totally forgot…I have no idea how we start…"

Bob tapped my shoulder. I didn't have time to calm Rory down. It was showtime, for better or worse. I gave her knee a gentle pat and rose, holding her hand.

As we stood, the crowd exploded with cheers, as usual. Suddenly, Rory seemed to have no idea what was going on. She looked around questioning everything, where she was, what she was doing, why people were screaming.

"Come on, these are for us," I whispered. I continued leading her toward Piotr and Xenia, to take their place. We were nearly there. There was no time for a pep talk now. She had to follow me. She had to.

After they stopped and let us pass, I did a quick spin to the side, then whisked Rory around in front of me, placing us in our starting position. The crowds were roaring, drowning out the music. I suddenly realized we'd always used music whenever we danced. That was how she knew to dance on the beat. She'd have no choice but to follow me now. I could see her try to concentrate on hearing the beats. No time for worry or self-doubt. I pulled her toward me, then whipped her out to my right, catching her with my right arm. The beginning move of our cha-cha. She was in her proper positioning. I shifted my weight and held my opposite arm out; she naturally cha-cha'd toward it. She was doing it right. She was no longer thinking. Her muscle memory took over. The cheering grew.

"Sasha!!!"

This was what set me on fire. Always. The crowd. The audience. My fans.

"Go Sasha, go Rory."

Make that *our* fans. People were chanting for both of us. A lot of people. I met her eyes. It might have been Valentin leading the cheering section; I hadn't asked that of him. Judging by the cheers, I think people had learned who she was and liked both of us. I had my sexy, cocky smile amped all the way up. The smile I always wore when I danced. I directed it to Rory, then out to the crowd, then back to her, telling her I belonged first to her.

I pulled her into a split, our snazzy ending position. She got there, ended perfectly, just as we'd planned. The music stopped abruptly and the crowd went absolutely wild. I pulled her up from the splits and wrapped my arm around her waist. Holding her beside me, I took a deep bow, bringing her torso down with mine, so she'd follow my movement and take her bow as well. I realized now we hadn't practiced our bows. As always, the cheering was making my ears ring. It was like being at a rock concert. Then, I couldn't help it; I turned toward her, my lips brushing hers ever so briefly, the crowd going even wilder. I turned her around, held her hand in mine, and led her back to our seats.

The music changed to a foxtrot, and we sat. The applause didn't completely die but toned down a lot. Latin was always more popular.

I caressed her knee. "You did very well. Really, really well," I said, a compliment that was a first for me.

"What? Are you sure? I couldn't remember anything," she said, trying to catch her breath.

"Your muscles did," I said, kissing her on the cheek, now unable to give a shit whether I smudged any bronzer. I had to kiss her. I had to.

Our second dance was the samba. The adrenaline still had us both on a high, but something had changed in Rory's demeanor. She sat up straight with all the confidence in the world, now like an old pro, used to the blinding lights and eardrum-shattering cheers, which happened the second I stood and reached for her hand. This time I didn't bother to wait to get to the center of the floor to begin our routine, since samba was a dance that traveled around the ballroom, and since she didn't need that preparation now. We faced each other and did hip/pelvic rolls toward each other. I went down all the way, and she held my hand while lifting her back leg beautifully in a high *arabesque penchée*. This was not a traditional samba move—it was one of the steps she and Greta had choreographed as something that would be unique and suit her balletic background. We were unsure how it would go down.

As her pointed toe rose to the ceiling, the crowds burst into applause. They were even louder now than with our cha-cha. They gave her—us—everything we needed with those cheers. They accepted us. They accepted her. And she knew it. She was on fire right along with me. She let the crowd in, let them fuel her. We barreled through the rest of the routine, giving it more than our all, putting our souls into the movement. Samba was a happy, fun, sexy dance. I'd never felt happier than now, dancing with Rory. *Never.*

Competition dance had always been a source of near-hysteria for me, so needy was I to win. And I still felt that drive. But I'm not sure how to explain it—Rory and I just had this human connection that went so far beyond anything professional. We were one, and now this partnership meant something on a different level. I was in love, truly in love with my partner for the first time ever.

We had another break, during which we watched the ballroom dancers tango. I could tell Rory was using up a lot of energy, which was a good thing but could turn into a bad thing fast. I handed her a bottle of water. "You keep getting better and better. I'm so proud of you, Rory."

She nearly choked.

"Are you okay?" I asked.

"No! You've never pronounced anything perfect. But that was damn close. For you, Sasha!" The fact she could joke showed how far she'd come in just two dances. She was at ease; she was herself.

Our next dance was rumba. I could feel her adrenaline going strong, but I could also feel her nervous energy dissipate. Our rumba went better than it'd ever gone before. I was brilliantly gentle, if I say so myself, giving her more than adequate time to make her gorgeous lines and do all her beautiful stretches and delicious leg lifts full-out. I couldn't deprive the audience of that by overusing my strength. The crowd went crazy again as she slowly lifted her leg up all the way until it was straight, toe pointed at the ceiling, when I grabbed it and wrapped it around my shoulder, before sliding her across the floor. It was one of our many signature moves: beautiful and sexy, what rumba was all about. And I could tell she felt both in that moment.

At the end of the dance, Greta stood and held her hands over her head, clapping wildly and hooting. I couldn't hear her, the crowd was so loud. But she was front and center in the audience. Her very satisfied face couldn't be missed. Rory saw her too, and waved.

The paso doble and jive were our two final dances. Rory was like a breathtakingly beautiful, free-roaming gypsy recounting a story of woe and passion for her people as she stomped out those flamenco taps. That got a lot of applause, as did her cape-flying multiple pirouettes during my mad high midair turning jump. Her adrenaline was really taking her to new territory, I could tell. And my love of her and immense admiration of her artistry were doing the same for me.

"You are doing stellar. But here, drink, drink, drink," I said during our next break, handing her the Evian. "They put the most physically strenuous dance at the end on purpose. To test your physical stamina. That's part of the competition. Take deep breaths. No matter how tired you feel out there, you just have to breathe deeply and keep going."

She sobered and nodded.

"Even if you have to open your mouth to get the air in. Don't feel stupid opening your lips as you smile. I'm serious. This is how people crash."

The jive wasn't our strongest dance. Rory's kicks and flicks and kick ball changes had not acquired razor-sharp precision until late. And her speed in that dance was never anywhere near as great as mine. What she lacked in speed and precision, the judges would have to see her make up for in artistry and originality. She did know how to spot from so much ballet, so where many others were lacking—in the supercharged multiple spins—she should do very well. That's why Greta had included so many in our routine. They were her strength. And the crowd realized that quickly, as the screaming became thunderous whenever she did one. I could tell Rory was so tired she was on the verge of collapse, but I saw her breathing deeply through her open-lipped smile. And, I could tell, the crowd's applause kept her going.

The music ended and it was over. I squeezed her hand. "You did it. We did it."

"I know," she said, out of breath. "I know!"

As the scores were being compiled, all the

couples rose again and took several bows, first individually, then as teams, and finally as a whole group. By the time we took our seats again, the emcee was ready to announce the winners. This comp was much faster than the others. Italy came in fourth, then Japan, then the U.S., and Britain won. As I'd predicted.

"The results mean nothing. But the individual scores will be very meaningful," I whispered in her ear as we made our way to the podium. We took our places on the second step from the top while professional photographers snapped away, along with everyone in the audience who had a cell phone. Which was everyone.

"This is fun," Rory said with a giggle as she posed for the onslaught of flashes.

Her attitude made me nothing short of thrilled. The fact that she was happy to get her picture taken meant her self-esteem had grown light years. She wasn't the least bit worried about any body part. I could tell from the way she moved.

When we finally all got back to the practice room, Bob's ecstasy level had definitely gone down a notch. "Ugh, I don't know if we'll ever beat them," he said, exasperated. "But here you go." He passed out copies of scorecards to everyone on the team.

I grabbed ours. These scores would give us a solid indication of how well the judges liked Rory and me, how accepting they were of our partnership.

I sat down, put my elbow on the table, hovered over the scorecard, and studied it for several minutes. I was pleased. Very pleased. They'd ranked us exactly the same as Micaela and Jonathan. So they liked us, thought we were just as good as the reigning couple.

We didn't beat them, but we were tied.

"Tell me!" Rory insisted. I felt Xenia's glare. I didn't want to reveal my thoughts to Rory with her watching.

With a deep breath, I rose and extended my hand toward Rory. I lowered my chin to her so Xenia couldn't see my face, and flashed Rory a quick but wide grin. Rory was so excited, she jumped up and put her hand in mine. So much for secrecy and discretion.

"Okay, we're going to go home and get a good sleep," I told Bob.

"Thanks so much, Sasha. Very, very good job. Both of you," Bob said, smile partially returning. "You did it, kiddo, you really did it." He hugged Rory. "Bless you," he added, kissing her head.

Nice guy. Very nice. It was a good night for us.

***

"What was that all about? What did the scores show?" Rory chirped after we'd left the Winter Gardens and were out of earshot of anyone on the team.

"England came in first for ballroom, which is why they won. But the U.S. came in first for Latin."

"That's us! We did?" she squealed, squeezing closer to me in our arm-in-arm walk home.

"Yes. But don't get too excited. It's mainly because Xenia and Piotr were better than their second couple. The scores they gave us and Micaela and Jonathan were very, very close. In fact, neither of us actually won. That's why I was taking so long to read the score sheets. We tied in samba, cha-cha, and paso doble and we scored one point higher in rumba and one point lower in jive. Xenia and Piotr were only a quarter point behind us in samba and paso. It's going to be a very serious competition tomorrow night, Rory. The judges like us. But we have to keep it up."

Her stomach jolted. I could feel it through our connection. "My adrenaline is doing crazy things with my body," she said, realizing I could completely read her.

I felt a crooked, mischievous smile overtake my face. I was so wholly in my element. I loved this. It wouldn't be Blackpool without it being this close. I would never be a ballroom competitor if it was easy. I lived for this.

"You really get off on this, don't you!" She laughed. She could read me as well as I could read her.

I stopped and turned toward her, planting my lips hard onto hers. I lifted her by the waist. She let her right leg brush off the ground, did a little *arabesque* in bent attitude position and pointed her toe. *Sweet*. Not to mention gorgeous. As always. I bent over and dipped her, wrapping my arms more fully around her. Just like that couple in the famous photograph of the lovers after the soldier had returned from war. But our battle was far from over.

CHAPTER TWELVE

"Oh my gawwwd, baby. You looked soooo gorgeous out there!" Paulina was sitting at a lounge table in the bar closest to the hotel entrance waiting for us to return, her legs crossed and her patent leather red pump swinging in the air. I loved this woman more and more each day.

Rory had texted her, Raj and Sam about the after-competition parties in our hotel lounge, while warning them she wanted them to come and enjoy themselves but that we couldn't stay for very long tonight. And she couldn't drink. The real party would have to wait until tomorrow night.

I was immediately rushed by fans, most of whom I didn't know, making me all the more glad Paulina was there for Rory.

"Honey, you took my breath away," I heard Paulina say. "I was actually jealous of you, and I'm not the jealous type."

"Seriously?"

"Never been more serious. I couldn't believe that was you. You've just…transformed yourself."

I kept one eye on Rory, not daring to lose her here again, and listened to them for a bit, while

201

signing autographs and posing for pictures. Valentin, Sergei and Max walked in. When they saw me occupied, they ventured over to her.

"Very, very good tonight," I heard Val tell her in broken English.

"Yes, splendid! Delightful! Brilliant. Lovely!" This was Sergei.

I had to laugh at them. These words—where did they get them? She giggled and introduced them to her friends. We now shared friends.

When nearly forty-five minutes had passed, I held my hand up, promising the rest of the crowd I would be available at Daiyu's tent in the Pavilion from two o'clock onward on Thursday afternoon. I assured them there would be plenty more time for signings and photos.

Rory said goodbye to her friends and took my hand. We walked together arm in arm to the lift.

"Well, what did they have to say?" I asked.

"They said I not only did all the steps right but that I looked good doing them! That I was actually in my element. Paulina insisted I totally owned that floor! More than anyone else. And we were on with Micaela! And Paulina looked so sincere. I mean, I knew I was doing the steps right, because I wasn't screwing us up, but I was so focused on that, I didn't know how I actually interpreted everything. Whether it came across, you know."

I laughed. "Of course it came across."

But she was on a roll. "And then Sam said she couldn't believe it was me out there, her friend, a recent beginner. She said I just looked like a huge star. Like…you! She swore I looked as much of a star as you!"

"Rory, you've got to realize, you're here for a reason…" But then I stopped. This wasn't an issue of her lacking self-confidence. It had really hit her that this was a huge stage, and she was on it.

"I mean, it just hadn't even occurred to me that we were on the floor the same time as they were. I couldn't see anyone else when we were dancing, so I'd plumb forgotten there were even other people up there with us! I got so lost in us!"

"Me too, sweet," I said, pulling her to me as we arrived at our door, and kissing her long and hard on the lips. "Yes. Me too."

**

The next morning, Rory went down to the breakfast lounge while I showered. I was standing at the mirror drying my hair when she walked in. I was wearing nothing but a towel. We exchanged mischievous glances, then simultaneously remembered our bargain. No sex until tonight. After the comp. It would be a present to ourselves for having gotten through it all. For having won. Before then we'd only have moments of smoldering passion, as we'd had when she'd only been my student. We'd so been there before.

But then my eyes traveled down to the item in her hand and my stomach dropped. She held a copy of the *Blackpool Daily*. "Oh no, Rory. Don't ever read those things during competition. Ever." I grabbed it from her and threw it in the trash. "I'm serious. You read it after the comp is over. Only after. Otherwise it will really screw with your head."

She pursed her lips and widened her eyes. It

already had. I took a breath.

"I see it already has. What? What was it?" I asked. Now I needed to know. If something had upset her, I needed to know it.

"Nothing," she said. But she knew I was right. She knew I could see it had already screwed with her mind. "It's only good."

"I don't even want to know that. Even being aware of how much critics like you can give you too much pride, get you off your game. We'll talk about it tomorrow. No more thoughts about it now."

"Okay, no more words, no more thoughts, I promise."

"Good girl," I said, cupping my palm under her chin, pulling her face toward me and kissing her lightly on the lips.

Of course I couldn't help glance at it, my curiosity now piqued. The headline read *Mystery Woman Steals Sasha Zakharov's—and Blackpool's—Heart.* There was a photo of her wrapping her leg around my waist in *arabesque*, our favorite move. I saw words—*mesmerizing, ballet background*, and *best partner yet.*

Wow. Okay, enough. I refrained from picking it out of the trash, reminding myself of my own words.

***

We had a setback on our way to the Winter Garden, and I blamed it on the paper. Even though it had nothing to do with our little tiff, our emotions were brewing.

"Tonight will be a lot different than last night," I warned Rory as we walked down the cobblestoned street. "For one thing, there will be a lot more people on the ballroom floor, especially in the early rounds. Floorcraft will become more important, and that's where following will come more into play. If it looks like we may run into someone, particularly on the traveling dances, I might have to change the routine a bit or move us out of the way. I need you to be amenable."

I felt her pulse race.

"What?" she said, stopping abruptly. "You can't change the routine on me now, Sasha. It's in my muscle memory."

"Calm down, Rory. We very likely won't have to. I'm just warning you it's a possibility. Anything can happen out there."

"Well, could you have thought to tell me this before now? So we could have practiced an alternate routine?" Her words were coming out fast and jumbled. She was getting way too worked up.

"We can't practice an alternate because I may have to change that as well, depending on what's happening on the floor. If we'd prepared alternate routines, I would have to think of every possible situation. That would be impossible."

I was getting too worked up as well. This was only a slight possibility. I stopped, tightened my grip on her hand, took a deep breath and closed my eyes. I was sure I'd told her all of this before. But no use fighting at this point. She didn't remember. I tried to shake off the stress.

"Okay, don't worry," I continued after a few seconds of deep breathing. "I am just telling you to prepare you for the absolute worst. Honestly, I've only once had to do it. If I have to tonight, I will alter just as slightly as I can."

She breathed heavily and nodded. We resumed walking but I could feel her pulse. It wasn't returning to normal. She was freaked out, to put it mildly.

"When did you have to change it before?" she asked.

"During paso. The floor was too crowded behind us for me to do a full-out *tour jeté*. So I did another basic and moved us over a few feet."

"Couldn't you just not have done it? Or done a less full-out jump?" Her voice was laced with panic.

"That's an important step, Rory. I couldn't do it half-assed."

"But wouldn't the judges have known what you were doing?"

"Yes, but in that case, if I moved us slightly it would have been fine. Which is why it was more important that I moved us. It was more important for the judges to see that Xenia could follow my lead. It would have looked worse if I just did a half-assed jump when there was a better alternative. Do you see?"

She threw her hands up. One was still connected to me, so my arm came up as well. "Sasha, Xenia is at a totally different level than I am. You need to not do that to me. We needed to prepare slight alterations if—"

"No, she is not. You are at a higher level. The judges told you so last night. There was no dance where she came out with a better score than you." My voice was firm, but not raised.

"Sasha, that's not what I meant. I'm relying on muscle memory here."

"And me." I looked at her, peering into her eyes with all the serious intensity I could muster. "You are relying on *me*. You need to trust *me*. Have I ever let you down?"

She looked up at me. Her eyes softened.

"Would you answer me, please?"

"No, of course you haven't," she said.

"And I don't intend to start now." I was now holding both of her hands. I caressed her palms with my fingers.

"It's not you who I don't trust," she said, her voice cracking with a threatening tear. "It's me."

"Rory." I rolled my eyes, then let go of her hands and turned away in frustration. "You have to trust yourself. You owe yourself that much at this point. Please," I said, turning back to her.

She blinked back tears and took a deep breath. Then she frowned. Her eyes darted around and she focused her gaze on something over my shoulder. I turned to look. I saw only tree branches.

"Rory, I'm sorry. I didn't mean to work you up. I want you to calm down. What I described has hardly ever happened. It's something that happens in standard ballroom a lot but very rarely happens in Latin. I just wanted to warn you in the extremely unlikely event—"

But she wasn't focusing anymore on what I was saying. She looked wary, and turned to glance over each shoulder.

"What is it?"

She blinked hard, took a breath, then forced her lips into a smile. "Nothing. Absolutely nothing."

There was a rustle in the trees. She gasped. We both looked up to see a small bird taking off. She laughed.

"Okay." She gazed up at me. "I'm sorry I got so

worked up. I'm done now. It's good you warned me, though," she whispered, seeming to recover from both the worry and fright.

"Okay, good," I said, kissing her forehead. We continued walking, past the bird-ridden tree. "There is just one other thing I need to remind you of. Tonight is going to be much more a test of endurance than last night. There will be a total of fourteen rounds. We have already practiced with that many rounds, so I think we will be prepared. Plus, we will have breaks in between. But I just wanted to remind you."

Her eyes widened again and her hand began to tremble. It seemed she couldn't shake something.

"Tell me what it is," I insisted.

She shook her head. "No. I'm just remembering bad things. I don't want to talk about them. Please, let's just go on. You were saying something. Please continue."

I wondered if the bad memory was of Uncle Oleg or Cheryl. But I wouldn't make her talk and relive anything if she didn't want to. "We will have plenty of time between rounds, at least for most of the competition. It gets more difficult from the quarterfinal rounds through the finals because there is only one heat per round. And they will still give us a few songs to recover while they open the floor to general dancing," I said, trying to get her mind back to dance.

She nodded, indicating I was succeeding.

"That's why it was so important to build up strength and endurance," I continued, softening. "Which you did, my love." I kissed her cheek. "And we have our big bag of food that we bought at the market. That will be kept in the tent. I need you to go to the tent and eat whenever you feel hungry or fatigued. We're moving so much there's no way you will gain a thing. I promise."

"Sasha, I'm so beyond the anorexia at this point," she said, matter-of-factly. She still seemed preoccupied by something else.

"You will need to go to the tent frequently for makeup touch-ups because we will be sweating so often. Plus, it's a good place to go to relax and calm down between heats. You might as well take advantage of the food while you're in there," I went on.

"I will. I promise. I'll go to the tent frequently." She began walking faster.

"And breathe with your mouth open, like last night. Your muscles need oxygen or you can lose balance and even faint."

She opened her lips as I said this, breathed deeply.

"Oh good, we're here," she said, reaching out for the doors of the Winter Gardens. I turned around. She was spooked by something outside? More than the bird-tree?

"Rory," I began. But she gave me a don't-ask-and-make-it-worse look. So I didn't. "We are," I said, and opened the door for her.

CHAPTER THIRTEEN

After we were made-up and costumed by Daiyu's assistants, we walked toward the ballroom. I wanted to stop off and wish Svetlana good luck. I'd texted her a congratulations on the Rising Star comp and she'd texted back thanking me, saying she was competing in the main Latin pro competition as well, and inviting me to stop by the main changing room. She and her partner had staked out a back corner.

"Should we be going through here? I mean, together?" Rory asked as I opened the door.

"Why not?"

"I mean, isn't this the women's room?"

"What? No."

"Sasha, it says right there." She pointed to the sign above the doorway.

I laughed, forgetting once again she was new here. "Rory, that's for the general public. No one pays attention to those things here. Everyone's all together. Come on."

We walked into the large room of men and women together in various states of dress, changing and helping their partners. Yes, there were breasts and men in dance belts, their asses exposed. She initially

210

looked a bit mortified, then recovered, and laughed it off.

"My modest American," I said, kissing her cheek.

She rolled her eyes. "I don't know if being American has anything to do with being a bit weirded out by seeing people out in the open standing around in nothing."

"Yeah but isn't it the same backstage at the ballet?"

She thought, then shrugged. "I don't know. I never got that far. I never performed." There was no sadness in her voice when she said this. No painful memories of things that hadn't ended up happening, like there had been when she'd talked about ballet before. Just matter-of-factness.

I kissed her again. She was over it. She was happy now. Here, with me, in the world of ballroom.

"Well, no one has any time to focus on each other's bodies. Everyone's too worked up about the competition, and too busy fixing buttons, pins, zippers. Everyone's hyper-focused on looking and dancing the best they can."

"Yeah, I see that now," she said.

Fortunately, Svetlana and her partner were both fully dressed.

"Thank you for coming!" Sveta said in Russian, hugging me.

"This is Josef, from Beverly Hills Dance," she said, introducing her partner. We shook hands.

"You were stunning last night," Svetlana said to Rory, in accented but good English. "You stole the show! Go you!" She pumped her fist in the air.

Rory blushed. "Wow, thank you."

"Seriously, oh my gosh, it's all I heard anyone

talk about everywhere we went last night. Even Cheryl and Luna were floored. And I mean floored!"

Rory momentarily froze, but then pulled herself out of it and smiled. "Thank you, Svetlana. That means so much, coming from you. I've always admired your dancing since I first saw you in the O.C." But there was a noticeable shakiness in Rory's voice now.

Shit. Sveta had left the studio before the incident during the mambo team performance and didn't know about the bad blood.

The emcee announced the start of the first heat and we all walked out to the floor together. I gave Rory's hand a firm squeeze. "Don't worry about anything. That meant nothing," I mouthed to her as we walked. She flashed me a worried smile. "Trust me," I whispered.

She nodded. "I do."

Squeezing her hand again, I turned my gaze from her and looked out at the fans, politely smiling and mouthing "Thank you" to their chorus of "Go, Sasha," "Good luck, Sasha," "Kill it, Sasha," and, finally, "Go Sasha and Rory!"

We weren't in the first heat but Sveta was. We wished her good luck and watched as she and Josef were called out to the floor, amidst the many, many others, until there was hardly a free square foot of space out there. I could feel Rory's heartbeat race, after what we'd talked about on the way here. I gave her hand another squeeze.

"Don't worry," I whispered.

"I'm not." She squeezed back, letting me know she was sincere.

The cha-cha began. Sveta and Josef could hardly

move, but they did brilliantly, as I knew she would.

The music ended and the usual chaos ensued as the couples from heat one exited the floor and the next heat entered. We weren't on for a couple more heats, but with every changing round, I inched us closer to the floor to minimize our need to scramble when we were called.

"It's getting tiring just watching," Rory said after the third or fourth heat. I'd lost count.

"Don't worry, your adrenaline will kick in as soon as soon as we're called. I promise."

***

By the time the emcee finally announced our heat, we were right at the dance floor, ready to go on. The audience cheered like mad when our names were called.

"Here we go. *Merde*, sweetheart," I whispered and gave her a peck on the lips.

When I did so, the entire ballroom erupted into a fit of screams. Even I was surprised. I swear, it was louder than ever before. Like aural fireworks.

The chants began before the music.

"Sasha, Sasha, Sasha!"

I smiled out at the crowd while I led us toward the middle of the floor. The other dancers parted for us, as usual. I could tell it surprised Rory. I could see her bemused expression out of the corner of my eye. Then, the audience wave began. People in the front area rose and roared as we passed. Rory laughed, now in bemused delight.

"Go Sasha! Go Aurora!" I could have sworn I heard someone say. I wondered if the *Blackpool Daily* article had referred to her by her full name.

No time to think about that now. The music began and we started with a bang. Well, as much of a bang as we could. The first rounds were always hard. The floor was so overcrowded we needed to make our steps as small as possible. We couldn't dance full-out at all. I realized I hadn't told her how crowded it would be. She'd been right. I hadn't prepared her. I blasted myself for it. Her muscle memory was used to dancing as expansively as she could. But, amazingly, she seemed to be a pro at making her steps the same length as mine, to match me. She was following. And she was doing so brilliantly. I knew she could do it. I knew she could.

The music ended before we were even halfway through our routine, and the emcee directed us to exit the stage. These early heats were short. I felt sorry for newcomers. They had so little chance of being seen. The crowd kept screaming until we were completely off, as usual. Rory didn't look happy. I squeezed her hand and led her back to Daiyu's tent where we could talk in private.

"*Sashaaaaaa!*"

"*You rock, you rock star!*"

I smiled at everyone and thanked them, trying to get Rory to the tent as fast as I could to calm her down.

"I feel like it didn't go very well," she said, once we were inside and out of earshot of anyone. "I was concentrating way too hard on not bumping into anyone. And how are we ever going to do the traveling dances like samba and paso doble, where we really have to move about the floor? We will definitely have to change everything!" Her voice was full of panic.

"No, no, don't worry about it," I said. "The first couple of rounds are always crazy, until they go through the first series of cuts. Half of those people won't make the first cut, and half of those the second. So by the third round, only a quarter of us will remain, and we will be more than able to dance everything full-out." Now that I heard myself voice my own logic, I realized I'd worried for nothing earlier. We wouldn't have to change our floorcraft at all. That was me being my typical over-concerned, cover-all-the-bases self.

"Yeah, but that's assuming we make the first two cuts."

Okay, now I had to shoot her a look of utter sarcasm. She laughed, finally.

"Okay, Mr. God's Gift, but—"

"No, I don't mean to be obnoxious, sweet. You know that. I just mean, that's why it helps to be known. They know we are finals material." I shrugged. "That's why it can be very hard to get your start here at the huge competitions. It gets more and more impossible each year for new people to be seen. I hope Svetlana makes it, but I'm not sure if she will."

I fanned Rory's beautiful face with one of Daiyu's ornate Chinese hand fans and handed her a bottle of Evian. "We can take our time to relax. We have several more rounds until we're on again."

We returned to the floor several rounds early, of course, to make sure we would be ready to go on when our heat was called. At the start of every other heat, there was a roar emanating from some side of the room. During one, it was for Xenia and Piotr, then Micaela and Jonathan, then Arabelle and

Andrew. We, the stars of Blackpool who returned year after year after year, to please the fans and try once again to win. Or, in the case of Micaela and Jonathan, maintain their champion status.

"Don't worry about dancing down since we can't dance full-out," I said to Rory when we took the floor to begin our samba. "Remember what I said. Just do the steps, follow me. You will be okay. I prrrromise."

That rolling r got her to crack a smile.

We managed to get through the first two rounds without having to alter our routine and without smacking into anyone. And, of course, we made it through to the second cut. We were home free. At least regarding the overcrowded floor.

Svetlana made it through the first cut, but not the second. She was thrilled nevertheless. And I was happy for her. It was a very good rank for a complete novice. She and Rory chatted a bit on the sidelines, between dances. They were both somewhat nervous and seemed to put each other a little more at ease. Sveta's praise was good for Rory's self-confidence. And there seemed to be no more mentions of the witches of Beverly Hills.

Speaking of which, after Sveta's mention of them, I'd texted Val to see what was up, if anything. According to our group of friends, Cheryl and Luna weren't doing anything suspicious. They'd watched competitions—last night's and tonight's, thus far—had eaten in the Italian restaurant with Xenia and Piotr, the diner inside the Winter Gardens, and the Japanese restaurant downstairs, and late last night had gone out to a bar at the Imperial Hotel—the fancy hotel by the sea, where they were staying. *Figures*, I thought. They wouldn't be caught dead in a bed and breakfast. It was where Xenia and Piotr were staying as well. They didn't have seats for tonight's performance, but were standing in the mezzanine aisles.

"Don't worry, we will keep watch," Val wrote.

It had taken two hours to get through the initial rounds, one hour for each. We would definitely be here well into the night.

If we stayed in the ballroom for too long, fans would start to approach. I welcomed them but I could tell they made Rory nervous at this point. I knew she'd be better after it was all over. So I gave Sveta a final congrats and a hug, and Rory and I headed to the tent for some downtime and snacks. Which gave Rory some time to read texts from her friends.

"Paulina said she could make us out the second we took the floor," she squealed, before madly typing her response back. "She said she could really see my hips moving madly in samba! She said I rocked it!" Rory sang. "She said Swan Lake Samba Girl—what Bronislava used to call me—is no more!"

"Bronislava used to call you that?" I asked.

"Yeah, 'cuz I looked like a ballerina *bouréeing* across the stage, like a swan. You know, mainly with the *voltas*. Gosh, that seems like a lifetime ago."

"And it really wasn't. That's the crazy thing," I said.

"Tell me about it."

***

The floor was still crowded during round three, but a lot less so. We were able to move much better. Now we could dance nearly full-out. And there was virtually no chance we'd have to alter our routine. Unless someone tried to sabotage us. I shook the thought from my mind. It wasn't going to happen. Not with Valentin's guys on the watch.

Rory was moving beautifully. I was so proud of her. She was adding so much to the steps, making everything as dramatic as possible, really entertaining the crowd and telling a little narrative with our dance. Her nerves were nearly gone.

Things started moving a lot faster after round five. Many of the couples had been eliminated so there wasn't as much waiting time between heats. I worried Rory might get worn out, so I had one of Daiyu's assistants wait for us near the dance floor with water and nuts in tow. But Rory actually seemed much better now that there wasn't as much waiting between heats. It meant her adrenaline was constantly pumping. As was mine. We really were so similar in the heat of competition.

And I could tell she was actually beginning to have fun. The cheers were getting wilder and were now always for both of us, not just me. I could tell her body was tiring, as anyone's would by this point, but her adrenaline was really coming through for her, for us, in a big way, driving her more and more so that she was actually getting stronger and faster with each passing round. Exactly like me. We were one and the same. My former partners would begin to peter out, no matter how hard they tried not to. Not so with Rory. We were so solid, so meant for each other.

"What's so awesome," she said at one point, out of breath after our round six jive, "is that the cheers seem to be for us, for our partnership, and not just our professional one."

I'd most definitely noticed that too. I was making it so, in my own way, though I didn't tell her. At the end of every rumba, I was now giving her a little kiss on her forehead, and it was getting longer and more pronounced each time. I wanted the crowd to know we were in love, that she was mine. As the rounds progressed, the crowd was coming to expect it and was starting to go crazy before I even did it.

"What took me so long to become part of this awesome world? I haven't lived until now!"

I laughed. "I know. I know, sweet."

I could tell her words of enthusiasm were due partly to nerves and exhaustion, and her absolute insistence not to let them, especially the latter, get the better of her. We were now nearing the end of the tenth round. Her face was red. I could see the blood pumping extra hard, to keep it all going. At the end of every dance now, she was downing practically a half bottle of Evian, a banana, and a bag of almonds or walnuts.

"The dances are getting shorter," she said, in the midst of chewing at one point. "I mean, the orchestra's not playing full songs, so it's going doubly fast as before."

I shook my head. "It's just an illusion," I said. "They're playing for the exact same amount of time; it just seems faster because we're now out there so much more."

She looked shocked.

"We just have to get through one more round," I said, not letting myself worry. I didn't need to. I knew she could do it. "Then we'll be on to the quarterfinals.

This is a very important cut, so it will take them some time to compute the scores to decide who will advance. They usually open the floor to general dancing so the audience has something to do. We'll have a good break. And we'll have another good break after the quarterfinals round, into the semifinals, and that's when we'll change costumes."

She laughed, a little too much. She was tired. "Your English is so damn perfect. It never ceases to amaze me!"

I laughed. "Yes, I think you've mentioned that."

"Seriously," she said, after swallowing a long swig of Evian. "Your impeccable grammar makes it clear that your emotions are totally under control, and that you're not feeling anxiety at all. I could always tell how stressed and frustrated you were when your English started to falter. It makes me feel so much better knowing how in control you are. And I won't faint. I'll get through it. I will. We will."

Which of course made me kiss her. Again. We were on the sidelines but people were still watching because when I did so, wild cheering broke out. She giggled. I laughed. Hell, the crowd was probably applauding that I wasn't fighting with my partner, like usual. It was an incredible feeling.

We made it through the last round before the quarterfinals quite well. Far from fainting, Rory danced the hell out of our routine. It went without saying now there were no foibles. But we were also dancing with such meaning, such passion. I'd never been so on fire, never happier with my partner.

We returned to the tent and Daiyu herself fanned Rory and me down. The makeup man returned and touched up Rory's hair and face, and Daiyu's assistant powered me off and gelled me back again. Rory and I took turns sipping Gatorade and she popped grapes in her mouth in between lipstick blots. She was downing so much food, it was hard to believe she'd been on the verge of an eating disorder.

Starting with the quarterfinals, all of the couples left took the ballroom floor at once. It was at this point that the audience really started to roar. Every single couple who would remain for the finals in a few short rounds was up there right now; all of the stars of the ballroom world were on the floor at once. There was so much screaming, so many names being called out at the same time. There were more cheers for Rory and me, but there were a good number for Micaela and Jonathan, Xenia and Piotr, and Arabelle and Andrew, which drove home just how close this competition was, what fierce competitors we were for both the judges' votes and the audience's attention. It began, as it always did at this point, to feel a little like a boxing match.

I felt Rory's nerves begin to prickle. I hoped her self-confidence would remain strong.

I squeezed and shook her hand, trying literally to shake the prickles off.

She nodded, understanding what I was doing. "Don't worry about me," she whispered.

Since we were all on the floor at once, without heats, we had no break time between the dances. If she lacked confidence or energy in the least, she definitely didn't show it. We killed it, dancing our best round yet. She'd become a true pro.

"I love you," I said this time after our rumba as I kissed her now on the lips, wrapping my arms around her and squeezing her close. The crowd went so completely nuts now, so crazy the band actually delayed the beginning of the paso for a few seconds to let all the cheering die down a bit. That was all we needed—that crowd and its encouragement. I looked at Rory, my eyes beaming into hers, my confidence radiating, setting her on fire.

She nodded. "Your fans—our fans—are the only ones I can hear," she whispered.

The band gave us a short break between paso doble and jive, which was customary, jive being the most difficult when you were dead tired. Micaela strutted around, waving to her fans. Arabelle stood in place, smiling radiantly to all the "Belle Arabelle" callers. I wrapped my arms around Rory from the side, and pressed my lips to her temple in response to our cheers, making them all the louder.

The orchestra broke into their jive music, which brought me back to earth. Judging by our scores in the team competition, this was our weakest dance. But my display of confidence in our partnership to the world made Rory's adrenaline surge through her entire body, from her small toe to the crown of her head. I felt it through our connection, through her fingertips. As soon as we started that backward slide, followed by our hyper-fast jive kicks, I knew she was going to nail it. We were going to nail it. And when we heard her name—"Aurora, go Aurora! Yes, Rory!"—I knew the audience knew it too.

After the quarterfinals we rushed back to the tent, the wild applause from the ballroom echoing all the way down the hall. Daiyu and her assistants had our new costumes all ready. Rory's took longer, of course. She didn't seem the least bit embarrassed this time by the assistant seeing her in a semi-naked state.

She was far too focused. After she was all zipped and buttoned in, she began shaking out her legs, stretching her hamstrings. I knew she was achy. I was too.

"Just two more rounds. That's all, honey. Then we're done. You can do it," I said.

"I know."

The applause was even louder as we took the floor for the semifinal round, owing largely to the costume change, which, as usual, everyone had done. Micaela even had a different hairstyle—a French twist that looked flawless. I read Rory's expression as she gazed at the intricate hairdo, wondering how she'd had the time. I kissed her again, on the cheek so as not to disturb her just-made-up lips. She giggled and, again, the crowd went mad.

The big band began their cha-cha and we were off, our muscle memory on super-drive. I could no longer feel the aches. I was numb to the pain. Rory was too, I could tell. If she felt any, she danced her best and her fullest right through it.

The cha-cha nearly blended right into the samba. I saw a kind of blur in Rory's eyes. She breathed deeply, nodded, telling me it was all right. Her muscles were in control. And they were doing the right thing. Thanks to the hundreds and hundreds of hours of practice we'd put into it all.

The crowd was going so wild now, cheering back and forth for the eight of us—Rory and me, Arabelle and Andrew, Micaela and Jonathan, and Xenia and Piotr. If they didn't have a live band we would never have been able to hear the music.

The samba ended and they gave us a few moments of rest to reboot for the rumba.

"Thank the lord for a slow dance," she said under her breath. Then, "Don't worry, I'll put everything I have, and more, into it."

Good girl.

The rumba music began. We did our opening move: my deep lunge/her slow leg lift, followed by me pulling her passionately toward me, and her backing slightly away so she could bow down to me while extending her leg up gorgeously high behind her. The crowd cheered like crazy. As I knew they would. It was one of our most beautiful moves and we could do it full-out now, with so few people on the floor. Then, our series of lightning-fast underarm turns. I led her into the first, then second, then third whipping spin. She was spotting by peering intensely into my eyes. We got so swept up in our little wind tunnel, we created a gust that emanated out to the front few rows of the audience. People laughed and now the applause was so loud it nearly blocked out the music this time, even with the live band.

Then, I saw it. Something large was coming down, right at us. Right at Rory. *What the fuck?* I pulled her back to me swiftly. My sharp movement took her off guard and she stumbled. She wasn't able to *développé* her leg all the way up, and she ended up sliding into me, her unfolding knee landing not in my groin but smack in my rib cage. It hurt like hell but I didn't allow myself to move a millimeter. Instead, I picked her up right off the ground and set her back on her feet, squarely. I had to, because things were about to go very bad. I saw Arabelle out of the corner of my eye, falling. The flying object had hit her. Or it had hit the floor near her, and was causing her to take a bad tumble. I heard a loud crack.

"Oh my God, oh my God!" people cried.

I stopped moving. As did everyone else. There were screams. But not the cheering kind. The horrified kind.

Arabelle was behind Rory, sprawled on the floor. Rory looked at me, bewildered. She backed up, looking at my chest, a terrified look in her eyes. I pulled her to me, not wanting her to step on Arabelle, who she obviously didn't see.

She followed my gaze and turned around. Arabelle was now completely prostrate on the floor, facedown. There was blood spreading out from under her hair. My first thought was that she'd cracked her skull. There had been very minor accidents before at Blackpool, but nothing ever like this.

"Call an ambulance," I yelled.

It all happened so quickly. The music was actually still going. I don't know if anyone could even hear me.

Rory struggled out of my grasp and ran toward her.

"Rory!" I yelled. I now saw liquid—not blood, but something clear, all over the floor surrounding Arabelle. Whatever was in that object when it exploded had created a liquid pool. Someone had intended for there to be a bad fall. Rory's heel skidded out from under her.

Oh no. I watched as she slipped and fell flat on her butt, sliding straight toward Arabelle. At least she fell in the best way possible, unlike poor Arabelle.

Rory slid toward Arabelle, moving her arms and pulling herself beside her. She lifted Arabelle's face.

"Rory, wait," I called out, knowing you weren't supposed to move a person who had a potentially serious injury. But, thank God, that didn't seem to be the case with Arabelle. She was crying and her nose was bleeding badly. It didn't look like she had any blood on her head. It seemed only to be her nose.

"We need ice and towels," Rory called out. She cupped her hand underneath Arabelle's nostrils to collect the blood. I knew where they kept emergency medical supplies near the practice rooms. I ran off to retrieve bandages and ice, yelling out for people to call for help. Andrew ran behind me. It didn't occur to me until I'd reached the room that I'd left Rory. I didn't have my phone with me. I trusted Valentin to keep an eye on everything though. I had to at this point.

When we returned with ice and bandages, Rory was holding Arabelle in her lap. Arabelle's white gown had a jagged line of crimson going down the front. It looked like she'd been stabbed in the heart.

I looked at Rory. Reading my mind, she shook her head. "It's just her nose," she said. "But it's bad. It may be broken."

I wrapped ice in a cloth and Andrew and I both helped Arabelle up. I handed her the ice right before a paramedic brushed me aside and took over.

"Clear out. Everyone please clear out," he said.

Rory began to get up. "Be careful when you walk," I said to her. "There's water everywhere and it looks like rubber pieces, maybe from some kind of a…balloon?"

The emcee came over the mike, announcing that the floor would need to be cleaned and Arabelle would need medical assistance. We would resume as soon as possible, he said.

I grabbed Rory's hand and walked her steadily

around the spilled water. It had created quite a pool.

"What happened?" she said.

I shook my head. "Someone apparently threw something containing water—maybe a water balloon bomb—at someone on the floor. Perhaps us."

"You know it was Cheryl," she shouted, stopping to stomp her Latin stiletto into the parquet.

"Please be careful, sweetheart. I don't want you to get hurt. There's still water."

She continued to look at me, not moving. Her lips were a straight line. She wasn't letting me tell her not to worry about Cheryl now. I didn't know what to say. I'd trusted Val's guys. Maybe they were watching the wrong person. Maybe Cheryl had someone else do her dirty work for her, somehow knowing I had eyes on her. I needed to get back to the tent to get my phone and text Val. Rory put her hands on her hips.

"I know," I said. "She missed you. She'll get hers. Don't worry. Let's get back to the tent."

Satisfied, her frown eased a slight bit and she walked with me.

***

Once we arrived at Daiyu's, I got into my bag and pulled out my cell phone. There was already a text from Valentin.

We're investigating, he wrote. *If she was behind it, she didn't do it herself. I was looking right at her as it happened. She looked just as surprised as everyone. Same with the other lady she was with. Sergei said the same.*

Thank you, I responded.

Rory had been texting her friends too. No one knew anything, apparently. We sat and waited for an update on Arabelle. Instead of being angry, Rory couldn't stop tearing up. I put my arm around her.

"I know it was meant for me, and glad as I am it didn't get me, I'm just so sorry for her, Sasha. She's the last person who deserved to have her Blackpool ruined, after everything she's been through. I just can't believe Cheryl would do this, would actually stoop to this level. I seriously want to kill her. How could anyone be that mean? What happened to her in her life to make her so evil?"

I shook my head. "I don't know. Let's just…let's not think about Cheryl right now, Rory."

She frowned sharply and moved out of my embrace.

"I mean, I don't want to be filled with anger right now. We need to be focused on ourselves. If we focus on Cheryl, she's won."

Rory considered this, and slowly began to nod.

I then noticed her dress had just about as much blood on it as Arabelle's. And this was her new one, for the finals. She'd have to change back into the old. It wasn't customary and judges didn't like changes, whether they be to rules or customs, but what could we do?

"Come on, just get changed. And don't think about that witch. Promise me you'll put it out of your mind. At least until the competition's over."

Her lips parted into a slight attempt at a smile and she nodded again. She got up and went back behind the screen with Daiyu, her assistant having already left by now.

"Oh shit," Daiyu said, zipping Rory up. I'd never heard Daiyu curse before.

"What?" Rory said.

"There's a tear."

"Oh no. I'm so sorry. It must have happened when I took it off earlier. I was rushing so fast, I hadn't taken off my shoes and I probably got the heel stuck in the fabric. I'm sorry. This is my first time here, Daiyu, and I'm so nervous," Rory spat out.

Daiyu laughed. "Don't be ridiculous," she said. "Everyone does that. I'm surprised there's only one tear!"

"Really?" Rory said, trying to laugh too, her face lined with worry. "But what are we going to do?"

"It's on the seam. It won't be hard to fix. But I'll need you to take it off first."

Rory stepped out of it, carefully this time, and sat in a towel, getting her makeup redone, as mascara now dotted her cheeks, while Daiyu sewed at the speed of light, like the consummate pro she was.

As soon as the hairstylist was done, I walked to Rory. "You were amazing, by the way. I forgot to tell you that. The way you took care of Arabelle. You didn't even think about damaging your dress, about slipping and getting hurt yourself. I'm so proud of you," I said to her, squeezing her shoulders, giving her back a mini-massage.

"I only did what I had to do. You ran off and called the paramedics and got her ice."

"You were the fastest thinker, though." I kissed her on each shoulder, then each side of her neck.

About half an hour later, Val texted me. *It was apparently some guy who threw the water bomb. Twenties, dark hair, short, stocky, wearing dark glasses, thug-like. Your ladies seem to have no involvement. At least they're not acting the least bit suspicious.*

My heart sank. That description fit my cousin,

Pasha, to a tee.

"What's up?" Rory asked, eyeing the cell phone.

"My friends are saying it was a guy who threw a water bomb. No word about any women involved," I told her, trying to calm myself. *It could still be someone they hired*, I thought. The description could fit a good many so-called "thug-like" persons. Maybe it wasn't my family.

"Really?" She looked dubious.

I shrugged. "That's what Valentin says."

About twenty minutes later, the emcee was back, announcing that the competition would continue. The floor had been cleaned, the culprit had been found, and authorizes had assured the organizers justice would be meted out. Most importantly, Arabelle was okay. She had a broken nose but no other broken bones or injuries, and would be able to continue in the competition.

I hugged Rory. "It's going to be okay. Let's just do it. They caught the guy. Security is going to be maximized now. Nothing more is going to happen now," I said, trying hard not to doubt my words and hoping like hell my uncle wasn't behind it. But why would he be, anyway? *He knows Rory is not Tatiana now. There's no one else on the dance floor whom he would confuse with her.* It would make no sense. It wasn't him. It was just some crazed nutter who hated either us or Arabelle. Or someone out there.

We all returned to the ballroom floor. Everyone cheered wildly, particularly when Arabelle entered. Myself included, of course. She'd changed costumes and was no longer all bloodied. Her nose was badly swollen and wrapped in a large bandage. She was still a beautiful woman. And her nose would heal. She took a gracious bow and smiled.

We began the rumba again. We were now more rested and less tired but, emotionally, Rory was way, way more worked up. Her face said it all: *Screw that bitch. We're going to win. Just let her try to stop us.* She still believed it was Cheryl. I could see it in her eyes.

Rory's fire returned, and so much more wickedly than ever. It was the most intense rumba I'd ever danced in my life. Again, there was so much cheering it was nearly impossible to hear the music when it stopped. I pulled her to me dramatically, and pressed my lips to hers, leaving them there for several seconds. People cheered, but there were far more chants this time for Arabelle and Andrew than for anyone else. And rightly so. I didn't kiss my love this time for the crowd. I did it for her, my brilliant, most wonderful partner. My partner who would never, ever let me down. Who would be there forever. Whom I was never, ever letting go.

We nailed the paso and jive as well. Rory's jive kicks had the most strength and sharpness and pizazz she'd attained yet. And she was very nearly as fast as I, very nearly so. It was her best jive ever. She wasn't the least bit overwhelmed by what had happened, or tired. Cheryl had clearly jumpstarted her. Or whoever had thrown a water bomb at us, for whatever reason.

We returned to the tent again before the finals. Rory ate another banana and washed it down with more Gatorade. "Potassium," she said. Which was good for sore muscles, we both knew. Gone entirely was her worry about how she looked, wholly replaced with concern over health, over repairing her stressed body.

One of the young men who was helping to

collect the judges' scorecards came to the tent. "Finalists are being announced. Return to the floor, please," he said.

"Already? That's fast," said Greta, who'd just arrived at Daiyu's tent to give us a pep talk.

"It is," I agreed. "I guess scoring was easy. Or they want to make up lost time."

"Probably the latter, now that you mention it," Greta laughed. "Nope, they really don't like to get behind here!"

On the way to the floor, we overheard the young man tell one of the judges a boy in his teens or twenties had thrown a water missile from the first row of the balcony. His friends had turned him in. Valentin had said Cheryl and Luna were in the mezzanine, nowhere near the balcony.

"He'd better turn her in. He'd better not take the blame for that witch," Rory said.

I simply squeezed her hand. Talking about it at this point was futile. We'd find out what had happened when we found out.

Unlike in the other rounds, finalists were announced by name and country, not number. First called were Arabelle and Andrew. The entire ballroom cheered, of course. Then, Xenia and Piotr. Less applause but still a great deal of it. Then, the Italian couple who was in the country team match, followed by a Chinese couple. The emcee then announced Micaela and Jonathan. Deafening applause again, for the current champs. I could feel Rory's heart skipping beats. I squeezed her hand again, letting her know she had nothing to worry about.

We were the final couple announced. *Of course.* Roars completely overtook the huge room as we took the floor. It was like an echo chamber. It was hard to make out any specific names this time. Just enormous loads of applause. For all of us.

Rory looked out onto the floor. Now that there were only six couples on it, its immensity was all the more apparent.

I pulled her to face me. I placed my palms on each cheek. She looked up into my eyes.

"I love you," I mouthed.

Her eyes sparkled. And laughed. There was no fear, no panic whatsoever. The music began. I swung her out and she was ready. We were off and going.

We moved like never before. We gave every little thing we had to every single step, no matter how basic, how small. We were on fire together, working each dance as hard as we possibly could.

The finals were a complete blur, as they usually are. We went from one dance right into the next, with only the emcee's words breaking the rhythm. I was never more in tandem with my partner. We were fast and flirty in cha-cha, playful and sexy in samba, romantic and in love in rumba, fierce and loyal to each other in paso. No fatigue, no pain, no fear, no worry. The cheers were so loud, so intense, it was completely impossible to hear the music this time. Rory followed my lead perfectly, even if I wasn't completely on beat. Lead/follow was way more important than us being on beat anyway. The emcee had to shout out the dance's end. No one could hear the music. It wasn't until the paso ended and the emcee gave us all some time to catch our breath before the jive that I started to realize Rory was tired, her center appearing to be on the verge of caving in.

"Mouth open," I whispered in her ear.

She smiled and parted her lips. Then nodded.

Jive was like a lightning-fast sprint at the end of a cross-country marathon. But we were athletes. Both of us. We'd trained hard for this. We were ready. We were invincible. I squeezed her hands and she squeezed back, indicating she'd heard my thoughts and couldn't agree more.

The swingy big band tempo began and I looked down into her eyes again. The picture of calm, right before all hell broke loose with our feet. I then raised my eyebrows, indicating that I was ready to begin. She read me, like always, and we were off.

I looked into her wide eyes, full of excitement and passion. For the dance. For me. I whipped her into her series of turns, rolled her out into a sweetheart position, led her in our side-by-side kicks, and finally wrapped my hands around her back for our final, ever-so-dramatic dip.

The emcee again called out the end of the dance, the music having apparently ended. But I didn't bring Rory up right away. I gazed down at her, held my hands around her back.

"I love you," I said to her.

"I love you too," she said back, still prostrate in my arms.

The crowds were going insane. They couldn't have heard us, but they likely knew what we were saying to each other. I saw Micaela out of the corner of my eyes. She was reaching for my hand. It was customary for all the dancers to hold hands, forming a line, and run to each side of the stage together, taking a group bow. I was late.

I pulled Rory up, then held her hand and reached for Micaela's, next to me, and directed Rory to hold

Piotr's hand, to the left of her. At first she looked confused—this was Xenia's partner—but Piotr's smile was genuine and seemed to indicate relief that the whole thing was over and we were all in one piece. She smiled and accepted his hand.

When all of us were laced together, arm in arm, we ran as one across the ballroom floor in a horizontal line, taking our collective bows, then did the same for each side of the room. Rory laughed the whole time. I'd forgotten to give her all the details of little things like this, like how to take bows, how long the wait would be between heats, and the like. We were always working so hard on the actual dancing. The important part, obviously. But she ended up adapting to it all perfectly, a brilliant woman, a true pro, my partner. And, looking into her eyes, I was just so happy she'd enjoyed herself throughout it all. *Competitions are serious, yes, but dance is about happiness.*

The wait to get the scores was now on. It was half past two in the morning. We didn't go back to the tent. We didn't really need to. We didn't need to groom or eat or rest. Instead we paced back and forth across the shortest perimeter of the ballroom floor. Rather, I paced and Rory followed me.

"They're taking longer than usual," I said, after a great many back-and-forths. I always paced at this point in the game. It helped me to keep control; I had to move to maintain focus, especially about something over which I now had no control. But I paced more than usual. It was actually getting tiring.

"Why?" Rory asked.

"Something's going on," I unintentionally snapped.

"Well, it seems like everyone's thinking the same

thing. You all have the same intense, confused looks on your faces."

She was right. I caught Piotr's gaze. He raised his brows and I shrugged. What the hell was going on?

Bob walked up, placed an arm around my neck for support. He had no answers either.

When I looked back at the floor, I saw Rory had stopped following me. She was now talking with Arabelle. It looked like they were saying supportive things to each other, as Rory pressed her hand against Arabelle's shoulder and smiled. Micaela soon joined them.

Arabelle glanced at me. Then she said something to Rory, and Rory and Micaela both turned to look at me as well. When my gaze met Rory's she gave me a serene smile. I knew exactly what they were saying. I was an asshole. A supreme hard-ass, slave-driving, hyper-control freak. But Rory had tamed me. Rory had tamed the beast.

I squinted at Rory, but my playfully wicked smile belied my mock-confrontational look.

Micaela said something else to Rory and now she giggled, and looked back at me again, shaking her head in disbelief. I'd have to find out what they'd said. But later. Because the emcee was back, announcing that the judges had made their decision.

He directed all of the finalists to proceed to the center of the floor. I caught back up with Rory, breathed deeply and gave her a long kiss on the cheek, then squeezed her hand, and held it tightly. I could feel her legs about to give out from under her as the emcee introduced the presenters of the medals, Greta and Dean. Of course the audience went crazier than they had all night when Greta floated out in her cinnamon floor-length gown. She did have that air about her, as if she was walking on water. Dean waved to the crowd, his typical, dimpled schoolboy grin covering his face, then did a very short series of *bachacatas* at the speed of light—his trademark. Rory laughed, and I was so glad he'd retired. He would be a total bastard to beat.

"Ladies and gentlemen, placing in sixth in the cha-cha, from Italy, Roberto Montecelli and Ariana Brushendi." Everyone clapped and Ariana went down the line one by one, hugging each woman, while Roberto shook the hands of each man, before proceeding to the winners' podium where Dean placed a medal around Roberto's head and Greta the medal around Ariana's.

I'd forgotten to tell Rory how this went too—the hand-shaking, the procession to the podium for the presentation of medals. I knew she'd watched Blackpool DVDs but I didn't know if she'd watched all the way through to the awards. But she was smart. She was a lawyer, after all. She caught on after the first go-around. The emcee announced fifth place, which was the Chinese couple. When he got to fourth place, Rory's legs were shaking again, so she started to bounce a little. I suppose akin to my pacing. She was right to get her adrenaline flowing right now. We were down to the big four.

The emcee paused. The room was silent.

"Placing in fourth, from the United States…" I felt Rory's pulse dip, and I squeezed her hand. "…Piotr Smekalov and Xenia Lupinski."

I'd known it would be them. Actually, I thought maybe Arabelle and Andrew might place fourth, but I knew we wouldn't place behind Xenia. I knew it.

Rory breathed a big sigh of relief as the crowd reacted. The throng seemed pretty evenly split into cheers and disappointed "ooooohs." Xenia and Piotr were higher-ranked than Arabelle and Andrew. So this was officially an upset, even after what had happened. It was a minor miracle Arabelle was able to continue. The judges knew that and were rewarding her. Xenia gave a curt smile out toward the crowd and cursorily hugged each of us. That was uncomfortable, for Rory and me equally, I think.

After Xenia and Piotr proceeded up the steps to get their medals, Jonathan grabbed Rory's hand. I'd forgotten to tell her to expect this too. She looked over at him, then realized this too was customary. We were all holding hands in a row, as a show of solidarity.

The emcee announced the third-place winners as Arabelle and Andrew. Arabelle nodded and smiled. Now, the entire ballroom cheered, no one uttered an "ooooh" at the placing, including Xenia and Piotr fans. In fact, the audience gave them a standing ovation. It was unanimous. *Good for her. Good for them.* No one deserved it more.

Rory was delighted. She held her hands high above her head and clapped, hooting loudly. Arabelle turned to the crowd and bowed graciously, her hands folded together as if in prayer, just like in the cabaret performance in the O.C., which she'd given in honor of her late husband. The gesture made the crowd go even wilder and brought tears to Rory's eyes. She sniffled.

"She's so beautiful. It's just so moving," she said as Greta placed the bronze medal over Arabelle's head.

I put my arms around Rory and squeezed, and kissed her cheek. This woman had such an amazing, warm spirit. I couldn't believe she was mine. No matter what happened, I told myself, I won. I had her.

"Placing second in the cha-cha…"

There was a long, drawn-out drumroll. You could feel the tension encompass the whole room. I remained still. Rory's bouncing intensified. It was completely silent, absent the drums.

"Ladies and gentlemen, from the United States, Sasha Zakharov and Aurora Laudner."

I took a deep breath. This wasn't what we were hoping for. I couldn't look at Rory, to see the disappointment in her beautiful eyes. I simply focused on shaking Jonathan's hand, releasing Rory to hug Micaela. When I took Rory's hand and turned us toward the audience to take our bows, downright cacophony erupted. A good half of the audience was booing the judges' decision, very, very loudly. Maybe more than half.

"First place, first, first!" went the chants.

I smiled gratefully out to our fans, our many, many fans, and nodded my head to them, mouthed "Thank you," and waved, before turning and leading Rory to the podium.

"You did tremendously well," Greta said to Rory, placing the silver medal around her neck.

Rory smiled at her but I could see the tears welling behind her eyes.

"It's okay," I whispered, kissing her on the cheek, which made the crowds erupt with louder cheers than ever before. I really loved this audience. I missed these people every year between Blackpools.

We'd lost the judges' vote, but the crowd loved us. Sometimes that was really what mattered.

Micaela and Jonathan were announced the cha-cha winners and, as they took their bows, that same chorus of cheers and boos emanated from the audience. I dare say there were more of the latter this time. That had never happened before. Not here, anyway.

We all descended from the podium and returned to the floor to hear the samba results. The placements were all the same as for cha-cha. The crowd had all the same responses: standing ovation for Arabelle and Andrew, a combination of boos and cheers for Xenia and Piotr's placement under hers, and a combination of boos and cheers for our second place results and Micaela's and Jonathan's first place.

"The boos seemed even louder this time," Rory whispered to me as we walked toward the podium.

"The audience likes us," I said.

"It's weird bowing to boos."

I laughed. "Yeah, it's one of the weird things about how awards are given out. Audiences are really responsive, and they really have their favorites."

She laughed. "I don't mean I felt it was a bad thing. It's rather awesome knowing how many people wanted us to win."

"It's not over yet," I said to her as I led her up the step. She shot me a bemused frown. Yes, I'd told her ad nauseam that the same couple almost always wins all five dances, and is named overall champion. Only a few times in Blackpool history had that not been the case. Our chances of winning any gold medals were almost zilch now. If anyone else would have said what I'd just said to Rory, I'd have laughed my head off and felt sorry for the poor, deluded soul. But somehow I actually believed my own words. Something made me believe it could happen.

But my emotions were all out of whack, as I was pissed and feeling defeated a second later. I could feel Rory coming to terms with this, with being the silver medalists. I knew how much she wanted to help me get to number one, to propel me past Micaela. I knew she felt she'd failed. I could sense it in her weakening pulse, her weakening hold on my hand. And her sweaty palms indicated she was scared that I was mad. I was, but not at her. Never at her again. Anything that happened now was totally my fault. She'd worked so hard, so amazingly hard, especially given her insane boss, her awful sister, that debilitating eating disorder, the sabotage-happy Cheryl, her knee injury, all that she had to deal with. And we still made it this far.

She was beyond amazing. She was my rock. My angel. If I was pissed at anyone, it was the judges, for rewarding the same exact couple it had for years. There wasn't a new champ until the old ones retired. That was always the case. I thought this year might be different with the new judges. But that was delusional thinking. I should have never gotten my hopes up, Rory's hopes up. I was pissed that the judges had let her down, had disappointed her so. That's what I was angry at.

As we descended the podium and returned to the floor once more for the presentation of the medals for rumba I noticed the crowd was beginning to get smaller. People were throwing their hands up and shaking their heads before exiting the ballroom. There were a lot of people who were that angry about the ultimate winners. It amazed me. Judging by that thinning crowd, there were more people who wanted to see us win than Micaela and Jonathan.

"Why are they leaving?" Rory asked.

"It's a show of disdain for the judges and who they're crowning the winners," I said.

"So they're leaving for us? That's kind of sad," she said.

I nodded. "It is."

The first four medals in rumba went to the same couples as in the two prior dances: the Italians, then the Chinese. The crowd that remained went wild again for Arabelle and Andrew. There was no special standing ovation for them now because everyone just remained standing throughout the presentation of awards. No one bothered to sit. But the cheers for Arabelle grew. She and Andrew were going to place third across the board, it seemed. They both looked thrilled about that. People were no longer bothering to boo their placement above Xenia and Piotr, but were politely clapping now.

"Ladies and gentlemen," continued the emcee, almost on rote at this point. "Placing second in the rumba, from the United…" The fact that he took a pause like that told me something was up. Something out of the ordinary was about to happen. "…Kingdom, Micaela Dermansky and Jonathan Banks."

Rory began to walk to the podium, out of custom. But I firmly gripped her hand and held her back. She tossed her head about and laughed at herself, then turned toward Micaela. She'd obviously thought she'd only forgotten to give Micaela her customary hug. When she saw Micaela approaching her, she looked taken aback. I turned to Jonathan and shook his hand, as Micaela kissed Rory on the cheek and congratulated her. I had to give it to her—Micaela was the epitome of grace and serenity. She transferred that shining smile over to me and shook my hand as well. She was not letting one loss get to her.

"Congratulations, Sasha," she said to me.

"Thank you, Micaela," I said.

She walked back to Jonathan and they held hands. Micaela was not Xenia. There was no jealousy, no anger. She was in love with Jonathan. Love overcame all those nasty emotions. Only now that I had Rory did I realize that.

I turned us to face the crowd, which was back to roaring. People who'd left were piling back in. There was a bit of cacophony at the doorway. The applause was suddenly deafening. There were no boos now, only cheers.

Rory still looked dumfounded. I whisked her toward me with such force—happy force—she twirled into me, my chest stopping her. I caught her, planting a long, solid kiss on her lips. Of course the crowds went even wilder at this.

It wasn't until the emcee introduced us as the first-place winners in rumba and she heard her name that she fully realized we'd actually won this dance. And what a perfect dance it was for us to win. Rumba was the most balletic dance, the one that most showed off Rory's attributes. The fact they'd given us the gold on this dance showed that I was wrong. The judges were not doing the same old same old. They recognized true talent and originality and brilliance. Even if we didn't win in any other dances, they'd gone against the grain. They'd championed someone who deserved to win.

I think Rory's obvious bafflement made the audience go even more nuts. She took her hands from me and used both to cover her mouth in a show of complete shock. I bowed. She had to look at me, to follow my direction, still in disbelief.

I wrapped my arm around her shoulder and practically pulled her to the podium, my lips pressed to her cheek all the way. I felt the audience was cheering for love. Not just for the winners of a competition—they were cheering for that too, of course—but for a partnership that was working so beautifully on two different levels.

There were so many flashbulbs going off when Dean and Greta placed our medals over our heads, I was temporarily blinded.

We returned to the floor, and the winners of paso doble were announced for the first four places. Everything was the same. I could feel Rory's heart pounding so hard, it pulsed straight through my skin, giving me a head rush. Again, we were the last two couples on the floor. Again, the emcee announced the silver medal winners, this time without a pause after United. The crowds erupted—all with cheers—when Jonathan and Micaela were named. Again, I had to hold Rory back from going to the podium. She still wasn't used to winning. As soon as Micaela and Jonathan were on their way up and we were the last ones standing, I took Rory in my arms, giving her the most passionate embrace of the evening, followed by the most heavenly kiss atop her heavenly lips.

The ballroom was now completely full again, back to capacity, when the jive result announcements began. I felt Rory's pulse return to normal, her faculties now fully operating again. Now my panic began to go into overdrive. But I wouldn't dare show it. This was the dance that would decide everything. Rory and I had won two dances, Micaela and Jonathan two. The winners of three or more dances were named the overall Latin ballroom champions. Jive had been our worst dance. Rory, with her lyrical adagio background, had had the hardest time learning it, and keeping up with the fast rhythms. And these judges knew that, as evidenced by our team results. But I sincerely felt that in our final, we really killed it. Rory's anger toward Cheryl did that for us. She'd been on like never before. Cheryl had inadvertently given her a strength she didn't know she had.

And then I heard the emcee say Micaela and Jonathan's names. My mind was so caught up in remembering our jive, how it had felt, how odd it was that Rory's anger toward Cheryl had driven her so, I hadn't kept up with which medal was being called. But I hadn't yet heard our names. Had I missed it? No. Jonathan and Micaela walked over to hug us, the crowd so boisterous I couldn't even hear Micaela congratulate us, though her lips were right to my ear as we embraced. They turned to walk to the podium, and I took Rory's hand and turned toward the audience. There was more raucous cheering, more cameras flashing than I'd ever witnessed here. We hadn't even gone to the podium yet. Perhaps people wanted to capture our completely stunned-silly expressions. We were the new champions. We'd displaced the reigning queen and king, a formerly near impossible feat.

For a split second I followed Rory's gaze, to a hazy figure out in the crowd. *Cheryl.* She was in the front standing area, in between the first two sets of seats. I didn't know how long she'd been there, whether she'd watched the awards ceremony from so close. The second I caught her gaze, she immediately looked down. But she didn't only lower her eyes; she bent her entire head down, haughty chin and all. Still, I could see the look in her eyes quite well. Her expression was one of utter devastation. Like something all-important had been taken from her. Was our failure really that critical to her? She'd made us the enemy. Unless she saw it the other way around. That I'd hurt her by choosing Rory. Maybe she actually had entertained that she had a chance at this, as a competitive dancer. She had nothing else in life. She had no career and was on the outs with her husband. For a split second, I actually felt sorry for her. She looked so defeated. I looked at Rory.

She was giving Cheryl the same gracious smile that Micaela had given us. She'd become Micaela, both in terms of temperament and, more literally, in terms of championship. I pressed my lips to her cheek, once again. Closed my eyes.

Then, chaos erupted.

"Oh, oh my God!" Rory screamed. "Sasha…I…Sasha, it's, it's me! Look!"

I opened my eyes. The lights were so bright. The cheers were so intense. It was hard to hear or see anything in the commotion. For a split second, I thought Rory had seen something that wasn't actually there. A ghost. Then I saw it too.

My sister.

Tatiana took one glance at me, one pleading glance, her big black pupils penetrating me to the core. Then she took off running, as if she were running for her life. She ran through the aisles. It took me a second to realize she was being chased. By my uncle? He'd broken his promise. *Fuck no.*

The last thing I wanted to do was leave Rory alone. But I knew my uncle knew she wasn't important to him now, Cheryl could no longer sabotage us, and Valentin was still looking out for us. He was there, watching everything. He'd keep an eye out for Rory—I thought. There was no time to text him. I had no access to my phone in the tent. And someone was going to abduct my sister if I didn't get to her first. I had to go after Tatiana. She was alive and well. At least for now.

"Tanya," I called out and sprinted after her. She'd gotten a head start but the crowd was so dense she didn't get very far. I clearly saw her run out the back door that led to the maze of practice rooms. I arrived at the door the same time as my uncle. He was too squat to gain any distance on me. I shoved him as hard as I could away from the door.

"Be careful, you don't want to do that. I am not the enemy," he said, turning to eye a younger man dressed all in black with long blond hair, running behind us, pushing his way through the crowd, quickly gaining ground.

I wanted to ask who he was but there was no time. I ran through the door, calling out Tatiana's name. I saw her at the end of the long hall, opening the door that led to the stairs, which in turn led outside. Her hair was long, loose and wild as she fled.

"Tatiana, please wait," I called out. She turned to look at me, right as I heard the door behind me open. She fled through the door. I ran as fast as I could after her. I ran all the way up two flights of stairs.

Damn, she was fast. I could see her hair trailing. I heard footsteps behind me. I didn't bother calling out to her again. She was scared of the guy following me, whoever he was. I knew she wouldn't stop.

I felt a gush of wind as she opened the door to the outside. It took me a few seconds more until I was outside as well. Where was she? I looked all around.

"Tanya," I called out, running down the street to the back of the building.

"Tatiana, Tatiana!" I heard my uncle behind us.

Then I heard the door slam shut again. Now voices. "Where is she? Where did they go?" These were American-accented voices. This was followed by more Russian—my uncle and cousin.

What the fuck? Had they hired Americans to help them kidnap her?

"Over there!" one of the Americans said. They took off running in the other direction. I began to run after them. But then I heard her.

"Sasha," she whispered.

I looked all around. It was Tatiana's voice. A voice I hadn't heard in so long. I recognized it. But it was so soft. Was it a ghost? Was this all a dream? I looked around and around, calling out her name. Then I saw it. A white arm reaching out from behind a large trash bin. I ran toward her, grabbed the arm, held her soft, cold hand.

"Come out," I said.

She carefully emerged. Her face was full of fear. Her eyes grew wider and she screamed as I felt an arm on my shoulder. I turned around and swiped full force with my fist, connecting with my cousin. I'd delivered a punch right to Pasha's chin.

"Fuck, Sasha, fuck," he yelled.

"Stay the fuck away from her. I told you that! I warned you!"

"Shut up. Shut up," my uncle said, running up to us, huffing and puffing, his large body nearly giving out. "There's no time for family fights right now. They've got Rory."

My heart nearly fell out of my body. Of course, Rory had run after me. All the way outside. Oh my God, I'd gained one and lost the other.

"Who? Who has Rory?" I yelled at the top of my lungs, throwing my cousin aside and stomping toward my uncle.

"I will explain in the car," he said, pulling me along. *Fuck*. I pulled out of his embrace and returned to Tatiana, whom my cousin was now pulling along behind me.

"Get your hands off her," I said. He did as I said and stepped away from her, with his hands up in surrender.

"Sasha?" Uncle Oleg called out. I turned back. He had his arm extended toward a black van waiting to the side. For a second I wondered if this was all a ruse to get me to release Tatiana to them. But who were the Americans, then? My uncle's face actually looked sincere. "Now we have something they want and they have something we want."

"What are you talking about?" I asked.

"Tatiana's husband," he said.

CHAPTER FOURTEEN

Tatiana nodded. They weren't lying about that part, anyway.

"Stay away from her," I warned Pasha again. "No one is to touch her except me." I held my hand to Tatiana. She looked at him, and my uncle, then took my hand. I pulled her to me, hugged her.

"Hurry up and get in or they'll get away," my uncle snapped.

I directed Tatiana to get in first, and I sat next to her. My cousin got in on the far side, so that Tatiana's skin touched only mine. Those bastards were getting nowhere near her. My uncle got in on the passenger side. A man I didn't know was in the driver's seat.

"Who are you?" I asked.

"Anton, a friend of mine," Uncle Oleg said, answering for him.

The man eyed me in the rearview mirror. Big black eyes, pockmarked face, skin yellowed from smoking. He definitely wasn't American. He was Russian through and through.

"How do you know they have Rory?" I said, my heart sinking just at the words.

"Because they just texted me. 'I have someone you want, you have someone I want.' And they gave me an address for where we can do the exchange."

"Give me that," I demanded, reaching for his cell. He handed it over. He wasn't lying, at least about what the text said. "Who is this? Who the fuck is this?" I yelled when no one answered me immediately.

You hurt her and you will die, I texted.

Tatiana placed her soft, delicate hand over mine. "He won't hurt her. I've never known him to hurt anyone." She spoke in Russian, which sounded soft and sweet to me for once.

"Who is this motherfucker? Is it someone from the agency you worked for? That sham agency?"

She shook her head and looked away, outside the opposite window.

"Tanya, please. They have someone I love very much. Rory is very dear to me. I need her back." I took a deep breath. My voice had started to break. As much as I loved my sister and was elated she was alive and unharmed, I needed Rory to come back to me. I didn't know how I'd live without her.

"He's my husband," she said, her face still turned away from mine.

"Yes, I know, but how did you end up with him? Who is he? You actually married this guy?"

"Please. I don't want to talk about it, Sasha," she said.

"Tatiana, this is my wife. My wife-to-be, anyway." I was yelling.

"Sasha, calm down," my cousin said. "We will get her back. We found Tatiana. We will find Rory. We will get her."

Anton was driving like he meant it, tires squealing, horn honking, flying over bumps in the road.

"Okay, can you just tell me how well you know this man, what he's capable of?" I asked, lowering my voice.

She shook her head, still not looking at me. "I met him at the club I worked for after I left the agency. He was a nice guy, an American. He gave me huge tips. He told me he wanted to take me out of there and take me away from it all. I told him what I owed the agency, that I couldn't leave till I paid them back. He said he'd pay them. He said he owned a big farm in north California. I was so sick of Tokyo. But I didn't want to go back home. California seemed like a good idea. And he seemed like a nice guy. And California was where you were." She turned her head in my direction now, though still not looking into my eyes.

"So what happened, Tanya?" I whispered, brushing my fingertips lightly over hers. I was trying to be gentle. I loved her dearly, but I needed to know who had Rory. I had to keep pressing and I knew she'd talk if I was kind and gentle.

"We got to California. He was nice. His farm is huge. It was boring, Sasha. I couldn't stay there forever. I wanted you. I wanted your life. I expected...excitement." She turned her head more toward me, still refusing to make eye contact.

"Did he hurt you?"

"No, never," she said.

"So this is a new behavior for him, then? Coming after you and committing a kidnapping?"

She said nothing. She apparently didn't know this

bastard very well.

"Well, how did he get you there, to the U.S.? Didn't you have to get a visa?"

She laughed and finally looked me straight on. "He's rich, and American, Sasha."

"So he got you fake documents?"

She shrugged. "He did whatever he needed to do to get me there. I didn't really ask questions."

"How did you get to England?"

"Same way," she said.

"He brought you? To see me dance?"

"No, I used his credit card and the documents he gave me to go to the U.S. He found out and followed me."

Her story didn't completely make sense. If he was such a nice guy, how had he violently kidnapped someone? He'd committed a crime bringing Tatiana into and out of the U.S. I of all people knew all the red tape hell you had to go through for that. There was something she wasn't telling me. But before I could ask anything more, Anton screeched to a halt.

"This is it," my uncle said. "Be quiet when you get out."

Anton quietly opened the door. When he did so, he pulled out a gun. My uncle did the same. I looked at Tatiana. She was unfazed. Like she was used to this. *What the fuck?* My cousin opened the back door and stepped out, pulling out a weapon as well.

"Stay here," Pasha said to us.

Like fuck, I thought. I went to open my side and struggled with the lock before realizing the van's doors only opened on one side.

"You stay here," I said to Tatiana, as I crawled out over her.

"Sasha, no! You can't go. You're not trained for this!" She grabbed my arm.

"This is my wife," I said, pulling myself out of her grip. "I have to go."

"Sasha," she called out as I began to run behind my cousin.

But then I realized what I was doing, leaving my sister behind once again. What if there was someone out here ready to snatch her? What the fuck was I doing? I was so focused on getting Rory back I wasn't thinking at all. Just as I turned around to go back to Tatiana, I saw her jumping out of the van. She ran toward me.

"Come on," I said, holding her tightly in my arms. So tightly she nearly disintegrated, she was so thin. We ran toward the warehouse the other three were standing in front of, weapons drawn.

"She's in the back," I heard a man say from inside, in English.

"Bring her out now," Uncle Oleg said to him.

Then I realized there was a man standing in front of the door. I hadn't seen him there in all the darkness. Tatiana spotted him at the same time I did. I felt panic flutter through her body. I held her more tightly. "I won't let you go," I said.

"I just want my wife," the man said, now pointing at Tatiana.

"No one will get hurt. We will do the exchange fair and square and no one gets hurt." This came from another man, another American-accented voice. I couldn't see him, and wondered how many were inside, whether they had weapons as well.

"Bring her out now," my uncle repeated.

I then saw another man standing off to the side.

I recognized him as the young guy with long blond hair I'd seen earlier running outside the Winter Gardens. He was pointing a gun at my uncle. So I guess the answer to my question was yes. Tatiana shivered again.

Seeing the man point at Tatiana, my cousin turned around. Huffing, he backed up toward us, holding his gun firmly aimed at the man with the gun. "I told you to stay in the fucking van with her," he said.

"Bring her out," the man who'd pointed at Tatiana said, turning to look inside the room, where there was apparently yet another person.

As the door opened, there was more light. I got a good look at the man who was apparently Tatiana's husband. He looked more like a businessman than a thug. He was dressed in an almost preppy manner, in khaki pants and a blue pressed linen button-down shirt under a brown corduroy jacket. He had a forlorn expression on his face. He was clean-shaven and had a head of thick but short brown hair, graying at the sides. He could have been in his sixties or even older but he clearly kept himself up. He had a sad face. He certainly didn't look like a thug. I could see how Tatiana had trusted him. But of course looks could be very deceptive.

Then I saw her. My Rory. A man who looked exactly the opposite of this man had his grimy hands on her shoulders. That man was big and muscular with a pockmarked face, and angry eyes that said he would easily break her neck if asked to. I looked more closely at the hand that held her left shoulder. It too was holding a gun.

Rory was still wearing her skimpy Latin toga. Her

wrists and ankles were tied together and she couldn't walk but for the man pushing her along. She was shivering. It was freezing out here. She looked terrified. Our eyes connected. Panic surged down my spine. And then I saw her glance down at her hand, then foot, ever so quickly. I followed her gaze. She moved her feet very nonchalantly into a perfect third position. When she did so, she showed me that whatever they'd tied her with—it actually looked like heavy duty tape—she'd broken through. She wiggled her fingers too, subtly indicating she had full use of her hands as well, though she was pretending not to. I looked back at Tatiana's husband. He was far too focused on my sister to care about Rory. Seeing Rory scheming, my brain cleared, and I was able to think.

I suddenly realized my cousin was no longer at my side. I heard movement coming from behind me.

"Keep quiet," Pasha said in Russian, indicating he had some sort of plan.

"Tatiana, please," said her husband. His voice was thick and cracking, as if he was about to cry. "I'm so sorry. Please come back. Please come back home. I promise you…I promise you I will give you what you want. Whatever you want, sweetheart."

"She is not going to go anywhere with you," I said, pronouncing every word, every syllable to its fullest, in perfect fucking English.

He stood still for a moment as if in shock. Then he shook his head in disbelief and laughed. "Well then, sonny boy, you are never going to see your girlfriend here again."

Sonny boy? Who was this guy? Certainly not from New York or L.A.

"Sasha," Tatiana said, now brushing my arm and

stepping around me.

What? "No," I said, softly but sternly. "You are not going back to him. We can do this. Rory can move." I said all of this in Russian, and whispered the last part so only she and Pasha could hear. But she eyed Rory's supposedly bound hands and feet for too long, and her husband followed her gaze, realization slowly dawning in his eyes.

Just then, a burst of gunfire rang out from behind me and I saw the man standing on the other side of Tatiana's husband jump back as if he'd been shot and Tatiana's husband jump to the side. I saw a flash of movement coming from my side and realized it was my cousin.

My only thought was to protect Rory, but I didn't know how to do that without leaving my sister. But then I saw her—Rory—slicing her legs through the air in a brilliant lightning-fast *grand battement* kick, aiming her stiletto directly at the face of the man who held her. The heel lodged in his nose and he flew backward, grabbing at his face. The gun went flying.

The man who'd been shot hadn't been taken out, but only wounded, because he took off running straight toward Rory. She made a hasty attempt to scramble around the man she'd just kicked, now stepping on his cheek. He was still lying on the ground.

"You bitch!" he said, grabbing her leg.

No. That was not going to happen. He was not going to get her.

"Go to the van. Hurry up and run," I ordered Tatiana as I ran as fast as I could toward the wounded man with the gun. I flew toward him with all my speed, and when I got close enough, I jumped, slicing my front leg through the air, in a massive *grand jeté*.

He hadn't seen me coming, and I kicked him good and hard in the chest, slamming him into the brick wall. Rory scurried out of the first man's hold and reached for the gun, grabbing for it just as I got to her, and whisked her up, one-armed, into the air, carrying her back to the van. I heard bullets going off like crazy behind us. *Oh my God.*

"Keep down!" I said to her, holding her folded over my arm, covering her head and torso with my body as I ran.

Just as I got to the van, the doors slid open and we flew inside. Anton gunned the motor.

"Tatiana!" I yelled.

"She's next to you, on the floor," my uncle said from the front seat. We screeched out onto the open road, the van swerving. I heard bullets still sounding behind us. I heard a loud clank at the back of the van. Followed by another very loud clank, like metal hitting metal. Or metal hitting the ground. Then there was a loud crash and glass went flying everywhere.

Fuck. "Keep down," I yelled, pushing Rory to the floor next to my sister, covering her head. I felt both of them now, held one hand over each little warm, blonde delicate crown. I could feel Rory's pulse beating straight through her skull.

"I think we lost them," my cousin said in the far back seat. He was facing the back of the van, gun raised and pointed.

I felt Rory breathing deeply, which slowly began to stop her heart from racing so.

After a while, the van slowed and proceeded at a normal pace. Rory peeked up at me.

"Can I get up now?" she asked.

I looked around. There was nothing but black night and silence. I nodded. She sat up on the seat next to me. I wrapped my arm around her. Tatiana got up and sat on my other side. Rory looked forward, out the front window. She turned around and, meeting the eyes of my cousin, jumped and gasped.

"It's okay," I said, realizing this was the man who'd kidnapped her, whom she'd seen chasing Tatiana in the ballroom. A man she hated, and rightly so. I caressed her arm and kissed her cheek and her chin. "I am so, so, so sorry you were pulled into this. So sorry, my love."

She looked up at me. Now she was flaming mad. I could see it in her pupils. They pierced my soul. I also saw she had a big dark spot on her cheek. *Shit.* They'd hit her.

I lightly brushed the darkened spot. "Oh my God, they hit you. This is going to bruise a little. Maybe swell. We'll get ice. I'm so sorry. So sorry." I continued caressing her cheek and chin, kissing her forehead.

She closed her eyes. "Well, I'm just glad the right people have finally kidnapped the right girl this time," she said sarcastically.

I had no idea how to respond, and said nothing.

"Are you going to tell me what the fuck is happening?" It wasn't often she used profanity. But I couldn't say I didn't understand her anger. Her life had been put in jeopardy twice now. By me and my family, all of whom, momentarily at least, disgusted me. Except, of course, my sister.

"Rory," I said after a few moments, "this is my sister, Tatiana. I had thought she was de…dead. If not, gone from our lives forever. Because of my…my fault. Now that she is here, she is never leaving my sight again. Nor are you. I will never let anyone hurt either of you ever again." My voice had started to crack but I forced it to be steady, and heavy, like lead. As much as I hated for people to see me cry, I felt tears welling at the backs of my eyes.

***

After we'd all given our statements to the police—at Rory's very correct insistence—I told Rory the whole story from beginning to end. Well, at least what I knew of it. I well knew it would be some time before I'd get all of the details out of my sister. The more I'd tried to talk to Tatiana, the more I'd realized she was really traumatized. And humiliated by things that had happened to her. She'd tell me in her own time.

We'd moved to the fancier Imperial Hotel, because there was now too much media at our hotel in town and because the Imperial had far better security. The police had caught Tatiana's husband and were holding him in jail, but we had no idea how much support he had, whether he could send anyone after us. Tatiana knew virtually nothing about the man she'd married. She'd been so desperate to get out of her situation in Tokyo, she didn't bother to find out a lot about the guy.

Of course poor Valentin had apologized profusely for letting me down.

"It all happened so damn fast, man. We couldn't figure out who was following who and we just couldn't keep up with everyone," he'd said when I first talked to him after we'd gotten back to Blackpool safely.

I'd laughed, and thanked him for trying. "Are you kidding? These are serious thugs. We're a bunch of professional dancers. You're a good man, Val. You helped me more than I can ever say."

The authorities had put us up in a large suite. There was a guard assigned to our room, keeping station 24/7 outside. As much bullshit as my family got into, this was surreal to me, being under surveillance, fearing for my safety and that of those I loved. It killed me to know I'd brought Rory, a do-gooder, law-abiding lawyer, down with them.

Tatiana slept in one of the bedrooms in the suite; Rory and I were in another.

But at the moment I told Rory all I knew about the events leading up to the previous night, we were up, unable to sleep, in the living room talking. We sipped sweet black coffee and gazed through a huge window out onto the sea.

"We grew up poor, very poor, in a small town. In Siberia," I said, looking away from her and out to the ocean. I was always embarrassed about this, particularly in front of Americans who I felt could never really understand poverty in Russia. "As I told you before, dance was my way out. So when I met Tamara's aunt and she offered me that, a more promising life in Novosibirsk, in dance, I jumped at it. My dad was pissed as all hell. I don't know why. He worked on a farm. I don't know that he ever wanted anything more. Maybe he did and I never got to know him well enough. I was too scared of him and his fists and his broken bottles of vodka…"

"Oh my God, Sasha!" She reached out and placed a hand on my chest, over my heart. I still didn't look at her. I shook my head.

"He never touched me. With the bottle. I always felt threatened though."

"Oh my God," she said again.

"He didn't want me to leave. I don't know why. There was no future there. I couldn't imagine spending long days on that stupid farm or in the factory nearby with your only salvation being a bottle of vodka at night. Maybe he was jealous, or I was showing him up by leaving. He could have left too. He just didn't."

"That's horrible to be jealous of your own children," she said.

I didn't want her pity. I didn't want anyone's pity ever.

"It's just how a certain generation of Russians are." I shrugged. "There are a lot of people, especially Eastern Europeans, like that."

She shook her head. I shouldn't have expected her to understand. Things were just different, more beautiful, here. She held my hand and rubbed her thumb along my fingers.

"At first it killed my mother for me to leave. Or I thought it did, because that's what my father and her brother—my Uncle Oleg—told me. But Tamara's aunt gave my family money every month for my services. I know she was happy with that. I know, because she got very, very mad at me when the money stopped coming in after I left Tamara."

"But, I mean, that's like child labor, if your family got paid. You were seven. You weren't a commodity!"

I continued looking out the window toward the vast ocean. There was so much that separated us. So much life experience. I knew she wasn't judging me.

Or my family. Or my country. She was just speaking her mind, thinking like a lawyer, speaking out for those she cared about.

She nodded, seeming to realize her words were harsh, at least against my mother, but unable to take them back. "So, how does your sister figure into this? Did she want to leave too?"

I shook my head. "Not then. She was a small child when I left."

"So why do you blame yourself for what happened to her?"

"Because after I realized there were better partners for me and left Tamara for Moscow, there was no more money. I'd cut off my mom's money supply."

Rory sighed and shook her head, but said nothing.

"It wasn't all about the money. She was losing her son for good. And she knew it. Moscow was very far away. It was another world. She realized I wasn't coming back. I received letter after letter from my mother begging me to come home to her, and very nasty calls from my father telling me I'd never get where I wanted, I'd come running back to them and then I'd be sorry because he'd beat the hell out of me for hurting my mom…" I trailed off, remembering those calls. My father seemed possessed, he was so angry. And he made it all about me hurting my mom, which pissed me off so much I always hung up on his bitter, cursing voice. God forbid he ever take responsibility and admit he was pissed for his own reasons.

Rory remained silent, and lightly ran her fingers up and down my chest.

"I wanted to be free. I wanted my life. I wanted to be a dancer. I wanted...nothing to do with them." It pained me to think how embarrassed I was of that feeling, of them.

She laid her head in the crook of my neck and transferred the gentle trailing of her fingertips to my arms. "And when Tatiana got older, she became well acquainted with the legend of her older brother. She wanted to be like him," she said softly.

"She fought with my mom a lot. And my dad. They always blamed it on me, said I put thoughts into her head during our phone calls. It wasn't entirely true. I always told her to be good, study hard. When she was older she could come abroad, to wherever I was living at the time. But like normal kids, she wanted things too soon."

"I can't say I don't know that feeling," Rory said with a light laugh. I was thirteen when I got accepted to the School of American Ballet summer intensive and was on my way to New York. If they liked me I was so prepared to stay, forget school, become a ballet dancer forever."

I remained looking out the window but grabbed her hand and held it tightly. We all had this hunger at a young age.

"But please go on," she said.

"Right before she turned eighteen, there was some so-called modeling agency in Japan that came to Siberia auditioning girls. It was located in Tokyo but it was run by Americans. Tatiana tried out and they offered her a contract."

"And it wasn't legit?"

"I'm still not completely sure. It wasn't a prostitution ring or anything. But it was a kind of scam. She signed and went to Tokyo later that year. She worked for them for over a year, almost two, got very few jobs. The organization told my mother she wasn't getting the level of work they expected and now we owed them all this money for her room and board and for acting as her agents. My mom had been so excited that her daughter would be sending money home now. She was expecting to receive money, not be told we had to pay. She didn't have the money they said we owed."

"How much was it?"

"Almost twenty thousand dollars."

"Oh, shit. Yeah, that's a scam to me!"

"Yeah but you don't know my mother."

"What do you mean?" she said.

"She can sometimes…embellish things. I mean, that's what she said the agency said she owed. I doubt she lied outright but she likes to get people riled up. She plays on people's pity…" I didn't want to go into it. I was talking too much about my parents anyway. Way too much. "Tatiana had no phone so I was never able to get the story straight from her."

"Well, I still think some journalist should look into this, possibly do an exposé."

Rory. Always the do-gooder, trying to right all the world's wrongs. But she was right. This organization was shady. I nodded. Then I breathed deeply and turned toward Rory, still without looking in her eyes. Time to come clean.

"What is it?" she asked.

"Tatiana had no phone, that's true. But I could have still found her at that time. When she was still with the agency. My mother asked me to go to Japan and get her. I could have. I had the means to do so. I was already abroad and I had money. But Xenia and I were working so hard at the studio, trying to get established, and training hard for Blackpool. I was so nearsighted. Winning that damn competition was all I could see. We were already having serious issues with our partnership. I just…truthfully, I didn't try all that hard to contact my sister. I didn't have time."

"But…" Rory shook her head. "She wasn't your responsibility. You were trying to get your own career started. She went to Tokyo of her own volition. How old was she?"

"Eighteen when she left home. About nineteen, twenty when things soured with the agency."

"So she was legally of age to be making her own decisions. Albeit young," she noted.

I was a bit taken aback, thinking she'd have more sympathy for a young woman out in the world. But then, I supposed it was Rory's feminist nature to think of Tanya as an independent being in control of her life.

"What?" she said.

"You're just not as sympathetic as I would have thought." I gave her a bemused smile.

She stopped stroking my arm and cocked her head. "I don't mean to be unsympathetic. I just mean, you had so much on your own plate. A grown woman isn't your responsibility and you shouldn't put her troubles on yourself. I totally understand why you care so much about her. I just don't think you should feel so responsible for anything that went wrong. It wasn't your fault, Sasha. Not in the least, and you can't keep beating yourself up over it."

I looked back out the window for several moments, thinking how vast the world was, how

Tatiana had been so lost in it.

"I'm sorry if I offended you," Rory said, placing her hand back on my chest.

"Please. Do you really think you could do that?" I turned toward her and let out a little laugh.

"Probably not." She smiled. "So, how did she end up marrying that crazy American, or how did he end up thinking she married him?"

"I'm not sure about that yet. We have to talk more, when she's ready. I know she got involved with some shady people, trying to pay off her debts. I think she at one point became an…how do you call…exotic dancer…if not a…" I couldn't say it. I couldn't call her a stripper, far less a prostitute. If she ever was. I really hoped not. I didn't want to think about it. It would probably take a while to find out, if she was as reticent as I to talk about things she didn't want to talk about.

Rory looked down. "Now I feel bad. I feel like taking back everything I said about her being old enough to take care of herself. Eighteen is certainly not very old. I was in my first year of college then… My tuition and room and board all paid for by my mom, and my dad's life insurance policy… I, I just don't know what it would be like to be on the streets…" Now it was her turn to gaze out the window.

But then I sensed her pity. I hated that. Even coming from Rory. I shook my head rapidly as if that would rid me of it without having to speak any words. "Anyway, apparently she found that American guy in one of the clubs. He told her he'd marry her and pay off her debts. She figured it would lead to a better life, in California. She soon realized she'd made a mistake.

She didn't love him, and wanted out. But she couldn't afford to go home. And she didn't want to. When the agency told my mother an American had taken her with him to California, she somehow assumed she was with me. Apparently Tanya had told my mother earlier she absolutely wouldn't go back to Russia. She wanted to find me and stay with me. My mother told my uncle to get her from me, bring her home. Those are the people who kidnapped you. They thought you were her since you look so much alike." My jaw began to quiver with anger all over again about my mother's family of fuckers snatching Rory.

Apparently Rory wasn't as overcome by anger as I was. "But, I mean, she's now an adult. It's her choice to marry, or to live with you. She's not a minor. Snatching her is kidnapping, plain and simple."

I sighed. "Exactly. That's my family for you. That's my mother. Tatiana has a heart condition, which I guess makes my mother all the more protective, but still. It's her life. I couldn't agree more."

"Heart condition?"

"Yeah. She had to have surgery as a child for a congenital heart problem. She has to take it easy. She can't run a marathon or anything but it's not that big a deal. She'll definitely survive."

Rory's eyes darted around and I could tell she was remembering something. And I knew just what. Those fuckers. That was why her clothes were all ripped when my uncle returned her to me.

"The surgery left a scar over her rib cage. That's why they were searching under your bra." I felt my face heat up, my hands ball into fists at the memory.

"Wow, it can't get more serious than that. What kind of congenital condition?"

"One of her heart valves was…twisted. I forgot the term. But really, she's fine. Never had any problems after that."

"Sasha." Rory's voice softened. "I was so scared. Why didn't you tell me then what happened?"

I took a deep breath. "I made a deal with my uncle that he'd bring Tatiana to me once he found her, not force her to go back to Russia. If he agreed, we wouldn't press charges. If he reneged, I promised him we'd turn him in and I'd hunt him down and he'd be in deep trouble with the American authorities."

"But why didn't you tell me?" she repeated. "You could have told me about the deal. I wouldn't have reported him unless he reneged."

I smiled, squeezed her hand. "I know, but I was scared that if you knew and he knew it, it would put you in danger. And it would also have caused you great internal conflict. You're a lawyer, sworn to uphold the law. I couldn't have put you in that bind. I needed you to trust me. That I'd take care of you, not let him hurt you ever again."

"Sasha, I'm not that fragile. You could have trusted me."

I thought about it. She was right. Maybe, if I was honest with myself, it wasn't about that at all, about needing her trust and protecting her from her own internal conflict. Maybe it was about humiliation, deep humiliation that my family, my own family, could have done such a thing to the woman I love.

"Rory, maybe…maybe I was just so embarrassed—no, that's not even a strong enough word. Just so mortified, and so horrendously angry at my family for doing that to you. For doing that to Tatiana. My family of thugs. My mother…I love her, I do. She's my mom. But sending them after her. I just didn't know how to tell you that those mobsters, those criminals, were related to me. And I assured them that if they ever touched you again, even if they mistook you for her, that I would kill them. And I meant it."

She laced her fingers through mine, and I held her hand tightly. "You are not your family, Sasha. You are not responsible for anything they do, for who they are. You are you, and you have so very much to be proud of. You left home as a child and you've made your own way ever since. Look at you now. You're a star. And you did it all on your own. They did nothing but try to stifle you. You owe them nothing."

I thought long and hard about her words, let them sift through my brain. She was right, of course. I'd spent practically my whole life trying to distance myself from them, from my past. How ironic that to this day they just wouldn't let me go. But that was partly my fault.

"Rory, I'm so sorry. It was wrong of me to let them go after what they did to you, regardless of whether they were family, regardless of my embarrassment of them, and regardless of my being terrified for my sister's safety. If you want to press charges against them, and me for being an accomplice, or whatever it's called, then I will understand. I will. I am so sorry. I deserve it. When they brought you to me and put you in my arms and you were all limp, my heart fell out of my body. It was the most devastating feeling I have ever experienced in my life. When I thought you were d— I just…" My eyes began to pool with tears. I wasn't a crier. "I reached for my uncle and nearly tore him apart with my bare hands. It is only because they soon told me you were only drugged and unharmed that…" My voice was cracking so, I couldn't get any more words out.

Still holding my hand, she inched as close as she could, lying at my side, wrapping herself in the crook of my arm. I reached around her with my other arm and held her.

"I can feel your whole body shaking, Sasha."

I said nothing. We sat like that for a while.

"It's okay," she finally said. "I don't think I'll be forgiving them anytime soon for snatching me up on the street and doing whatever they wanted like that. It is a crime. And it's equally wrong for them to just take it upon themselves to go whisking your sister back to Russia against her will. Despite her heart condition. But I would never turn you in. Don't be ridiculous. I love you. And I forgive you. You are not your family."

I pressed my lips into her head, and released our handhold so I could wrap my other arm around her body. She melted into me, my body still shaking. We rocked each other side to side.

"It is really eerie though," she continued after a few moments. "I mean, that Tatiana and I look so much alike. Is that why you looked at me like you did when you first saw me?"

I laughed lightly. "No," I said firmly. "I mean, yes, okay, you reminded me of her. But I knew you weren't her. I looked at you like that, Rory, because you captivated me. Your presence. I don't know what it was, but I was just completely spellbound. Somehow I just knew."

"Knew what?" She wiggled herself farther into my side, then looked up at me. Her eyes were now bright, twinkling.

"That we would work together," I said.

"What do you mean? How did you know that?"

"I just did. Just one of those things you know. It's...unexplainable."

"I believe you." She giggled.

The most wonderful sound in the world: Rory's laugh. Especially after the hell we'd been through. Then she yawned. It was well into the morning and we needed to get up in only a few hours to sign autographs and pose for photos at Daiyu's tent. This seemed like a good note on which to snuggle up together and go to sleep.

In bed, we held each other tightly under the covers. Even though it had only been a few days since we'd arrived at Blackpool, it felt like an eternity. We'd waited so long for this night. But we'd been through way the hell too much drama, to put it extremely mildly, for mad-crazy hot sex.

"We'll make up for it tomorrow night," I whispered in her ear, nibbling her earlobe.

"Mmmm, you'd damn well better believe it," she said. "I mean, after everything that's happened, let's not forget—we frigging WON Blackpool!"

Damn true! The night had gone on for so long, it seemed like weeks ago that we were on that ballroom floor.

CHAPTER FIFTEEN

We ordered room service for breakfast. Rory was finally tired of the traditional English breakfast with the fried, greasy sausages and breads. So we splurged on Eggs Florentine, home fries and mimosas. Tatiana ate toast drenched with butter and jelly and a bowl of Fruit Loops cereal. She was twenty-two but in some ways she seemed much younger. She grew up fast, like you had to where I was from. Maybe she was demanding the childhood she never had. She wasn't speaking a whole lot. I think she was intimidated by Rory because whenever she was around, Tanya was silent. She spent a lot of time in her room, alone, watching TV or playing with my iPad. Despite the fact she'd been in the U.S. for several months, her English remained very weak. I caught her eyeing Rory several times. I couldn't read the look—whether it was a bit of envy or adoration or inquisitiveness. Or all three.

I hadn't completely decided what to do about the apartment situation back in L.A. I definitely had room for Tatiana in my house but she might come out of her shell better in her own place. And I'd love more than anything for Rory to move in with me. I planned somehow to broach the subject with both of them soon.

As much as I didn't want to let her out of my sight, I let Tatiana talk me into allowing her to stay at the hotel while Rory and I went back to the Winter Gardens for the signing and photos in Daiyu's tent. The police assured me our suite would be constantly guarded. I still wasn't sure I completely trusted my uncle yet, despite the fact he'd come through on finding Tatiana and on getting Rory back. I couldn't imagine they'd subvert the police security guards though.

I gave Tanya my credit card so she could use the hotel's amenities, like the spa and indoor pool and sauna. She deserved to pamper herself, for once. She hadn't yet told me and I really didn't want to think about all that she'd been through.

Her husband and his men were all in a holding facility. The prosecutor told us they'd likely go to trial here for kidnapping Rory, attempting to kidnap Tatiana, and for illegal possession of firearms and charges related to that crazy shootout, in which, miraculously albeit not surprisingly, no one was hurt. My uncle told me they clearly had no experience with weapons, the way they shot. And they'd tied Rory up with duct tape, failing to see she'd get free a lot easier than with something like rope. And it was the husband's son who threw the water balloon onto the dance floor. *A water balloon?* He'd told police he'd aimed at me, thinking if Tatiana saw her brother hurt she'd come out of hiding and they'd pounce on her. But how much damage could a water balloon do? It was like they wanted to be thugs but were too stupid to do it right. Well, I guess we should be thankful for that or it could have been a lot worse. The man seemed to be a farmer who became really desperate to get his wife back and would stop at nothing. I'd told the prosecutor I'd gladly offer to pay the husband everything he'd given the Tokyo agency for Tatiana's debt. I wanted him to leave us alone for good. She waved me off, saying it was beyond her jurisdiction and I could talk to his lawyers at a later point if I so desired.

"I still can't believe Cheryl had nothing to do with this," Rory said to me on the way to the Pavilion.

"I can."

She squinted at me. "I know she's a no one here, as you and Greta said ad nauseam, but after what she did to me at the studio, you still didn't think she wouldn't try anything?"

"I didn't say that." I looked at her straight on, eyebrows raised. "No. After what she pulled before, I made sure she wouldn't hurt you again. After you saw her here, I made some calls, had Valentin and our friends watching her like hawks. Believe me."

"What? You coulda told me!" Rory squealed, play-jabbing me in the arm.

"I didn't want you to worry in any way, and I knew you would if I let on I was concerned about her. So I acted like it was nothing. And see? It was."

She laughed and rolled her eyes. "Well, I'm glad you were looking out for me."

"Of course. I want nothing more than to look out for you for the rest of your life." I said the second sentence under my breath.

"What?" But her rosy cheeks indicated she'd heard.

She turned to gaze out the window, leaning her

forehead against the cab's door. I squeezed her hand. She squeezed back.

"So, Tatiana will live with you, I assume?" she asked after several moments. There was worry in her voice.

There had definitely been moments of awkwardness and tension between her and Tanya so far. They'd get to know each other, I was sure. It wouldn't last. At least I desperately hoped it wouldn't. They'd come from vastly different places, geographically and psychologically. Sometimes it took a while to connect with someone whose life experience contrasted so sharply from your own. Rory would never have gotten herself into the mess Tatiana did. I was sure of it. I knew she didn't judge her for it though. Rory wasn't like that. But for some reason I felt the need to defend my sister anyway. "Tatiana is young but she is a very complex, complicated person. I mean, we all are."

"I know that. I guess I will never learn to penetrate the deep, dark Russian soul." She took my arm and wrapped it around her tightly, but still looked out the window. There was going to be weirdness between her and Tanya for a while perhaps. Hopefully only a while.

"I actually meant all human beings," I said with a laugh.

"Oh, yeah. Very true." She laughed with me briefly, before changing the subject. "The sea really is beautiful here. I'm actually kind of looking forward to coming back to testify. I mean, not to relive everything but to see how a criminal trial here is different from one in California."

I smiled. "No matter how many competitions we

win together, how much we perform, I will always love the lawyer in you, my sweet. Always." I bent my head around hers and kissed her forehead. She giggled and her laugh was genuine this time.

***

The signing was a blast, as always. This despite the fact that there were absolute loads of paparazzi because of what had happened. Reporters from the main news stations and papers, far outside of Blackpool, all wanted to talk to us, but fortunately, Blackpool personnel—along with police—were there to insist they refrain until after our scheduled signing. We couldn't talk to them anyway, with the criminal investigation happening.

Fans were just as excited to get Rory's signature as they were mine. Since we'd never actually posed for pictures as the champions, because of what went down immediately prior to the naming of the final winners, Daiyu chose a photo of me kissing Rory on the lips after one of our rumbas. The crowd had gone so wild whenever I'd done that, I thought it was an excellent idea. It made me so amazingly happy to see that photo every time I signed. I didn't want to cover our lips in any way, or any of our connecting body parts, so I signed in the white space over my head. Rory must have felt the same way because she continuously signed over her dress.

Rory looked beautiful, of course, despite the bruise on her cheek. Icing it all night had decreased the swelling tremendously, and Daiyu's excellent makeup artist was able to cover the purpling.

Even after everything that happened, it was still a

bit surreal to know we were actually the Blackpool Latin Champions. *Finally.* What I'd waited for all my life. I was sure it would take weeks for that to fully sink in.

"My face is beginning to hurt from smiling so much," Rory whispered with a giggle. "But of course I'm loving every second! I'm a Blackpool champion!" She was in disbelief as well.

The second we signed our last poster and posed for our last picture, the reporters descended on us. Every single newspaper and TV station wanted an interview, and they could have cared less of course about our lives, our path to glory. They just wanted to hear all the gritty details of the kidnapping and shooting. It was like we were being attacked by killer bees. It definitely wasn't a good kind of being the center of attention. I didn't want to relive everything or force Rory to, and we couldn't talk about specifics anyway. We certainly didn't want to do anything that might result in a defense attorney's claim that Tatiana's husband—who, we now knew, was a billionaire from Napa named Arnold Tucker—had his right to a fair trial prejudiced by our blabbing to the press about factual details. With the police's help, we managed to fend them all off.

Rory did grant an interview to the *Blackpool Daily*, so long as no questions were asked about the criminal incident. She'd wanted to clear some things up that were said in that article that I'd never read.

We went into one of the back practice rooms. The guy—a youngish English gent—didn't ask any prying questions. Could've been because I was sitting next to Rory, my arm around her protectively, shooting daggers at him in warning every time he opened his mouth. He asked her where she grew up, how she met me and how she felt her ballet background helped her to learn ballroom so quickly. She told him she wanted to make it clear she'd been accepted to the School of American Ballet in New York but wasn't ever able to attend because of her father's death, followed by her developing a nasty case of anorexia. Her mother wished her to stay at home to overcome her eating disorder, which she did. She'd told me she wanted to be honest and open about her illness; didn't want skeletons in her closet coming back to haunt her later.

"It's very generous of you to be so forthcoming about this," the reporter said. "A great many young dancers—particularly females, and particularly ballet dancers—have a run-in with an eating disorder. You are definitely not alone. And congratulations to you for overcoming." His face was full of sincerity.

"Thank you very much," she said.

I couldn't be prouder of her in that moment. I knew she'd been embarrassed by the mental illness. Probably as embarrassed as I'd been about my family, before she set me straight on that. I put my arm around her and squeezed her whole body, planting a big kiss on her cheek.

When she told him she'd met me because she'd joined my studio after moving to Los Angeles to work as a lawyer, he was quite amused.

"I know of some amateur competitors who are in other professions," he said with a chuckle, "but not many pro dancers. And lawyer—it uses quite a different mental skill set from dance, no?"

"To make a massive understatement!" she practically shouted, glancing at me. I shot her my crooked, loopy smile. "You don't know how hard he made me work on using my muscle memory over my analytical mind. You really have to shut off that part of your brain and just force yourself to feel. To feel the music, and the movement, and your body and your partner's body. It's a huge challenge not to think everything out all the time. Huge!" She squealed with delight that someone else had finally understood her.

He chuckled. "I also can't imagine working a full-time job—any job—and training for a competition like this."

"Yes, well, I decided to take a hiatus from my job. I thought, I'm young now, it's now or never for me if I want a career in dance, and I had to know what I was capable of. I fell so in love with ballroom—and with Sasha..." She giggled and nodded in my direction. "I found myself so much more impassioned by the art of dance than by the art of lawyering that I decided...I decided to leave the legal profession and give this my all." She shrugged and held her head down.

Had she really decided to leave the legal profession for good and dance full-time with me? We hadn't had a chance to discuss it yet.

"Well, that decision paid off quite well," the reporter said.

"Yes. It most certainly did," she said, holding her head back up, her eyes moist and happy.

***

We stayed in Blackpool for the rest of the week, to speak with investigators and to watch the other competitions. Valentin, along with Maurizio, from our studio, competed Friday night and we'd planned to stay to cheer them on anyway. Awesomely, Val won his comp too. The two of us were both world champs now! And Maurizio finaled. It was a good night, a happy ending to a quite crazy comp. The police guarded our room 24/7 as long as we stayed. We had such a gorgeous view, overlooking the ocean. We had to invite our close friends—Paulina, Raj and Sam, Greta, Val, Sergei, and Max—to have our final Blackpool toast out on our lovely balcony.

"So what now?" Samantha asked Rory. "You guys going to keep competing and give Greta and Dean a run for their money?" She giggled.

"I haven't thought it all out. My life in L.A. seems so far away right now. But that's what I'm thinking," she said, raising her eyebrows, confirming what she'd said to the reporter.

"Well, that would be some feat," Raj said. "They were on top for, what, ten years?"

Rory laughed. "Crap, I hadn't thought of that. In ten years we'll be thirty-five and thirty-six, respectively. According to the Blackpool organizers, we'd be considered seniors!"

"You can do it, honey. If anyone can do it, you can do it!" Paulina sang.

"Are you going to teach at Infectious Rhythm? Or are you just gonna be a, you know, kept woman?" Sam cackled. Then both Rory and Sam looked at me.

I raised my eyebrows, letting them know Rory was more than welcome to be the latter.

"Oh you're such a goofball!" Rory shook her head. "Definitely a kept woman. I don't want to ever have to work for a living. Hell no! I mean, gross!" she joked.

"I could see you as a teacher. I'd love to be in your class, honey," Paulina said.

Rory's light began to fade a bit, and a slight frown took shape on her face.

What is going on?

"I can't really see myself as a teacher. I'm just a consummate student."

"But you're a champion now, silly. So you kind of know what you're doing!" Samantha chirped.

But Rory looked around the room, now lost in thought. I followed her gaze, first to Tatiana in the corner, snuggled into the plush cushions of the sofa, happily entertaining herself with my iPad, which now had a pink Hello Kitty cover. Then she looked at Greta, in the opposite corner, wearing another of her magical floor-length dresses, surrounded by people, her champagne flute held high in the air. She threw her head back laughing at something someone said. Rory seemed dazed.

"Rory, oh my gosh, what's wrong?" Samantha asked.

"Yes, a penny for your thoughts?" I echoed, wrapping my arms around her waist, rubbing my lips on her cheek.

She laughed.

"What?" I said.

She turned to me, her eyes sparkling. "You know what I'm laughing at. You and your Americanisms!"

I rolled my eyes.

"They are pretty funny." Samantha giggled.

Rory continued gazing into my eyes, her jade irises soft and dreamy. "I'm just so happy you've achieved your life's goal. At twenty-six. I mean, that's so amazing. How many people can say that?"

"What about you? You're only twenty-five," I said.

"Yes, me too, of course!"

But I spied a smidgeon of doubt in her eyes. Would she really be completely fulfilled being a competitive ballroom dancer? What about me? There were more competitions to win, for sure, and we could give Greta and Dean a run for their money, as Samantha had said, and try to go for more than ten wins in a row. But did I want to do only that? Was there more?

"So where do we go from here? Is that what you're thinking?" I said.

She laughed and threw her hands up. "Exactly. Your ability to read my mind is a bit unnerving, you know!"

"Well it's not hard, given I'm thinking the exact same thing. Plus, it's my job," I said, my facial expression now completely serious.

"Your job? How's that?"

I responded with the only thing I was completely sure of in our future. "You are the woman I love, Rory. The woman I am meant to spend my life pleasing. I want nothing more than that now. So, see, it works that I can see into your soul."

"Aaawwwww!" Samantha wailed.

"Okay, sweetness overload. Methinks you two need to be left alone right now!" Paulina sang.

Just then a loud mambo began to blast over the speakers. Hips began swaying out on the balcony.

"And that's our cue!" Paulina said.

"Okay, so tell me what it is I want?" Rory asked me after the others had gone to join the fun.

I looked around the room and squinted, thinking

hard, then said, "I think right now you just want to go home. To our house in the hills."

"Our house!" she squealed.

"Yes, our house," I repeated.

She closed her eyes and swayed from side to side for a few moments. "Yes, that's exactly what I want," she whispered. "Take me home to your...to *our* castle in the sky."

CHAPTER SIXTEEN

As it turned out, we soon had an abundance of choices. We hadn't even left England when the emails from L.A. started flooding our inboxes. I'd received a phone call early in the morning of the last day we were there from one of the Blackpool organizers, saying their office had been inundated with calls from Hollywood agents requesting our contact information, which of course hadn't been public. She said she initially directed her staff to take names and numbers so we could return their calls but there were way too many and it was becoming too much to handle for them. She wanted to know if she could give out my email or mobile. I'd said no to the phone, but yes to the email, and within hours I had far too many to even read, let alone respond to. The agents had heard about the events in Blackpool and had seen our pictures and seen us dance, and apparently thought we'd be perfect for TV or a feature film.

"You turned down the reality shows before," Rory said. "They think that now that you've won the championship, you're going to reconsider?"

"The shows asked me directly. I don't know that the agents would know I rejected them."

"Well, would you reconsider?"

"I don't know." And I honestly didn't. Like Rory, I wasn't sure what I wanted now that I'd achieved what I'd wanted for so long. I definitely needed some down time to process everything that was happening.

But I felt I had to respond, to be professional. I ended up spending the entire day reading emails, writing back, and organizing times to meet when we returned to L.A. A total of three different projects were in the works that one or both of us were wanted for: two longstanding reality competition TV shows that paired celebrities with champion dancers—one based here, one back home—wanted to offer us an insane amount of money to become pro dancers on the shows. More than any of the pros had been paid before, according to the agents.

The second option was a new reality TV show that took a behind-the-scenes look at the world of competitive ballroom dancing. We'd of course be the first showcased pair of champion dancers. The program would follow us for the next year as we prepared for the World Championships, the U.S. National Championships, and Blackpool again next year, to see if we could continue our winning streak.

The third project was for me alone, as they already had the actress: a movie with kind of a Cinderella storyline about a young woman from the wrong side of the tracks who meets a glamorous, sexy ballroom dancer and is whisked away to a fairytale world where she completely remakes herself and falls in love.

Rory laughed when I told her this storyline. "It sounds just like my life."

"You're not from the wrong side of the tracks," I said. "You're a lawyer."

She laughed again, but this one was lighter. "Funny, it doesn't seem that way. It seems like I'm...just...I dunno, lower class..."

I finished her thought for her. "Than who? Than your sister." Jeez, her family was as bad as mine, albeit in different ways. Mine was physically abusive, hers emotionally. We needed to put them behind us once and for all. We were working on it.

The last project was already underway. The screenplay had been written and the lead actress had been cast. And she was a pretty big deal. She was such a big deal that they were having a hellish time figuring out who would play the dancer. No one seemed strong enough to hold his own opposite her, they'd told me.

"Oh please," Rory said. "I don't care how unknown you are right now in Hollywood, you have so much charisma and personality as a dancer, you could hold your own against frigging Angelina Jolie."

The thing that appealed to me most about this one was that, as written, the male lead wasn't Russian. It meant I'd have to be passable as American. It couldn't be overstated how huge a deal that was. That was my second dream in a way, now that I thought about it: to be American. To truly belong.

"That you are!" Rory shouted, pumping her fist in the air.

I looked at her dubiously.

"Oh my God, I'm so serious. Unless and until you get all upset and worked up about something—like, say, an imperfect practice before a dance competition—your accent is one hundred percent

American and your grammar is impeccable. It's crazy! You can so do that role, Sasha!"

But this project lacked one thing. I cocked my head to the side and squinted my eyes. She read my thoughts.

"Yeah, I know. I would love to do a project that we can both participate in. But…I don't know. This is so you. The actress is huge. And it's on the big screen. It could lead to so many other things. Sasha, I know how much you want this. You turned down the TV shows before for a reason. Do the movie."

***

I thought about it the whole flight home. I made it clear to Rory I'd do whichever one she wanted. She was the one to choose. She said she'd think about it, but knew she wanted the latter for me. She couldn't imagine trying to teach a celebrity to dance. "If I can't envision myself as a teacher at a little ole ballroom studio how'm I gonna teach someone famous?" she said.

"Because you have confidence now," I said sternly.

"Yeah, but seriously, Sasha, that kind of thing just isn't for me. It just isn't."

"What about the middle one?" I said.

"The documentary?" She thought about it and nodded. "It would be the life we've lived for the past several months, only we'd now be followed around and filmed. I mean, if they really do want to film the Tucker trial, I don't know how well that's going to go down with the English courts. But even if they couldn't get that footage, they might be able to gather pieces of the story separately. You know…" Her eyes darted about the plane, in thought.

"What? What's going through your mind?" I asked.

"I mean, I'm just thinking about Tatiana's journey. All she's gone through after Siberia, in Tokyo, in California. I mean, I wasn't joking about that exposé someone should make about the agency. Maybe that reality/documentary project could be about more than just the world of professional ballroom dancing, and could put some focus on something larger."

I squeezed her hand tightly. "You are brilliant. My beautiful, brilliant lawyer dancer," I said, kissing her.

***

As it turned out we were able to do both of the latter two. The movie casting crew auditioned me and told me the very next day they wanted me. But they did want me to work with a dialect coach and take elocution and acting lessons. I wanted nothing more than to make my American English beyond perfect. Rory was so right to insist on this project. It was perfect for me.

Amazingly, when the reality TV people found out I'd accepted the movie offer, they were even more excited about casting us than before. They broadened the scope of the documentary. They would now follow me around as I took all these lessons and prepared for the role, and as I struggled to do my work for the movie and still have adequate time to rehearse for competition.

I'd made Rory mention to the director the ideas she had for including the—let's face it, flashy and sensationalistic—criminal activity we'd been inadvertently involved in. She suggested we could do so without violating any fair-trial issues by focusing more on Tatiana's story and what she'd been through.

The director was young and biracial, and the more Rory spoke with her, the more she realized the director had a genuine interest in expanding the story so it wouldn't just be about glamour and fame and the hard work of a dance competition, but about what happened to the people left behind as well, and the families and backgrounds of some of these international stars. The director interviewed and really connected with Tatiana, and Tatiana liked her, compelling the director to accept all of Rory's suggestions. They even wanted to accompany Tatiana and me back home and film some footage there. I wasn't too thrilled about that, but I knew how much Rory was, and Tatiana was game, so long as she didn't have to stay. So, I agreed to do it. For them. The two women in my life, whom I loved more than anything.

The director had additionally decided to film Rory as she prepared to be second chair in Jamar's trial! Yep, it all worked out for her. She was going to get to work on the case she so believed in after all, despite that asshole, Gunther.

James and Jacqueline had called Rory after we returned. Jacqueline in hysterics, of course. But instead of berating her for getting herself involved in criminal activity, as Rory had expected, her sister was actually supportive, congratulating her on having won the biggest ballroom competition in the world, and being genuinely happy for our new projects.

Moreover, James had excellent news. The court had pulled Gunther from Jamar's case for some kind of ineffective handling of evidence. It was all over the legal news dailies, he'd said. The court happened to have transferred the case to a friend of James's. James called the friend and explained Rory'd worked hard on the case, truly believed in the client's innocence and had a lot of knowledge about him. The friend decided he wanted her to assist. So the ass of an ex actually did something good in the end. Not that it made up for all the shit he pulled, but, okay, maybe some.

Rory still wasn't sure if she wanted to return to a career in law, but if she did, it was going to be representing the underprivileged, not helping rich people find tax loopholes. Jamar's case would be excellent experience and might give her options.

"I've never really stopped thinking about his case," she'd said to me, snuggling into the crook of my arm after her meeting with James. "I need to help."

"Of course you do, my sweet, brilliant little do-gooder," I'd said, kissing her yet again.

James had more interesting news, she told me. Though he'd changed firms, he'd heard Mitchell and Cheryl were undergoing divorce proceedings. Cheryl had moved in with her new, much younger ballroom instructor.

I raised my eyebrows on hearing this. "Well, I hope he can give her what she needs." And I meant it. She was obviously profoundly unhappy with Mitchell and wanted more out of life than he gave her. Rory and I had both been there. We hadn't tried to sabotage anyone else by seriously injuring them, of course, but I felt like this meant Cheryl was now otherwise occupied and would stay out of our business for good.

***

After a couple weeks of staying with me, Tatiana moved into Rory's old apartment and Rory moved into my place—our place. I hired permanent bodyguards for Tatiana and Rory—you just never knew the power of someone like Tucker—who remained stationed outside Tatiana's apartment building and our house. So I didn't worry as much about not keeping both of them under my watch 24/7, which, with my now crazy-busy schedule, would have been impossible.

Tatiana was still shy around Rory, but she liked living on her own and being self-sufficient. She took classes in English as a second language and prepared for the S.A.T. She'd told me she wasn't too keen on being a non-traditional college student but wasn't sure what else to do. She wanted to be an actress but I wasn't sure how long it would take for her English to be up to par. Her linguistic skills were a lot weaker than mine. She definitely didn't want to dance and follow in my footsteps. I certainly understood wanting to be your own person.

"Following in someone else's footsteps always means you're one step behind," Rory agreed. "I'd know. I lived in Jacqueline's shadow for way too long."

I was sure Tatiana would find her way eventually. She'd find what was right for her and what she was brilliant at. I had faith.

***

Rory returned to Infectious Rhythm once a week to take an advanced class with Bronislava, simply to keep her mojo. And so the filmmakers had a reason to film at the studio where it all started for her. She'd really wanted to give her friends—Paulina, Raj and Sam, Kendra, Pepe, Mitsi, and Bronislava herself—little cameos on the show. Their personalities were all so over the top, the filmmakers had a blast capturing it all.

Josie, Kendra's girlfriend, never returned to the studio. Instead, she ended up with a role in my movie. She'd play a former dance partner of mine. She'd wanted to be an actress too, but had never revealed it to anyone out of fear her dream would never come true.

After Rory began working second seat on Jamar's case, she called Melinda Berenson, the appeals attorney for her former client whom she'd thought was mentally ill. The psychiatrist had indeed found him to be a paranoid schizophrenic, just as Rory had suspected. He was currently in a mental hospital, on medication, and would go to trial after he was declared—by a mental health professional, this time—mentally fit to stand trial.

"If he would have gone to prison and remained untreated, he almost definitely would have deteriorated, making him all the worse—and far more dangerous to his ex-wife and to everyone else when he got out. Now he'll hopefully get the help he needs," Rory said.

"Once again, you were right. You knew better

than your so-called superior. You're very intelligent, very intuitive. Don't you ever dare doubt it again," I said.

"I won't!" she said with a little laugh.

***

One night as we were rehearsing with Greta, the documentary director ordered the camera operators to stop filming. We all did as she said, and looked at her. She seemed truly distressed.

"It seems like you guys are on your best behavior whenever we're around?" she asked, though her statement wasn't a question.

"We can't be on our *best* since you're always around," Rory said. I heard tiredness in her voice. I knew she was getting sick of being followed.

"Well, I guess that's true. But I mean, how can you guys get along so well? You never argue. You never have any disagreements over anything. I've filmed dancers before. I know what it can be like, especially before a big competition. This is the Worlds, you know!" The director threw her hands up in exasperation.

We three stood there dumbfounded. I was so used to getting along with my ladies, I hadn't noticed we were doing so. It was natural now *not* to fight. Greta and Rory burst into laughter.

"Sasha used to be a huge problem." Rory pointed at me.

What? I widened my eyes at her.

"He used to be a horrible perfectionist," she continued. "We had to teach him to calm down and see dance as an art form and not an Olympic competition all the time, and actually have fun with it. And to stop trying to make me into a replica of himself and allow me to do more of my own thing that allowed me to shine."

I looked at her, mortified. She was making me look like a crazy, megalomaniacal control freak. Okay, I'd been bad, but not that bad.

"Because obviously," Rory continued, "I will never, ever be as fast and strong and razor-sharp as him." She finished with a cutely playful pout directed at me, followed by a wink. I realized she was blabbering, making crap up on the spot so as to refrain from giving away our real techniques for developing a partnership. They included, after all, me blindfolding her so she'd learn to follow me, and then doing…other things while blindfolded to get her to use her other senses. And then her demanding we dance naked so I'd be gentler with her body. Yeah, no, the director wasn't getting all that.

"I remember we decided I would act as go-between," Greta said. "So Sasha wouldn't get out of control. They weren't allowed to say anything negative to each other. They had to say it to me."

The director looked back and forth between Rory and me like we were children. Okay, time to fess up.

"I-I was a perfectionist," I admitted. "I'd always fought with all of my partners. Badly. And Greta did act as mediator when we got out of control. Which helped immensely. But…" I walked toward Rory. "I just, I don't know how to explain. Rory and I were the right partners for each other. I fell in love. Really, madly in love. That's how we became true partners." I wrapped my arms around her back and kissed her forehead. "And with that naturally came respect," I went on. "Respecting each other's boundaries and limitations and strengths and weaknesses, both physical and mental. It's only if you respect each other that you can listen to each other. You can't work together without respect."

"Respect, and dancing naked together," she whispered in my ear.

"Stop it," I whispered back, now trying hard to keep my emerging hard-on at bay.

"Seriously. When are they going to leave so we can do our naked rumba? We're never alone anymore," she play-groaned under her breath. Which was not making my…little issue…any better.

"Rory."

"What?"

"Don't say that. Don't talk about that."

"Why?"

"Are you guys having a conversation?" the director asked. "Because I should have the sound on if you are."

"No, no conversation at all," Rory said. "We're just…cuddling."

"Because I'm thinking about it now and…it's just not good," I said to her under my breath, pushing my partial erection into her lower abdomen area. She almost laughed, but managed to restrain herself.

"With all these crazy cameras? What are you, a porn star?" she whispered.

The director continued to look at us quizzically.

"It's just that I'm not feeling very well," Rory said. "I'm really not. I think I need to finish for the night. Please?"

The crew took what seemed like an eternity to

pack up and go.

The filming was generally fun, don't get me wrong, and I couldn't complain about how exciting our lives were now with all that was going on, but I was beginning to see how actors could get annoyed with the lack of privacy.

"Thank you!" I exclaimed, throwing my hands up in the air the second the door shut behind them.

"I know," Rory echoed. "Not that I'm complaining about being a kind of celebrity or anything, at all. But I mean…"

"I simply need time alone with the woman I love." I looked into her beautiful, ethereal eyes, full of wonder as ever. We penetrated each other with our pupils, just as we had the first time our gazes had connected. I could feel the muscles in the lower half of her body clenching. Along with mine.

I stood in the corner, near the doorway, holding a remote control. With one click, I dimmed the lights and played the music to which we'd first danced naked together, "*Bésame Mucho*."

I held out my hand. She skipped toward me. I would have ordered her to do her sexy rumba walks but it would have taken far too much time. I took her hand and whisked her around so we were facing the floor-to-ceiling window. I stood behind her in shadow position, my arms wrapped around her, my lips to her creamy, rose-scented nape. We gazed out over the canyon. With the room so dim, you could see the lights from the houses below. This was my favorite time of day because of that view. It was simply breathtaking.

"Let's see what you have really learned," I whispered in her ear, sucking gently on her earlobe.

"I beg your pardon?" she said with a giggle.

I placed my hand before her eyes and softly closed her eyelids. "Keep them shut!" I commanded. Then, with lightning speed, I whisked her around again, to face me.

I knew it was dizzying. But in a good way. I made her want to fall into me, on purpose.

"Good," I said. I gently placed my lips on her still-closed left eyelid. "I was expecting to have to get the blindfold."

She began shaking, in a good way. I could feel her whole body tingling with wonder about what I was planning to do. "Sasha—" she started.

"Shhh, no words. Just follow. Just feel me."

I led her into a series of underarm turns. They were slow and, in and of themselves, not very dizzying. But then I pulled her toward me. I pressed my lips ever so gently onto hers, then whisked her back out again into a step called a natural opening-out.

"Quit being a tease." She giggled, her eyes still closed.

Now I pulled her in and turned her in the other direction, a bit more quickly. I could tell she was getting a little dizzy with her eyes closed. But now she deserved it for telling me not to be a tease. I turned her faster and faster, whipping her around me. She opened her mouth and began to speak, but before she could tell me to stop I took her down quickly into a deep dip, where she could relax for several beats and get her bearings. Amazingly, she still managed not to open her eyes. For that she deserved a reward.

I pulled her up toward me. She let herself fall into me, leaning all the way, letting me support her weight as I'd begged her to do during our first dance in my private ballroom. Her body weight issues were a thing of the past.

I wrapped my arms around her. We stood in a quiet, still embrace for a few beats before I placed her solidly on her feet, making sure she was upright and balanced before letting go.

She remained standing with her eyes still closed. I walked to the kitchen and very, very quietly, opened the top drawer, removing the box. I could tell she expected me to return to her. She waited. And waited. The music ended. She didn't dare open her eyes. She had amazing self-control. I didn't. I couldn't wait any longer. I needed her answer. I walked up to her, standing inches before her.

And then I knelt.

"I have a prrrroposition for you."

Her eyes bolting open, she looked down at me. I was kneeling before her, on one knee, the view of the canyon behind her, its lights producing a glow around her, making her look like she was encircled by a heavenly halo.

"Rory, you've completely changed my world. Life since I met you, life with you is just…filled with…crazy. But in good way. In wonderful way."

Her eyes began to tear. Yes, I was getting caught up in emotion. To hell with perfect English.

"You are the only constant in this ever-changing landscape," I continued, after a deep breath, making up for my grammatical flub. "You make me so happy. You make me sane." My voice began to shake. "Who knows what the future will bring us. All these…TV shows and movies." I shook my head and held out my hands. "I just know that whatever comes next, I want to share it with you. I want you always to be in my life."

I pulled a small midnight blue velvet box from behind my bent knee and held it up to her.

"Oh my God, yes!" she cried out before even taking it.

"Ahhh…" The words *I think you are supposed to open the box and I am supposed to ask first* were what I'd intended to say, but instead I just said, "Yes!"

She grabbed the box and giggled as I scooped her up and twirled her around in the air. When I finally brought her down, she opened it. I so loved the ring, and knew she would too. Sadie's nephew, the tattoo artist, had given me the name of a jewelry designer in West Hollywood. She was Russian and knew exactly what I wanted. The diamond in the middle was cut into the shape of a star, and it was flanked on the sides by two sapphires, close to the color of my eyes. Above and below the diamond were two radiant green stones. Those gems represented her eyes.

"Oh my gosh, I've never seen such gorgeous stones!"

"If you don't like it, we can definitely exchange—"

"Shut up!" she screamed. "It couldn't be more perfect and you know it!"

She was right. I did know it. "You told me you like sapphires. And the beautiful green, it is called Russian jade. It reminded me of your eyes."

She teared up as she slid it on her finger. Where it fit perfectly, of course, since I'd measured her ring finger in her sleep.

She held her hand up. The ring glowed in the

light of the canyon.

"I am glad you like it," I said, hoisting her up.

She wrapped her legs around my waist. I circled us around for a few beats, then stopped, and in one motion, swung her back and flipped her sideways, so that she was now in a cradle position in my arms. I nudged her chin toward mine and kissed her softly but deeply.

Holding her in that position, I carried her up the winding staircase, down the hallway, and over the threshold into our paradise.

The End

ACKNOWLEDGMENTS

Thank you to Julia Ganis, my eagle-eyed editor, Marisa-rose Shor, my fantastic cover designer who can do absolutely anything, publicist Liz Donatelli, my friend and fellow romance enthusiast, and all the wonderful people in the Los Angeles chapter of Romance Writers of America for their generous advice, encouragement and words of wisdom. Thank you to my parents for their never-ending support.

But mostly, thank you to you, dear reader. To an indie author, reader support is absolutely everything. There are so very many books out there and I am so beyond grateful that you chose to read mine. I would really appreciate it if you would leave a brief review on Goodreads or wherever you purchased this book. And I love to hear from readers. So please do connect with me at www.tonyaplank.com!

ABOUT THE AUTHOR

After working for many years as an attorney in New York and Los Angeles, Tonya Plank returned to Southern Arizona, where she grew up. A former amateur ballroom dancer, she wrote the dance blog, "Swan Lake Samba Girl." Her first novel, *Swallow*, won several awards, including gold medals in the Independent Publisher and the Living Now Book Awards, and was a finalist in ForeWord's Book of the Year and the National Indie Excellence Awards.

When she's not hard at work on her next dance romance, she enjoys taking road trips with her rescue dog, Sofia, devouring Mexican food and Cadillac margaritas, cuddling up with her cats and a good book, and watching dance performances of any kind.

To connect with her, please find her at www.tonyaplank.com where she tries to blog regularly, or visit her Facebook page at www.facebook.com/tonyaplankauthor.

www.ingramcontent.com/pod-product-compliance
Lightning Source LLC
Chambersburg PA
CBHW070654180626
46817CB00006B/2362